A THYMELY DEATH

A THYMELY DEATH

LILY ROCK MYSTERY
BOOK 4

BONNIE HARDY

eBook ISBN: 978-1-954995-06-2

Paperback ISBN: 978-1-954995-07-9

Cover Design by Ebook Launch

Editing by Proof Positive

GET A FREE SHORT STORY

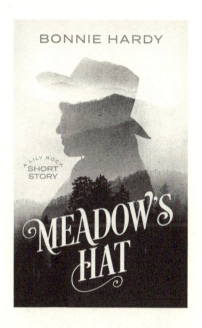

Join my VIP newsletter to get the latest news of Lily Rock along with contests, discounts, events, and giveaways! I'll also send you *Meadow's Hat*, a Lily Rock Mystery short story.

Sign up on bonniehardywrites.com/newsletter

"Death is only the end if you assume the story is about you."

WELCOME TO NIGHTFALL PODCAST

CHAPTER ONE

Olivia Greer took a lick of her ice cream, closing her eyes to appreciate the vanilla bean flavor. Michael Bellemare laughed.

"You do enjoy a good ice cream cone," he said, glancing over his shoulder to add, "and it's a pleasure to watch your enjoyment."

"Ice cream is a favorite," she admitted, taking another lick. "Having an ice cream feels more decadent before lunch. Better get to yours or it will melt." She pointed to his strawberry double scoop on an oversized waffle cone.

He took a large bite, licking his lips. She watched him, transfixed by what she saw. He stood in front of her with his easy smile. *I'm so happy we finally got together.*

"Here, let me get that," she offered, dabbing at a drip at the corner of his mouth. When she was done she offered a quick kiss.

"What's going on over there?" Michael pointed down the street where a bulldozer had been parked on the side of the road.

"Let's take a look," suggested Olivia.

We've been together every minute, so much so that I've lost touch with the comings and goings of Lily Rock.

With her spare hand she took his, pulling him toward the opposite side of the street. After another lick of his ice cream, Michael spoke. "I've been kind of tuned out, not keeping track of Cookie's new bakery and the new nursery next door," he said sheepishly. "If you remember, we had our first date and then things got a bit more interesting, and frankly, it was all I could think about. You know, when I'd see you again."

"And now you're less preoccupied?" she asked, her voice teasing.

"I'm totally locked into you licking that ice cream, if you must know." Michael stopped on the boardwalk in front of a gate. "So this is Mother Earth..." The gate had been constructed with horizontal redwood boards set with sturdy posts. On each side more fence had been built with a bit of light showing through each board, but not enough of a gap to actually see what lay behind the barrier. "I like this design." Michael ran his hand over the wood. "Very professional," he added.

"And not your idea for once," Olivia said.

"You're right. I had nothing to do with this place. Check out the signage." Right over the gate, "Mother Earth" had been etched into a board that looked like a slice of a tree trunk. Michael examined it more closely. "It looks as if the bulldozer finished its work and Mother Earth is ready to open her doors to the public."

Olivia appreciated her last lick of the ice cream cone. She also appreciated Michael, who shoved his hands into the back pockets of worn jeans, his lean body and broad shoulders inviting her scrutiny. When he turned around he smiled, and her heart took an extra beat.

That smile gets me every time.

She stepped forward to take the napkin from his hand, then deposited her napkin and his in the trash receptacle. When she turned back around, Michael had moved down the street toward another storefront. He gestured with his head for her to follow.

"Look," he said, staring into the window. "Cookie told us he was up and running and sure enough, he's holding a baking class."

Olivia glanced into the window of the storefront. Several people sat in folding chairs, paying close attention to Charles Kravitz, aka Cookie, who stood behind a counter, his mixing bowl in his hand.

Next to the bowl was a canister labeled "Flour". Next to that, freshly cut herbs lay on a paper towel. A wooden spoon and a whisk looked like props in a baking show.

Cookie stood behind the counter. Keen ice-blue eyes stared at his class, pausing to assess each student individually. He wore jeans and a very white apron over a chambray button-up shirt. A chalkboard rested on an easel at the end of the counter. Scratchy writing told the name of the class: Baking with Thyme—A Cookie for All Seasons.

"I guess that's the class he's teaching today," Olivia said. "The vibe is playful and cute."

"I don't think Cookie plays. He's all business when it comes to his craft," Michael said. "His audience is a bit older, not that there's anything wrong with that. I wonder if they even bake in a kitchen or if they just needed a day out?"

"I bet some of those people were already excellent home bakers. That's why they came to the class. Not so much to learn but to share ideas." *It's good to include the retired and elderly. Otherwise they get stuck in some back corner waiting to die.* Olivia's thought went immediately to her mother. *She wanted to be active until the very end.*

"Hey, isn't that one of your Tone Rangers?" Michael tapped his finger on the window. Olivia had coached the Tone Rangers a cappella group at the music academy a few months ago.

She stared at the back of the class once again. *All I see are older people, no one young enough to be a Tone Ranger.* "I don't know who you mean," she told Michael, still looking through the window.

A movement behind Cookie caught Olivia's attention. Sure enough, a young teen, dressed in a baggy shirt over a flowered prairie-style skirt, stacked measuring spoons and cups. They watched Cookie as if waiting for directions.

"I think that's Raleigh," Olivia said.

"I had forgotten the name, but I think he sang tenor." Michael paused, then he grinned. "I mean they sang tenor. Raleigh is non-binary, right?"

"They do sing tenor," she said with certainty. "A bit tricky to remember they and them when my eyes tell me he and him. Anyway, let's step inside and say hello."

She reached for the door, pausing when she heard a large vehicle rumble from the street. She turned briefly to see a bus pull up next to the curb in front of the bakery.

Michael whispered in her ear, "I think that's the transportation for Cookie's class." He pointed to the print on the bus. "This must be the bus that transports residents from Lily Rock's Hello Age retirement community."

"I think you're right. So this probably is a baking class arranged for the people who live there. I've heard the fancy retirement communities make all kinds of opportunities for their high-paying clients to be entertained."

The door to the bus swung open, revealing a bald-headed bus driver behind the wheel. Olivia squinted in the sun. "Do you know the driver?"

"I don't know him. Let's go introduce ourselves, shall we?" He walked toward the open door of the bus and then stopped. "Well look who it is."

The first seat on the passenger side was occupied by none other than Mayor Maguire. He sat on his back haunches, his tongue hanging out of his mouth. As soon as he saw Olivia and Michael he greeted them with a bark.

Olivia walked up the two steps to ask the driver, "May we talk to the mayor?"

"Do what you need to do," the man said, sitting back in his seat. She felt his eyes following her from behind.

Before she could greet the dog, he asked, "Actually I have to take a break, would you watch the bus?"

She glanced around at him to find that his smile revealed a broken front tooth.

"Sure, go ahead." Olivia turned to the dog sitting in the front passenger seat.

"Hi, M&M." She reached to pat the labradoodle's ears. "Haven't seen you in a day or two. What have you been up to, silly doggo?"

The dog leaned his head into her fingers, lifting his chin for more pets as Michael watched from the boardwalk.

Olivia heard him call to the driver. "How long until the class is over? You're here to pick up the seniors, right?"

"Yah, I'm here for them. Just a waste of time if you ask me. Nobody I brought has a kitchen, so they can't bake cookies. Want to help with the wheelchairs when I get back?"

"Sure," said Michael. "How long will it be?"

The driver looked down at his cell phone. "Only about ten more minutes. We gotta load them quick because they eat at noon and you don't want to get in the way of a resident's midday meal."

"Midday meal, not lunch?" asked Michael.

"That's what the old folks call it." The man shrugged. "These seniors appreciate good gossip and lots of food in the middle of their day."

Olivia gave Mayor Maguire a goodbye pat. She walked to the steps, moving onto the boardwalk. The bus driver and Michael were still talking. She took Michael's arm, nodding at the bus driver. He paused mid-sentence to look at Olivia, his eyes lingering. "I gotta go, if you know what I mean. Be back in five. Thanks for watching the bus." He hurried away, disappearing through the partially constructed entrance to Mother Earth.

Olivia and Michael were staring at their phones when the bus driver returned. She didn't look up right away. Scrolling on her phone, she pretended to be preoccupied with her texts. *If I look busy, I won't have to talk to him. Maybe Michael can handle this.*

"I read upside down," the man commented, watching Olivia closely. "It's a gift of mine. Looks like you've got a few texts there."

Michael took over. "I see the Lily Rock mayor is riding with you. If you're new to town, you probably don't know about him."

The driver dragged his eyes away from Olivia and her phone. He offered up his hand to shake with Michael. "I know the dog, but I don't know you."

"I'm Michael Bellemare and this is my girlfriend, Olivia Greer. We live in Lily Rock. And your name is?" asked Michael.

"Carl Million, but everyone calls me Flex."

As if to prove ownership of his nickname, Flex held both arms in the air, bending at the elbow. He flexed his exposed biceps in the sleeveless T-shirt. Muscles rippled up and down both arms.

I can't believe a guy in his fifties would actually flex his muscles for another man. Michael will have an opinion about this later.

She looked over to Mayor Maguire, who continued to stare from the open bus window. She called out, "See you later, M&M, we're gonna help get people back on the bus."

On cue the door to the bakery opened, revealing a woman in a wheelchair. Raleigh stood behind her, a smile of surprise on their face. "Olivia!" they called. "Good to see you. Remember me...Raleigh Ulrich?"

Olivia stepped behind the wheelchair to give them a hug. "Of course I remember you, Raleigh. You and your marvelous tenor voice. What are you doing here at the cooking class?"

Raleigh looked around, eyes stopping on the Hello Age bus. "I'll fill you in as soon as I get Mrs. Green in her seat. Be right back." They pushed the wheelchair toward the bus. Olivia held the bakery door open as a person with a walker came closer. The elderly woman wore a small waist bag, her gray hair closely cropped.

"Such a nice young girl," the woman commented, pushing past Olivia.

Michael waited for the woman to roll the walker forward out of the doorway. "I'll see who else needs help," he told Olivia over his shoulder.

"I'll just hold the door," she added with a grin. *I wonder what happened to Flex?*

After Michael and Olivia assisted the five remaining seniors onto the bus, he stayed behind to wait for Flex while she walked into the bakery entrance. Cookie Kravitz came around the end of the counter, wiping his hands on the front of his white apron. "Well look who's here," he said with a big smile. "I saw you both at the window but didn't want to abandon my class."

Olivia heard the bell above the door jingle as it closed behind her. Standing in the middle of the bakery, she examined it, checking out every nook and cranny. The carefully placed tables and chairs, each more distinct than the next, caught her eye first. "You've been antiquing," she commented to Cookie.

He smiled, watching her appreciate his choices.

Olivia kept commenting. "I like the way you took all of these tables and chairs and refinished them in the same oak stain. They look intentional but not the same." She turned to face him. "Thyme Out is a great name for a bakery."

"Since I bake with herbs and spices, it felt suitable. I like that play on words. What do you think?"

"It works, especially with the new place next door. Mother Earth and Thyme Out—very Lily Rock."

"Yeah, about the lady next door," Cookie started. Then as if thinking better of it, he changed the subject, a vague look coming to his eyes.

Cookie has some opinions about that woman.

Before Olivia could ask, Cookie cleared his throat. "The Mother Earth owner did a lot of work taking out dirt, adding dirt, taking out trees, adding trees. I'm kind of curious how things ended up."

"I haven't met her," said Olivia. "I'd like to know if she's planning on a nursery or a garden, or a venue that looks like a combination of both. She got her plans past the town council. That's amazing considering the people here hate any tree being removed."

"I know, I learned that the hard way." Cookie nodded. "I got rid of a large overgrown bush in the parking lot behind the kitchen, and you would have thought I'd stolen a puppy from Mayor Maguire and sold her on the black market. Big

8

brouhaha. We finally worked it out. I planted four smaller bushes to replace the ugly old one."

"I bet Meadow convinced the town council planning committee to let this one go," Olivia remarked. "She's often the most rational of the Old Rockers."

"I believe it was Meadow who helped negotiate the impasse. Funny the old townies call themselves the Old Rockers. They must have been something back in the day."

A shrill voice interrupted Olivia's laugh.

"Help me! Come quick."

A woman stood in the doorway of the bakery, frantically waving her arms in the air. When Olivia and Cookie turned to look at her, her eyes landed on Cookie. "I need a man. There's a dead..." She burst into tears.

CHAPTER TWO

Cookie took the woman by the elbow. "Show me where," he said urgently. "I'll come help."

Olivia raced out of the door. "There's a problem!" she called to Michael just as the Hello Age bus closed its doors and pulled away from the curb.

The frantic woman turned around to yell at the driver, "Come back! You've left someone behind!"

When Olivia realized what she was saying, she waved her arms in the air to stop Flex Million. Hydraulic brakes hissed, the doors swung open, and Flex appeared in the open doorway. "What's going on?" he asked, a look of annoyance on his face.

"That lady," Olivia pointed to the woman, "says you've forgotten one of the residents."

"I counted everyone," he insisted. "Give me a minute." Flex stepped back into the bus. Olivia watched him walk up and down the aisle, taking his time.

"I can't wait any longer. There's an emergency," she yelled into an open window. He hurried his pace, walking swiftly toward the front of the bus.

Taking two steps down he said breathlessly, "You're right. I think I was supposed to pick up Mr. Ulrich on the way home. His daughter-in-law dropped him at Mother Earth while she went shopping. Sorry about that."

"There's a problem," Olivia hastily added. "Come with me. We may need an extra set of hands."

"I can't leave all those folks alone on the bus," he stoutly insisted.

Michael, who had followed her to the street, intervened. "Okay then, how about this. Don't leave until we find Mr. Ulrich. Just stay put."

Olivia looked over her shoulder. She saw the frightened woman disappear behind the gate into Mother Earth, with Cookie following. Michael waited for Olivia, and they approached the entrance together.

Once inside, Olivia saw Cookie and the woman running ahead. Michael and Olivia sprinted to keep up. She led the way past the jungle of trees and potted plants.

Olivia could hear Cookie soothing the woman. "It's going to be okay," he said. "You call for an ambulance, I'll check for vital signs." Olivia heard the woman still sobbing.

Pushing their way through the greenery, they emerged into a clearing and found Cookie hovering over a man in a wheelchair. The sobbing woman stood to the side holding a cell phone to her ear.

Eyes wide with fear, she said, "I'd like an ambulance sent to Mother Earth in Lily Rock. We're located at 222 Main Street." Her hands visibly shook. "We have a senior citizen who's unconscious and we cannot detect a heartbeat."

When the call ended, Olivia stepped forward. "Hello," she said softly. "I'm Olivia Greer. I was talking to Cookie when you came for help..." She waited for the woman to reply.

Cell phone still clutched in trembling fingers, the woman

had streaks of mascara running down her cheeks. Her violet eyes opened wide, enhancing her childlike appearance. She lifted her hand. "I am Echo Kravitz. I own this business." She glanced toward Cookie then back to Michael. "Such a terrible thing to happen just when we got up and running."

Echo Kravitz? The same last name as Cookie. What are the chances of having two Kravitzes owning two new shops next to each other on the same street...

Instead of pointing out the coincidence, Olivia skipped over the matching last name, choosing to engage the woman instead. "You've created a beautiful place."

"I did it all myself," she admitted. "I don't suppose anyone will visit now that my first visitor turned up dead."

Olivia looked out of the corner of her eye at Cookie, who pressed against the chest of the man in the wheelchair. *Echo Kravitz feels a bit off to me. I wonder why she's more concerned about her business than the old man in her garden?*

A quick glance at Echo made Olivia want to look more closely. *No lines or wrinkles. Her eyes are huge. The hat covers her hair. Her neck looks older than her face, and I bet she has extensions.*

Echo gave Olivia an appraising glance. Her eyes quickly shifted as she stepped toward Cookie. A quick breeze came up, blowing her hat off her head. It landed in the dirt. *Yep, extensions. Look at all her hair.*

Olivia hung back, watching Echo stare at Cookie.

He held the tips of his fingers on the old man's neck. Echo's hands trembled. Cookie ignored her, his eyes focused on the man in the wheelchair. Cookie shook his head in frustration.

"It doesn't look good," commented Olivia.

"I checked his vital signs before I called for help," Echo

admitted. "They may be able to revive him if they get here quickly, though I doubt it."

"Were you a nurse in a previous life?" Olivia asked.

"No, not a nurse. I was a caregiver for my father before he died. It took years and left me penniless."

Michael, who waited a few feet away, took that moment to edge closer to the two women. He stood next to Olivia and she touched his hand briefly. Now all three of them watched Cookie.

I wish they'd get here. Every minute feels like forever.

Echo glanced at Michael, her eyes lingering for a moment. Olivia watched as she nervously folded and unfolded her hands. Then Echo lifted the hair off of her neck with one hand, her eyes darting to the ground as if she'd misplaced something valuable.

Spotting her straw hat, she bent over to dust it off against her pants. Then she plopped it back on her head. She tucked flyaways from her blondish hair under the brim.

Olivia looked down at Echo's worn sneakers.

"And your name is?" Echo asked.

Olivia felt Michael's arm around her shoulders. He pulled her close to his body before answering. "I'm Michael Belle-mare, Olivia's boyfriend." He looked at Olivia for approval, a bright smile on his face.

"You just started dating?" asked Echo, a hint of hope in her voice.

"Oh, we're way past dating," Michael said with a chuckle. And then as if he'd thought better of telling a stranger about their personal life, he looked at Olivia for confirmation. "Aren't we...past dating?"

Olivia shrugged. *You're on your own, buddy. We have a possibly dead guy right here in front of us and you've somehow gotten into a conversation with another woman about our personal life. Have at it!*

Avoiding the awkward conversational turn she said, "I'm going to talk to Cookie for a minute." Disengaging from his arm around her shoulders, she stepped closer to the man slumped over in the wheelchair.

Cookie rocked back on his heels before standing to his full height. He stared at the body, then shook his head. "I hope the ambulance gets here soon." Olivia watched him rest one hand on the shoulder of the motionless man, as if afraid to let go.

"Hello? Anyone here? I'm coming, Robert," came a shrill voice from the front of the garden. A woman rushed from the thick jumble of greenery into the clearing. Her eyes widened at the sight of the wheelchair. "Robert, I was a little late but you didn't have to fall asleep. I can explain..." Her voice faded away as she stared with wide eyes at the body. Olivia watched as comprehension came over her. She screamed, "Robert, darling!"

Cookie stepped closer to offer an explanation. The woman rushed past him babbling, "I only left him for a little bit. He's always loved gardens and he wanted to rest here while I ran a few errands in town. It took longer than I expected, but I came right back. I was going to wheel him onto the bus. I told Flex I would." Her chin quivered as she stared at the man in the wheelchair.

Michael stood beside Cookie. "I'm afraid Robert may have passed away. Cookie tried to revive him. The paramedics might be able to help."

She raised a hand to her forehead. "I know this shouldn't be too big of a surprise. He's suffered a decline with his Parkinson's for several years. I know it shouldn't be a surprise," she repeated.

The woman walked around Michael and Cookie to stand

closer to the wheelchair. She spoke softly. "Robert, it's me, Sasha. I want you to know that we all love you." She braced her hand on the blanket folded over the man's lap, leaning over to give the pale cheek a kiss.

"What's this?" Reaching under Robert's hand, she pointed at a sprig of greenery and a cookie lodged between his thumb and the blanket.

Michael bent over the body. He tugged at the green sprig trapped in the old man's fingers. He set the cookie aside, holding up the sprig in his hand. "Is this a weed?"

Echo spoke quickly. "That's a member of the Thymus vulgaris species, used for culinary purposes, and one of the herbs I grow and sell. Look, you can see over there." She pointed to a raised bed where plants grew. "The top row is thyme, many varieties. If you roll the leaves in your fingers you can smell the lemon. It's the perfect herb to put into the Mother Earth bag of herbs de Provence."

And that's way too much information about a twig.

Michael sniffed at his palm and then bent over to tuck the sprig back into the hands of the old gentleman. "I guess passing away in a garden with a fresh sprig of thyme and a cookie in your hand isn't the worst way to go," he said.

Sasha looked away, her eyes falling on Echo. "Did you call Hello Age to let them know about Robert?" Before she could answer, an ambulance siren wailed from a distance.

"I hear an ambulance now," Echo said. "I did not call Hello Age. I didn't know if he was...really dead." Her hand went to her throat.

Olivia listened to the siren, her heart thumping. Along with the siren she heard an answering cry, a prolonged high-pitched yowl from the street. *I think that's Mayor Maguire. He's signaling the ambulance. I bet he's waiting outside the gate.*

They all stood quietly, listening to the siren and the dog.

Within a few minutes, two paramedics ran down the path, a stretcher between them. "Did you call 911? Is this the guy?" one said, pointing to Robert in the wheelchair.

"Yes, yes, that's him," said Echo quickly. "I called and I think the man is dead."

"I'm his daughter-in-law, my husband is the next of kin," said Sasha. Then she began to explain again. "I just left him for a few minutes to get some shopping done and..."

Olivia watched one paramedic lift the man's wrist to take his pulse. The green twig dropped to the ground. She blinked.

"There's a twig and cookie under his hand," she said. "I bet the cookie came from the baking class next door."

Cookie took a step closer. "I'll be damned. He died with one of my signature cookies. Kind of beautiful if you ask me."

"I'll take that," said the daughter-in-law as she snatched the sprig and the cookie. "While you're at it, you can look in his pocket for a cell phone."

The paramedic slid a hand into the old man's pocket. He held out an iPhone to Sasha. "Is this the one?" he asked.

"It is. He never used it. We just gave it to him to make him feel better. He hasn't talked for months." She slipped the phone into her purse.

In a rush of activity, the paramedics moved the man from the wheelchair to the stretcher. One leaned over to push a few times on his chest. "We have to call time of death," he said with a shake of his head.

"Oh, you don't have to worry about that," insisted Sasha. "My husband is the next of kin and he has a DNR, a do not resuscitate, in his medical file. He didn't want to be revived, so you don't have to do any of that last-minute life-saving stuff. Just pack him up and get him to the funeral home."

Olivia shrugged. *DNRs and time of death are not the same. Is she deliberately trying to hurry this along?*

She reached into her purse again, and this time she pulled out a card. "Here you go. The Rest in Peace Mortuary. I'll call ahead so they expect you. Down the hill in Temecula, only an hour away. Tell them Sasha Ulrich sent you."

One responder took her card, looking at the details. "Do you need this for the number?" he asked her.

"Oh no, I have another card. Just move along," she said, her voice filled with urgency. Gone was the distraught daughter-in-law, replaced by a woman who planned ahead.

Olivia's stomach clenched. *Now isn't she the efficient one... Wait a minute. Ulrich. The old man's name and his daughter-in-law's name, and more importantly...Raleigh's name—all the same?*

A chill ran up her spine.

That's one too many coincidences.

CHAPTER THREE

Up early the following morning, Olivia looked toward the window where the sun appeared suddenly as if released from a jar. Branches from the pine trees stirred, bringing a smile to her face. *What a glorious day.*

When she went upstairs, she saw Sage and Michael sitting at the kitchen table, both scrolling on their phones. Sage in pajama pants and a loose T-shirt, her feet snugged up in lamb's wool slippers. Michael, barefoot, dressed in jeans and an untucked cotton button-up. He looked at Olivia and gave her a wink.

"Do you like the slight taste of peppermint?" he asked, holding up his Carpe Diem coffee mug and offering her a sip, which she gratefully accepted. He then took back his mug and sipped, raising his eyebrows at the sisters.

"I do," Olivia said, pouring a mug for herself. "It tastes like you waved a candy cane over a deep roast."

"It's okay," mumbled Sage, eyes still on her screen.

His lips turned down in a playful pout. "I do my best for the ladies," he mumbled. "I spend so much time at your house, I need to bring gifts, something original, my A game. The coffee blends are my signature offering, so to speak."

"You do feel like a roommate." Olivia sat at the table.

"Silly man," said Sage, looking up from her phone. "You don't need to bribe us to hang out. You're a fixture like...Mayor Maguire. You wander in and we feed and pet you."

Michael sighed. "For once I don't want to be compared to the mayor."

Is he serious or just trying to make us laugh? Sweeping her concern aside, Olivia focused on the coffee. "I, for one, love the flavors. Will peppermint coffee be your go-to blend?"

Michael took a sip, swishing the coffee in his mouth as if it were a fine wine. "I have flavor plans, blends, and mixes. In fact, I have an entire file I keep on my computer. Maybe I'll name the blends, you know, like Michael's Paschal Pastiche for early spring. I like that. Has panache..."

He continued with his theme. "I'm expressing a new side of my personality that I call *the barista archetype*." Michael raised his mug as if to toast the women.

Olivia suppressed a giggle. "So I'm not an expert, but I don't think there is a barista archetype. A hero archetype, maybe, and a jokester. You might even pass for an artist, what with your architectural chops. But a barista?"

Michael tapped his temple with a forefinger. "I've been thinking very hard on these coffee blends. Once I got into this new persona, I transitioned the peppermint from mid-December to my early spring concoction. No one does peppermint for spring that I know of. I would be original." He jokingly puffed up his chest.

Olivia, who never doubted Michael's originality, raised her eyebrows. "Architect turned barista...interesting. Plus I didn't know you were so liturgical. Paschal, really?"

"Oh, I have hidden depths you never dreamed of,"

Michael assured her. "I don't go to church, but I know the seasons. My mom was a cradle Episcopalian."

"From my perspective it sounds as if you've been talking to Meadow," sighed Sage. "She's the tea woman and now you are the coffee guy. What will be next, Mayor Maguire's seasonal dog bones?"

"Not a bad idea," Michael instantly agreed. "I bet Cookie has a few nutritional dog bone recipes up his sleeve. That could be a thing. Dog bones for free with every purchase at the bakery. He could advertise bake-your-dog-a-bone classes." Michael's eyes brightened. "I know, the mayor could be a special guest at the bakery. He would sample all the bits and pieces that were left over, get his photo taken. He'd like that."

"That could work. M&M is always hanging around for dropped goodies in the restaurants. I think our mayor has a sweet tooth and I know sugar isn't the best for dogs." Olivia frowned. "Cookie could put together a recipe specifically designed for a dog's good health."

"Cookie must be excited about his new bakery," Sage said. "I thought I saw a sign in front of the business yesterday: Thyme Out. That's the name?"

"That's the name," Olivia confirmed. "Kind of cute, don't you think? Speaking of Cookie, we spent a lot of time with him yesterday. I suppose that's all over town." Olivia leaned closer to Sage. "Any news from Meadow about the guy who died in the garden?"

Sage took another sip and then spit it back into the cup. "Too much peppermint for me," she said, lunging to the sink. "No, but Mom told me that you two were there when the paramedics arrived. She was sorry to hear that the old gentleman died."

Sage's mouth turned up at the corner. "It's a burden and a gift being Meadow's daughter. There aren't that many people left who have lived in Lily Rock long enough to be called an Old Rocker." She rinsed the remaining coffee out of her mug before placing it in the dishwasher, then turned back to say more.

"Mom found out about the death when someone checked out a book." Sage sighed. "Of course, Meadow took the sudden death as an opportunity to talk about herself and her end-of-life concerns. Last night she called and talked for over an hour to tell me about wills and directives. The dead guy is Meadow's new hero. She's all for exiting her mortal coil in a similar circumstance—in a garden with a shortbread cookie, at least that's what she told me."

"Meadow is Meadow," Olivia said.

Sage pushed her chair under the table. "I'd better finish getting dressed. You two have a good day."

Taking a moment, Michael leaned toward Olivia, staring at her lips. He reached out to pull her chin closer and then kissed her. He nodded and leaned back in his chair. "I will excuse Sage for tossing my peppermint coffee. She's been through a lot; her job was threatened only months ago. I didn't want to ask her directly, but any more trouble at the music academy?"

Olivia licked the taste of peppermint off her bottom lip. "Not really, the school board dismissed Simon Court as soon as they could and left Sage as the principal. She may have been a bit shaken after all the publicity last fall, but she's still on the job."

"She's good at her work and the students like her. I was hoping it would turn out that way." Olivia watched him stare into the empty mug, as if it were an unfathomable abyss. *He seems preoccupied.*

"Is something on your mind?" Olivia asked in a gentle tone.

Her cell phone rang before he could answer. It wasn't a number she recognized. She held it up to her ear. "Hello?"

"It's me, Cookie," said the hurried voice.

"We were just talking about you. I didn't know you had my number. Now I have yours. What's up?"

"I was wondering if you would drop by today, you know, just to go over what happened yesterday? I could use a little emotional support."

"It was pretty awful, the poor man dying right next door in the garden."

Cookie sighed. "So I've had a little employee fall out since yesterday, that's why I wanted to run it past you. Raleigh has been ignoring me since the death at Mother Earth yesterday. You coached the kid at the music academy, I thought you could help."

"I coached Raleigh while I was undercover for Janis. In all honesty I didn't recognize them yesterday until Michael pointed them out."

"Did you get a chance to connect again?"

"We started to talk, but the Hello Age bus drove up and your class needed help out of the door."

"So would you come over in a bit to talk to the kid? They haven't said a word to me all morning, just walking around in kind of a daze. I have to repeat every question to get Raleigh to do simple stuff. We opened fifteen minutes late because I couldn't find them. Finally I discovered Raleigh sitting in the back patio looking into space. I'm confused why the death of a random old man would cause them so much grief."

"I'll come over in a bit," Olivia said. "See you soon." She clicked off the phone and then filled Michael in.

"Do you want me to go with you to the bakery this morning?" Michael asked.

"That would be good," she sighed. "Plus I might have an

idea why Raleigh is so upset. Did you hear the old man's name?"

"I heard Robert something or other."

"The old guy's last name was Ulrich, the same as Raleigh's."

Michael put down his coffee mug. "Now that strikes me as more than coincidence."

"It would explain why Raleigh seems so upset," Olivia explained.

Michael leaned over to take her empty coffee mug. He stood, making his way to the sink. Olivia thought about her conversation with Cookie. A twinge of sadness came over her. *Maybe the old guy in the garden was related to Raleigh.*

Michael finished rinsing the dishes. He called out, "Going to get dressed. See you in a few minutes." She walked to the sink, placing her hands on the porcelain to look out the window toward the garden.

Michael's small cabin was visible in the distance. Since he rarely spent time there, leaves had piled up on the front porch. Olivia looked at the vegetable garden, noting the weeds that had grown since the last snowfall.

Since receiving the unexpected inheritance of the home from Marla, Olivia had spent hours staring out the kitchen window. The woods, especially the squirrels running up and down the tree trunks, brought a smile to her face. Inhaling the scent of pine through the open window cleared her thoughts.

But this morning something felt different.

A lot has happened to me in the past couple of years. Every time I look out this window, I think about finding Marla's body in the garden. And then I think about Mom, the weeks we spent before she died.

She remembered one of the last conversations she'd had with her mother.

"You're not to worry when I go," Mona said, lying back against the pillows, a scarf covering her bald head. She looked worn and very thin.

"But I'll miss you," Olivia cried, tears rolling down her cheeks. "What will I do when you're not here to listen? When you go, I'll be lost."

Mona gripped the sheet. When the pain passed she took Olivia's hand. "Then let me leave you with this method I have for making everything okay. It's a practice that I've used over the years. Say thank you whenever you can."

"You mean for gifts and presents, that kind of thank you?"

"The thank you should come from your heart, but not necessarily for presents. Say thank you for small things, like for the sun rising every day. Say thank you for a clean sink and a mug of black coffee just the right temperature to take a sip." Mona's voice grew weak, but she continued. "Say thank you for the dog next door and for the wind at your back. All of those things and more require your attention. Attention is love, Olivia. Begin by saying thank you."

Thinking of her mother, Olivia's eyes welled with tears. Then her heart quickened as Michael walked back into the kitchen. He stood behind her at the sink. Wrapping his arms around her middle, his chin touched the top of her head. "You thinking about Marla?" he asked.

She turned to face him, still in his arms. "How did you know?"

"You get that look on your face whenever you're standing at the sink," he explained.

"It's not just Marla, I've been thinking about my mom lately. Whenever I come across death, even when it's a stranger like yesterday, I think about my mom and how much I miss her. Does that happen to you?"

Michael sighed deeply. "I think about my son every day. It

seems unfair that he was taken so young, but then I realize I got him for a few short years. I'm lucky."

Olivia buried herself in his chest. "'Thank you for that. It helps." In a few minutes, wrapped in his arms, the sadness lifted. She pulled away from his embrace, determined to change the subject. "Since Cookie wants me to talk to Raleigh, we'd better get going."

Michael reached behind her to grab a dish towel. He dabbed at her eyes, then tossed it back to the counter. He placed his hands on each of her shoulders to lean in for a quick kiss. When he drew away, he smiled. "You're getting to be quite the Lily Rock helper these days, and not just with music."

"Is that a bad thing?"

"You aren't the same woman I met coming up the hill that day. The beautiful edgy one who had no interest in getting close to anyone."

Olivia wrapped her arms around his middle. "I'm close to you and I know where I belong. Thanks for your patience."

CHAPTER FOUR

Michael pulled his truck into a parking space in front of Thyme Out. He turned off the ignition and jumped from the driver's seat. Olivia knew the ritual of opening her door was important to him.

"I'm feeling like a pastry or a muffin," he said, waiting for her to jump down from the truck before closing the door and locking it.

"That does sound good," Olivia agreed. "Maybe we can talk to Raleigh and find out what's going on without making too big of a deal about it."

Once inside the bakery, Michael nodded toward an empty table with two chairs. "We could sit outside if you prefer," he remarked, "or over there."

"Let's go outside," Olivia said.

As they headed to the back door, she glanced to the right. Cookie stood behind the counter smiling. "Hey, you two. Pick out something from the baked goods, on the house."

Walking to the counter, Michael leaned to look inside the glass case. "Everything have thyme in it?" he asked.

"Not everything. Just my signature bakes. I have to have

cookies and muffins with thyme, otherwise why name the bakery Thyme Out?"

"Anything with spices, like cinnamon?" Michael wanted to know.

"Yep, here's my cinnamon swirl coffee cake. Sound good?"

Olivia jumped in. "Make that two slices. I love cinnamon."

"I hope other people like thyme." Cookie frowned. He gingerly lifted the freshly baked coffee cake from the display case. Cookie cut two slices as he continued to talk over his shoulder. "I considered renaming the place something entirely different after you found that sprig and a cookie in the dead man's hand. That was creepy. Anyway, do you want tea or coffee with that?" He set the plates on the counter within reach.

"I've had enough coffee this morning," Olivia said.

Michael looked around and then asked, "How about water?"

Cookie smiled and shoved two tumblers across the counter. "You can fill them up over there." He pointed to a bottle in the corner. "I'll be out in a minute to chat with you guys. Let me look for Raleigh to take over the front."

By the time Olivia and Michael situated themselves at a small table at the back of the garden, Cookie walked from the kitchen, still wearing his apron tied around his waist.

"Raleigh's good with customers," he said, pulling over a chair, "just not a fan of talking at the moment."

"That's what you told me on the phone. I may have some insight about their odd behavior."

Cookie's brow wrinkled. "Do tell."

But before she could tell him about the name, Michael cleared his throat. With a lifted fork, he took a bite of coffee cake. He rolled his eyes with an exaggerated appreciation.

"You use some fine vanilla and cinnamon, my friend. Great piece of cake."

Cookie smiled and then chuckled. "I knew we had something in common: treasuring the best ingredients."

"It's good to see eye to eye on a baked good," commented Michael, taking another bite.

"I like the cake too," Olivia added hastily, "especially the swirly part."

By the time Michael finished his last bite, Cookie started talking. "You might want to know how Raleigh came to work at my bakery. I hired Raleigh as soon as I left the music academy, after the arrest. They seemed like a nice kid."

"But Raleigh was still a student," Olivia commented. "Did they finish high school?"

"Raleigh didn't finish at the academy. At the time I was unemployed. I was busy figuring out how I could stay in Lily Rock myself. Then a week ago they showed up early in the morning. I saw them looking in the window. Once we got talking, I learned Raleigh loved to bake. I couldn't offer a lot of money, but I could teach them about baking. So I hired them on the spot."

"Does Raleigh live in town?" asked Olivia.

"They rent a room and bike to work," said Cookie.

Olivia's eyes settled on Cookie's face. *He looks genuinely worried about the kid.* "As I mentioned to Michael earlier, Raleigh and the man who died at Mother Earth have the same last name. I'll go back inside the bakery. I'll see if I can get Raleigh to talk to me and then report back."

With her water glass in hand, Olivia sauntered toward the back door. She stepped inside and caught sight of Raleigh pouring coffee into the mug of a customer sitting close to the door.

Olivia waited by the counter. As soon as Raleigh turned around and saw Olivia, they nodded a greeting.

"Hi, Raleigh." Olivia smiled. "Sorry we didn't talk more yesterday."

Nearly colliding with Olivia, Raleigh didn't look up until rounding the corner to stand behind the bakery counter.

"Want anything?" they asked, looking slightly to Olivia's left to avoid eye contact.

Olivia glanced into the glass case. "How about a dozen of the dinner rolls," she said. "I can use them for dinner and freeze the extra ones for later."

Raleigh reached for a paper bag. With tongs they reached for the rolls. Folding the top of the sack, they handed it to her. "I think there's a friends and family discount. Better check with Cookie. Be right back."

At least they're talking. She waited until Raleigh returned from the back patio.

"Six dollars even."

Olivia reached into her wallet. "Did you ever find another a cappella group?" she asked when they took the money from her hand.

"Nope," they said shortly.

"Did you go to another high school to finish out the year?" Cookie had already given her that information, but Olivia wanted to hear Raleigh's version. *I get to ask nosy questions because I was a Tone Ranger music coach. That gives me license.*

Raleigh's shoulders slumped. "I didn't finish at the Lily Rock academy. I took the rest of my senior year classes online and got my GED. My parents didn't care."

"Good for you," said Olivia. "You live here now, in Lily Rock?"

"I live in a cabin right on the other side of town...kind of a last-minute decision."

Olivia put her wallet back in her purse. "So what do you think of your new neighbor, the owner at Mother Earth?"

"She comes in a lot." Raleigh looked toward the door.

"I just met her yesterday," explained Olivia. Before she could say more, Raleigh's face clouded over.

"I know," they said, abruptly turning away.

Is Raleigh crying?

She could hear them sniffing.

"Are you okay? You can tell me if you're not."

They rubbed a sleeve across their eyes. "It's just that my granddad died yesterday." Tears fell down their cheek. "The old man that everyone's talking about? That old man was my granddad."

"The man in the garden, the one who passed away. He was your granddad?" Olivia felt her stomach drop. *Just as I suspected, they were family.*

Raleigh's lower lip trembled. "My granddad lived at Hello Age. That's why I rented a room up here, to be near him. He gave me money until I could find a job. And now he's gone."

Olivia reached into her purse to pull out an unopened tissue packet. "Here you go." She shoved it across the counter, tucking it underneath one of Raleigh's hands.

Raleigh blew into a tissue and then reached for another.

"I can't imagine how awful yesterday must have been for you," Olivia said. "You must have been so shocked when it turned out to be your granddad next door."

"I tried to call him on his cell phone. We talked most mornings."

Olivia felt a prickle up her neck. "I'm surprised to hear your granddad had a cell phone. It's nice that you spoke so often."

"Sometimes we talked several times a day," Raleigh offered. "We were like pals. Granddad was a musician when he was a kid. He sang and played percussion in a band. Just like Paul in your band, Sweet Four O'Clock. He bought me my first drum kit."

The ice is broken, just keep him talking, Olivia.

"I didn't know you played drums," she said with a smile. "I thought you were just an amazing tenor. This is good information."

Raleigh returned a slight smile. "I don't have my drums with me, but I'd like to. Don't think the neighbors would approve though, too noisy. But Granddad? He never complained when I practiced as a kid. He would stand outside the door and if I got frustrated, he'd come inside and encourage me just so I wouldn't give up."

Olivia cleared her throat. "I was told your granddad had Parkinson's disease. I assumed it had advanced to the degree he couldn't speak. The cell phone calls surprise me a little."

Raleigh's smile disappeared. He glared at Olivia for a moment and then their expression changed. "I guess you think you know everything about Parkinson's?"

Olivia felt her face freeze. *Oh, now I've offended them. And things were going so well...*

Before she could respond, Raleigh looked at the door. He walked past the counter toward two new customers. Olivia felt dismissed. *I'll go back and sit with Cookie and Michael. At least I can tell them why Raleigh is upset.*

She took her dinner rolls and made her way to the back of the bakery. Olivia found Michael and Cookie right where she'd left them. The men were deep in conversation. She sat down but didn't interrupt.

"So I'm blending flavored coffee for the seasons," Michael explained.

31

Cookie leaned toward him, his eyes bright. "You just started doing this recently?"

Michael laughed. "Kind of a defense on my part. Olivia here," he reached over to take her hand, "loves plain black coffee. Me? Not so much. I did learn that flavored coffee goes down a little easier, especially certain flavors like pecan and peppermint."

"He actually has a signature winter solstice blend," added Olivia with a smile.

"Your coffee and my thyme baked goods might make a good combination," Cookie said. "We can talk about this later. Right now I want to know if Olivia had any luck with the reluctant young adult in my kitchen."

Olivia nodded. "I kind of did and I kind of didn't. Raleigh talked all right, but then I asked the wrong question and they clammed up again."

She explained to Cookie and Michael about Raleigh's granddad and how they got angry with her about Parkinson's disease. "I wasn't trying to be a know-it-all," she said glumly. "But whatever I said certainly made Raleigh angry."

"'The kid is really moody," Cookie said. "But at least now I know the cause. So the dead guy was their granddad. You also got information out of them about living arrangements, and then who knew the kid played drums?" Cookie smiled at Olivia. "Man, you do get people to confess to you, just like they say."

Olivia shrugged. *It's because I ask questions and then listen. Nothing special.*

Michael smiled. "She wasn't even singing. You should see what people do after they've heard her voice. They just spill their guts. One time a woman did a dance and lifted—"

"That's enough, Michael." Olivia's face turned bright red. "You don't need to tell Cookie about that time."

How was I to know she'd pull up her shirt on stage because of my song? Good thing Cookie didn't live in Lily Rock then.

The baker shook his head, disappointment showing on his face. "I wish I could have been there."

Olivia glanced away from the men, hoping to hide her self-conscious blush. She took a minute to look more closely at the back patio. Bistro tables with chairs all painted the same bright blue sat on stamped concrete. Each table stood apart from the rest, with evergreen bushes delineating the space.

At the far end of the concrete patio, a trellis hung over a wooden gate. Rose vines showed young green leaves with scattered buds not ready to open.

"Where does that go?" Olivia asked, pointing.

"To the woods. There's a path that wanders behind all of the shops on our street, each with a separate back entrance," explained Cookie.

"Does that mean you can walk from Thyme Out to Mother Earth?"

"You could if you wanted to." Cookie's lips tightened.

"That's convenient if you like your neighbor. Do you know Echo?"

Cookie shrugged, his hands falling to his lap. "Sort of, I guess you could say we know each other. She calls me her was-band."

"What was that?" Michael asked. "What's a was-band exactly?"

"I am her was-band, you know, her ex-husband."

"You and Echo were married?" Olivia barely contained her surprise.

"Yep," admitted Cookie. "Some twenty years ago. She found out about my new bakery and just moved herself next door without me knowing. You can imagine my surprise."

"Do you two get along?" asked Michael.

Cookie shrugged. "Let's put it this way. She did everything she could to take everything I had, even though the marriage didn't last five years. She even wanted my Porsche, my baby."

"Did she get the car?"

"Hell no. I still pay her spousal support after all of these years. I know the courts would let me off the hook, but I decided not to go back to court to get it changed. I'd probably win, but then I'd have to deal with her. Until a month ago I thought I'd seen the last of that woman."

"Then you were surprised that she opened a business next door?"

"Shocked. I thought I'd avoided her successfully, after we settled the divorce. But an old friend of ours told her my plan for a startup bakery and wouldn't you know it? She's back."

I wonder why he's acting so embarrassed. Maybe because he married Echo and it was a bad decision? "I have an even more interesting story of an unusual divorce," she offered. "Michael and his ex get along great. They go camping every year." Olivia did not add that they took the week away to talk about their son who had died. *Michael can tell Cookie himself.*

Cookie turned toward Michael. "Does she call you a was-band?"

"Nope." Michael smiled. "As of our last camping trip she calls me Bellemare."

Both men stared at each other.

Male bonding right before my very eyes.

34

CHAPTER FIVE

"Why don't you two share old wives' tales while I go out back for a stroll to Mother Earth?" Olivia gave a little wave. When they didn't look over, she smiled. *Good. Michael needs another friend besides me.*

Admiring the stamped concrete designs along the pathway, she stepped under the rose trellis, through the wooden gate. Stooping to inspect a delicate array of early crocuses, she inhaled deeply. *Spring is just around the corner.*

A spongy dirt path overlaid with mulch ran in front of the woods. Old tree trunks, lined up end to end, created a walking path. Olivia looked to her right. As Cookie said, the back entrance of Mother Earth beckoned only a few feet away.

As she walked closer, a squirrel skittered up the trunk of a tree. *Too bad M&M isn't here. He'd love a good chase.*

A wooden gate with horizontal boards held the sign for Mother Earth.

Olivia tried the handle, but the gate did not budge.

I can walk around to the front. Maybe she'll let me in that way.

Instead of heading back to Thyme Out the way she'd

come, Olivia continued on the path through the woods. Past three more shops, she made her way to Main Street.

First she tapped her boots on the boardwalk, knocking away the mulch. Then she walked down the street, stopping in front of Mother Earth. Unlike the back, this entrance gate stood ajar.

I'll just poke my head in to say hello.

Once inside she stopped to appreciate the beauty of the garden. *I missed all of this yesterday.* She looked around, her face filled with wonder. *Part garden, part wonderland, like a secret garden, or what I imagine a secret garden would be like.* Memories flooded her thoughts.

"Here's my favorite book," her mother said, handing her a worn copy of Frances Hodgson Burnett's The Secret Garden.

Olivia snuggled close in her mother's lap as she listened to the words. When her mother closed the book, Olivia begged, "Read more."

"We'll pick up tomorrow," Mona had replied.

Olivia closed her eyes now, savoring the memory. *Thank you, Mom.*

When she opened her eyes, she still felt delight as she stood in the midst of the lush green oasis.

Even though a man died here yesterday, I feel peace. But where's Mother Earth herself?

Walking along the gravel path, she saw a pergola on the left side of the garden. As she came closer she saw a rustic table built in the center of the structure. Constructed around a tree trunk, the tree branches stretched upward to the curved top of the pergola.

Turning back, Olivia could see that each section of the garden ran seamlessly into the next. Noting the empty pots and containers, she concluded, *I bet Echo displays her more tropical plants when the frost is over.*

36

A small kiosk next to the main path displayed an array of pots, each filled with loose dirt. A nearby baker's rack held a variety of plant foods and sprays, all organic. No one stood behind the counter.

She gulped. In a flash, her mood shifted. Memories of the previous day made the hair raise on her neck. *That's the path the paramedics took after they hoisted Raleigh's granddad on the gurney and rolled him away.*

She called out, "Is anyone here?"

When no one answered, Olivia stepped past the kiosk, making her way farther into the garden. All along the path she saw ropy vines that snaked across the branches of taller trees. *I bet Mother Earth could create a wonderful Halloween garden here. The trees are kind of spooky.*

"Is anyone here?" called Olivia again.

Still no answer.

She finally reached the clearing. To her relief she found Echo sitting on a bench, her laptop perched on her thighs and earbuds secured in both ears. When Echo raised her eyes from her screen, she immediately slammed her laptop closed, pulling out the earbuds. "What are you doing here?" Her voice was shrill.

"I'm so sorry. I didn't mean to frighten you, but the gate was open," Olivia explained. *I wonder if she recognizes me from yesterday?*

Echo's jaw set as her chin tucked in. Then she blinked. "Don't I know you? Weren't you with Cookie yesterday when I came for help?" Her eyes grew wide. "You were here in the garden when they took Mr. Ulrich away."

"Yes, I was. I'm so glad you recognized me. Such a difficult day."

Standing up from the bench, Echo tucked her laptop under her arm. "I don't remember your name."

"I'm Olivia Greer, good to meet you."

The woman did not offer her hand, but she did nod. "Did you come to look at the garden or book an event?"

"Oh no, I came to see you, to make sure you were okay," Olivia said hastily. Casting her eyes around the space she added, "And to look at the garden. You've done an amazing job here, creating such a tranquil space in so little time."

"Not my first plant business," Echo said dryly. "My last garden, in North Hollywood, was quite popular. Then I got bought out, so I had a lot of cash to put into this place."

"But you said it's not just a garden, also an event space?"

"That's right. I'm booking for spring right now. I want people to know they can have a garden at their disposal but not have to do the work involved. They can book the space for celebrations, weddings, birthday parties, even small business events. I've had book signings at my other place, along with craft demonstrations. Some people sign in just for a day away. The Wi-Fi is fast and the garden can serve as an outdoor workspace when the weather cooperates."

She pointed to her right. "Back over there I can set up tables and chairs for crafters." Then she pointed behind her. "And over there is a small venue for music with a stage."

Olivia nodded her appreciation. "Just being here...it's like an oasis in the midst of a town, like a secret garden."

Now Echo smiled. "That's right, what I planned on from the beginning. Mother Earth is a vibe. An earthy, landscaped sense of mystery."

Olivia turned around again, taking in all the pathways. "I want to look at everything at once. You've carefully designed the space to unfold, arousing curiosity, at least it does for me."

"You're sensitive to your environment," Echo observed dryly.

Olivia inhaled. "I'm sure you are too. By the way, have

38

you heard from the family, the Ulrichs? Are they doing okay? I imagine they're in shock with Mr. Ulrich's unexpected death."

"Not exactly in shock. I mean, he had Parkinson's and could have gone any time. I suppose it was odd that he went here in my garden."

"So you just opened and Mr. Ulrich showed up?"

"This was the first time. His daughter-in-law called to ask if she could leave him here while she did errands in town. I told her I didn't think it was such a good idea. I'm not a babysitter. But once Mrs. Ulrich, Sasha, explained that her father-in-law loved herbs, I couldn't say no."

"I suppose she paid you," Olivia said.

"Of course she did, quite a lot if you must know, more than the going rate for rental space. Like I said, I'm not a babysitter. She didn't pay for me to take care of the old man, just to provide a space for him to sit awhile." Echo took out her cell phone to check the screen.

Is that my cue to get going?

When Echo looked up she said, "Mr. Ulrich was quite cordial. He told me all about growing herbs from seeds when he was younger. He was especially fond of thyme. Reminded him of his youth and his mother's kitchen."

A chill came up Olivia's spine. "He spoke to you?"

"Oh yes. His hands trembled when I cut the sprig for him to smell, but he talked just fine."

Looking past Olivia's shoulder, Echo made a move forward as if she needed to leave. "Sorry to cut this short, but I have another appointment. Someone wants to rent the space for a flower arranging class. If you'll excuse me."

She brushed past her, walking toward the garden's entrance. Before Olivia could call out a goodbye, Echo turned around and headed back. "You can walk with me if you like.

Sometimes people get lost. I'll be posting maps next week, but until then it can be confusing."

As they walked, Olivia observed Cookie's ex-wife more closely. *She has the sense of style of a younger woman, with a few flourishes but not trying too hard. Just enough effort to look well put together but not contrived—like her garden and nursery.*

As Echo walked into the kiosk to stand behind the counter, Olivia called out, "I'll be saying goodbye then."

The woman opened her laptop. She didn't look up.

"I'm heading next door to Thyme Out," Olivia added, sounding more friendly than she felt.

With a head snap, Echo stared back at her. "You're going to Thyme Out? I'd be careful if I were you."

"What do you mean?"

"That odd kid works there."

Olivia felt her eyes harden. "That odd kid, as you call them, is my former student. Cookie hired Raleigh and I, for one, am delighted."

Echo's mouth tightened. "I knew Charles Kravitz, the owner, before, back in the day. We were...quite close."

Instead of acting curious, Olivia shut down the conversation. "I have to go. Cookie and my boyfriend must be done talking by now." She moved toward the open gate.

By the time she walked next door, several people waited at the bakery counter. Olivia watched as Raleigh waited on each one, delivering pastries on small plates along with a napkins. They took the money, moving on to the next customer without a smile.

Olivia tried to catch Raleigh's eye. When they didn't acknowledge her, she walked past the bakery counter to the patio beyond.

Still seated together, Michael caught sight of her first. "I really enjoyed our chat," he said to Cookie, "but I've got to get going. Olivia's back." He looked around at the assembled customers, seated in all the available chairs. "I think you have a hit here. Lily Rock needed a good bakery and a place to hang out."

Cookie stood, offering his hand to Michael. "I want to talk more about your coffee blends. Maybe we can get something going, you know, as a part-time deal while you're figuring out your blends."

"I also have some ideas about homemade dog bones if you're interested," Michael said.

Cookie laughed. "Why not? Sounds like a plan."

Michael moved closer to Olivia, a smile on his face. "Glad you got here. I was getting a bit restless. How about we head back home? I need to make a few phone calls before lunch."

They walked through the bakery toward Main Street. The inside area was also filled with people sipping coffee and sampling baked goods. Raleigh was nowhere to be seen.

Olivia took Michael's elbow on the way out the door. "Do you know anything about Parkinson's disease?" she asked. "Raleigh was so sensitive on the subject and I couldn't help but feel curious..."

CHAPTER SIX

The next morning Olivia considered her options. *I can look for another Lily Rock temp job or I can make a batch of Michael's favorite lemon muffins.*

As she reached for the mixing bowl, she heard footsteps from the doorway. "What do I see here? A woman baking fresh muffins for breakfast?" Michael looked over her shoulder with interest.

Olivia inhaled his fresh shower smell, a combination of soap and woodsy aftershave. "Hey you," she said, concentrating on the bowl in front of her. After several stirs, she watched him out of the corner of her eye as he poured water into the coffee reservoir.

She stepped forward to kiss his cheek. "I am baking lemon poppy seed muffins for our breakfast," she said, pulling the baking tin from the shelf.

"And I will make an appropriate blend of coffee. A dark roast with a touch of orange flavor. How does that sound?"

"Perfect."

After pouring batter into the individual cups, Olivia set the timer and rinsed the bowl in the sink. While the coffee brewed Michael sat at the kitchen table looking at his cell phone. When she sat down, he clicked his phone off and placed it on the table. "I'm a man on a mission," he explained to Olivia.

She watched him go to the counter and return with the coffeepot and two mugs. As he poured he explained further. "Cookie wants me to stop by after the morning rush at the bakery." He placed a mug in front of her. Then he sat down and took a sip of his own coffee. "Nice with the orange. Do you like?"

"I do like this blend, especially for the early days of spring. Makes me look forward to warmer weather, smelling the orange flavoring." She smiled at him, patted his hand, then stood, looking toward the oven. "I think we're ready. One muffin or two?"

Olivia placed the muffins on a cooling rack while she rinsed the baking tin in the sink. Then she placed three muffins on an empty plate and took them to the table. "You might need this," she told him, handing him a calico cloth napkin. He unfolded it with a flourish and tucked it under the collar of his T-shirt.

"Thank you, ma'am," he said, choosing a muffin. "Cookie's bakes are good, but yours are the best." He took a bite. "Like these poppy seeds for instance; good choice with the lemon."

Olivia sat down at the table, watching Michael select his second muffin.

"I love a man who appreciates my cooking," she admitted.

"That's not all I appreciate about you," he said, his left eyebrow lifting.

"Good to know." She ducked her head, feeling her cheeks grow warm.

Once Michael finished eating, he took the napkin out from under his chin to dab at his lips. "So Cookie wants to meet with me after breakfast to talk about our new venture; coffee and cupcakes or some such notion. He thinks muffins are just cupcakes that you eat earlier in the day and that my coffee blends would bring in business."

Olivia nodded. "That may be a winning combination. I didn't realize you were looking for a new business venture. I thought you had an architectural project you'd been considering."

"You might have seen plans out on the table, but I'm not ready to move forward with that idea yet. It's in the conceptual stage." The tone of his voice sounded guarded.

She reached for his empty plate. "I think I'm going to see Meadow at the library today while you're talking to Cookie." She looked over at him as he scrolled on his phone. "Maybe I'll drive myself. If she has any ideas about job openings I'll follow up."

He put his phone down again. "I've got a busy day, why don't we catch up later? We haven't been to the pub in a while."

"Sure, sounds good."

"See you tonight for sure."

When she turned from the sink he'd already gone.

Once Olivia was in her car, her thoughts wandered. *Something feels odd about Robert's illness. According to his daughter-in-law, he was very near the end and not speaking. According to Raleigh and Echo, Robert spoke to them on the day he passed away. Raleigh seems evasive to me, like a person who's not telling the entire truth. I think Sasha took Mr. Ulrich's phone along with the thyme twig and cookie.*

I'm stopping in to talk to Meadow at the library. She'll know if there are any Lily Rock jobs that I can look into. Maybe she'll point me to a book about Parkinson's...

Olivia slowed her car down around the next curve, then

accelerated. She caught a quick glimpse of Lily Rock, the impressive namesake shining above the town. Then she reminded herself to focus on her driving. *Look out for the next curve.* By the time she navigated the remaining windy road, she drove under the Welcome to Lily Rock sign, a guide for tourists into the heart of the town.

She found a parking spot directly in front of the library and spotted Meadow's head through the window. She got out of the car, locking it behind her.

Olivia stood on the boardwalk, glancing to the right toward the constabulary. *I've been avoiding Janis since she fired me. I suppose that was her prerogative, but I still don't understand. I solved the murder for her and that was the thanks I got.*

Olivia pushed open the library door. As soon as she walked in a familiar voice called, "Hello, dear, good to see you this morning." Meadow McCloud stood behind the counter, a pair of glasses perched on the end of her nose.

"Sage was up and out early this morning," Olivia explained before Meadow could ask. She made it a point to say something about her sister whenever she ran into Meadow.

"That's my Sage, all ready to take on the world," Meadow answered, holding a book under the scanning machine. "I did hear that you and Michael found another dead body this weekend."

"We didn't actually find the body. We were asked to help by the owner of Mother Earth. She found the body."

"Of course, dear, if that's how you want to tell the story. But we all know that you and dead bodies seem to go together like milk and cookies."

Olivia nodded.

"How are things going with you and Michael?"

"We're hanging out a lot." *I don't want her in my business with Michael.*

She stood to the side, watching Meadow at work. *Why did her comment about Michael trigger me?* Then her mind rolled back to the scene in the early days, when she and her emotionally abusive boyfriend first got together.

"I'm the only thing you need," Don had said, nuzzling her ear. "Forget your music. Stay with me and be my roadie."

At first she'd resisted, playing her small gigs on the side, in between his more important concerts. Then she'd made an inadvertent error. It started with a last-minute decision to go with a friend out to dinner. Once Don found out he was furious.

"I don't want you hanging out with other people," he screamed.

She ignored his tantrum and went out anyway.

That night when she came home she found him already in bed. "I missed you," he said, turning his back on her.

The next day he was all smiles. But she couldn't let go of the sense of rejection. So after that first time she gave up. Her girlfriends eventually stopped calling. For years she'd arranged her life to keep the peace, hovering in Don's shadow. She'd quit working and let her music go. After eight years she didn't know herself any longer.

Because I gave in to him that first time...

Olivia took a deep breath. She stepped in front of the library counter to talk to Meadow. "I wondered if you've heard of any part-time temp jobs in town. I'm kind of out of work at the moment."

Meadow closed the book she'd scanned and placed it on the metal cart. "I heard that Hello Age is looking for a part-time administrative assistant. You don't have to have any nursing experience."

"Interesting, I'll think about it," Olivia said. "I met a guy named Flex, the Hello Age bus driver, just this weekend. Plus Mr. Ulrich, the man who passed away, lived at Hello Age. Which brings up another topic."

"Hold on to that thought." Meadow took a piece of paper and began to write. She handed it to Olivia. "Hello Age is a bit off the highway. Here are directions."

Since GPS it must be hard to give up the role of direction giver.

"Thanks." Olivia read the paper quickly and then shoved it into her front pocket. "And my other question is do you know anything about Parkinson's disease? I mean how long people live after diagnosis and what happens as they decline?"

Meadow stopped shuffling books to consider Olivia's question. Her brow wrinkled as she assumed the role of research librarian. "In the old days, I'd have referred you to Doc. But now I think everyone gets most of their medical information on the internet. Why don't you go right over there and google your question?" Meadow pointed to a row of computers across the room.

Olivia nodded. "I'll do some research and then go check out that Hello Age job. Maybe I'll drive by and introduce myself. Talk to you later."

She walked past overstuffed chairs and long tables, sitting down at the first available computer. Reaching into her purse, she pulled out a small notebook and a sharpened pencil.

After an hour of staring intently at the computer screen, Olivia felt a slight headache starting at her right temple. *I'd better knock it off and go outside for some air.*

She closed the notebook. Walking past the front desk, Olivia waved at Meadow before exiting the library onto the boardwalk.

"Well look who's here," said a familiar voice. "If it isn't the girl detective right in the flesh. How are things going?" Janis Jets stood in front of the library on the boardwalk, wearing her police officer uniform: tan slacks, a white-collared shirt, and a navy blazer.

"Hey, Janis, it's been some time. How are things with you?" Olivia forced herself to smile.

Jets looked her up and down. "Maybe not as good as they are with you. All rested and sparky in your cowboy boots and fresh smile. You and Mike still dating or is there trouble in paradise?"

"Yep, still dating. How about you and Cookie?"

Jets grinned. "Couldn't be better. He's good company and very independent, which I like. I have a job to do and I don't need a man hanging around all the time."

"Of course," said Olivia. "We women have lives."

"I don't have to tell you, as my former assistant, how busy we are at the Lily Rock constabulary. In fact, why don't you come in and meet my new permanent assistant? He's good at the job and minds his own business."

"I'm sure he is. Can't say I miss the constabulary. The downtime felt endless once I reorganized your filing and everything."

"And I can't say I miss you hanging around getting into my business, so we're even," said Jets, her jaw tightening. "I do, however, miss the occasional chitchat at the diner. Are you up for lunch?"

Olivia stopped to think. "I would love to catch up with you over a burger, but how about another time? I want to ask about a temp job before everyone scatters for their lunch break."

Janis's eyes narrowed. "And where would that be, pray tell? Cookie says you've been hanging out at Mother Earth. Is she hiring? Are you getting to know what's her name, his ex?"

Olivia felt the hair on her neck raise. "You worried about that relationship?"

"I'm not one bit worried about my man. What concerns me is that his ex is a lunatic and that she chose to move her new business right next door to his."

Olivia nodded. "I'm not looking for a job at Mother Earth. I'm looking into the temp job at Hello Age. Meadow just told me they're hiring. I thought I'd go look at the place to get a feel for it before applying."

Janis leaned closer. "Don't you get any ideas about the dead guy and try to stir up trouble, Nancy Drew. Robert Bartholomew Ulrich Sr. died peacefully with a cookie in his hand, surrounded by his favorite herbs in a garden. Even I can't make a murder out of that one, especially since he suffered from Parkinson's."

"How did you know all of that?" asked Olivia. "About the death and everything..."

"Even if no one suspects foul play, I hear about people dying in Lily Rock. Not just people, I hear if someone's cat takes a turn for the worse or gets a hair ball. It's just part of the job."

Olivia chuckled. "I suppose that's part of your adjunct duty, hearing everyone's troubles even if they don't require police attention. Maybe we can have lunch later this week?"

Janis nodded. "Sounds good. Text me. See you later." She spun around, taking purposeful steps down the boardwalk.

Olivia headed toward her car. To her delight Mayor Maguire stood by the passenger side. He wagged his tail as she came closer.

"Have you been waiting long?" asked Olivia, bending to scratch behind his ears. She unlocked the door and opened it for the labradoodle to jump into the passenger seat. Olivia made her way around the car to sit behind the wheel.

Mayor Maguire faced forward, his tongue hanging out the side of his mouth.

"I'm going to Hello Age," she told him.

The mayor looked straight ahead.

She leaned over, reaching in front of the mayor to lower the passenger side window. He immediately stuck his head outside.

Settling back, she shoved her key into the ignition. Olivia looked over her right and left shoulder before backing up.

"Bork," the dog commented.

"Oh, look at the cute doggie." A woman from the board-walk pointed at Mayor Maguire.

"You're still the best politician ever," Olivia commented, shifting out of reverse. "You greet all constituents with the same enthusiasm."

CHAPTER SEVEN

Mayor Maguire drew his head back into the car. Adjusting his body to fit against the seat, he lifted his chin to look straight ahead.

"Too much air up your nose?" asked Olivia, glancing over at the dog.

He looked at her and shook his head. With one twist he curled up on the seat, his nose tucked into his back haunch.

"So you're sleepy then." She turned away to focus on her driving. After her first precarious days in Lily Rock, she had adjusted to the mountain terrain. She enjoyed driving the curvy roads, learning to gently brake into the curves and accelerate out of them.

The rhythm had become automatic over the past months. As she maneuvered the steering wheel, keeping her foot ready, she remembered the directions Meadow had written for her.

Olivia drove past the Webster place just as Meadow had instructed. Alerted by Meadow's careful directions, the sign and driveway for Hello Age was plainly visible. This made her left turn easy. She slowed the car on the driveway as

Mayor Maguire leaped up, thrusting his head out the open window once again.

"Bork, bork," he called.

"You saw those squirrels, didn't you, buddy? Nothing gets past you." Two squirrels sat on a tree limb, tails twitching as Olivia drove slowly past. The mayor growled, squeezing himself through the space between the two seats, where he barked furiously out the back car window.

"That's enough. We're here," Olivia scolded him, pulling her car into the first space behind the Hello Age main building. She slid out of her seat, slamming the door behind her. On her way around the car to release the dog, she remembered his open window.

While Mayor Maguire pawed from the back seat, she opened the passenger side door enough to crank the passenger window closed. Only then did she let an impatient Mayor Maguire out of the back door, not bothering to lock the car. *It's a retirement community. No one wants to steal my old Ford anyway.*

The dog bounded away at breakneck speed. She followed his tail with her eyes as he ran toward an old barn at the far end of the lot. "M&M," she called out to him. The dog ignored her, racing past the old barn into the woods. Olivia shrugged. *Okay then, see you later.*

Olivia reversed directions, walking toward the main building. She stopped a few feet away to look at the Hello Age structure from the outside. Contractors had done a good job of keeping true to the original farmhouse structure. Fresh paint and new siding made the building look invitingly familiar and very tidy. When Olivia stepped onto the porch, she felt welcomed.

Straight ahead the front door had been widened to accommodate wheelchairs, though the double doors were closed.

Half glass and half wood, Olivia could see inside to a spacious entry area.

I wonder if they'll open the door for me since I didn't call ahead?

She walked closer, past two rocking chairs and a large potted fern. On the side of the pot a sticker had been attached: *Attended by Mother Earth. For plant care and advice inquire within.*

Mother Earth again. I guess Echo makes plant house calls as a part of her new business.

Olivia was unsure if she should knock on one of the doors or try the handle. In the end she decided to try the handle, which easily moved under her grasp. Once inside, the door closed behind her.

"May I help you?" came a voice from behind a long counter. A woman, wearing a pink oversized T-shirt, smiled in a friendly manner. The words Hello Age had been embroidered over the left-hand pocket. Her name badge, Elsie Meyer, Resident, had been pinned over part of the embroidery. She rested her hands on the counter. All of her short nails had been carefully manicured with a shade of pink that matched her shirt.

Olivia stepped closer. "I'm Olivia Greer. I'm here to inquire about the part-time temp job."

"Has it been advertised?" asked the woman, her smile faltering.

"Not exactly. I heard about the job from Meadow McCloud. She's the one who brings Mayor Maguire over to visit with the residents. She's also the Lily Rock librarian. She said I might be a good fit."

The smile returned to the woman's face. "I see. Of course. I'll let Agnes know. Why don't you sit over there in the living room and I'll get back to you."

Olivia looked to where the woman pointed. Two over-stuffed sofas had been placed facing each other with an enormous coffee table in between. Magazines and brochures lined the tabletop, spread as if to attract attention. She walked toward the sofas, picking the magazine closest to the entrance to read before she sat down.

With one leg crossed over the other, Olivia waited. Doubts niggled at her, as she second-guessed her last-minute decision to inquire about a job. *I could have worn a dress. Maybe I don't look professional enough.*

After a few minutes the entrance door swung open, revealing Mayor Maguire and Flex Million. They walked together, the dog breaking away as soon as he saw Olivia.

"Hey M&M," she said softly, letting her arm drop to her side. He nuzzled her fingers, and she lifted her hand to scratch under his chin.

The dog sniffed her boots. He looked back over his shoulder at Flex before he lay down on the floor, his head resting on his paws.

Looking very tan, Flex had rolled up his sleeves to show bulging muscles. He lifted his sunglasses to scan the room, and his eyes lit up when he saw Olivia. Mayor Maguire made a low growl in the back of his throat as Flex came closer.

"Calm down, big boy," Flex said in a no-nonsense voice. He offered a hand for the mayor to sniff. Maguire refused but he did stop growling. Rising up on his haunches, he moved over to stand between Olivia and Flex.

She reached to pat the dog's head. "Don't worry, M&M, he's a friend."

Maguire stayed in place, staring straight at the man in front of him.

"I thought we were friends," Flex said to the dog.

Maguire growled.

Flex turned his gaze toward Olivia as if looking for sympathy. "The mutt has been hanging out around here all week."

"Maguire is the Lily Rock mayor and pretty much chooses where he goes and who he befriends. Maybe today it's my turn..."

"Okay." Flex nodded. "Maybe I'll bring him a piece of meat or something. No dog turns his back on steak."

"I wasn't sure you'd remember me," Olivia said. She took in his appearance. Flex Million wore a green Hello Age T-shirt identical in style to the one worn by the resident behind the reception desk. The Hello Age name tag included his name and title: Flex Million, Staff.

"I wouldn't forget you or your boyfriend," Flex said. "Plus I saw an unfamiliar car in the back lot. Your Ford Focus, right?" He grinned. "I may forget a face, but now that I know your car, I'll never forget what you drive."

"Yes, that's my car," she said. "Monday was such a difficult day. How did the residents react as you drove them home?"

"The residents took it pretty hard. Most of them liked Robert. But the one they really felt sorry for was his daughter-in-law. Sasha spent a lot of time with the old man. She'd speak to all the residents when she was here. She visited nearly every day.

"The staff liked to use Sasha Ulrich as an example. She has the reputation of a family member who really cares. So we not only lose Mr. Ulrich but his family. That's how it goes at Hello Age."

"I saw Mrs. Ulrich briefly at Mother Earth. I do know the deceased's grandson though."

"The kid, I know him," muttered Flex. "Kind of a problem, if you get my drift."

When he didn't elaborate, Olivia ignored his opinion.

Flex kept talking. "The only one I haven't met is old man

Ulrich's son. He's never been by to visit so far as I know. But we'll see everyone at the funeral to say goodbye. They're holding it right here at Hello Age in our chapel across the way. I bet there will be a big crowd."

"When is the service being held?" asked Olivia.

Flex scratched behind his ear. Instead of answering he looked intently at Olivia. His eyes shifted to look at her chest.

I hope he's not trying to flirt with me.

Olivia glared at him.

To his credit Flex grinned, holding up his hands in surrender.

Olivia stood, making herself feel less vulnerable. She avoided Flex's gaze. Mayor Maguire moved aside. He waited and then stood next to her.

"I'm here to inquire about a job," Olivia said, looking toward the reception desk.

"You want to work here?" Flex moistened his lower lip with the tip of his tongue. "The manager can be found in the dining room." He pointed. "She sets up a special spread for new families while she sells them on the Hello Age lifestyle."

"I'm supposed to wait for her," Olivia said.

He kept talking. "While you wait, I can introduce you to Mrs. Ulrich again. She's down the hall cleaning out Robert's room. After a death, families have forty-eight hours to box everything up to make way for the cleaners and then the next resident." Then he added, "I'm a big help around here for lots of things."

"It's a difficult time, right after a loved one dies. There are lots of decisions to be made. Coping with a death and then having to go through personal belongings and box them up so quickly... I don't envy them that process."

"Sounds like you have some experience," Flex said.

Olivia had no intention of mentioning her recent losses.

Then Flex added, "This is a business, you know. Assuming you become one of the staff, you'll see that all the sentimentality wears off. People come and go. Our job is to make the process as smooth as possible. Now the Ulrich family, they've hired me to help with the packing and moving. I'm handy that way."

"So you can do that? Work for individual families?"

Flex came closer to Olivia. He leaned in close enough so that she felt his breath on her face. "Like I said before, I'm available for pretty near anything you want."

Olivia spoke firmly. "Good to know. See you later."

As she turned away from him, a woman hurried around the corner from the dining room, calling out, "Mr. Million, may I have a word?"

"Hi, Sasha," he responded. "So happy to see you. You've already met Olivia, right?" Flex pointed at Olivia.

Sasha Ulrich turned toward Olivia, a half-smile on her lips.

Olivia looked at her closely. Sasha's face showed very few lines or wrinkles, her eyes wide and very green. Dressed in a pair of slim-fitting black slacks and a white fitted shirt, Sasha looked well preserved and like a person who took good care of herself.

In a quick glance, Olivia understood.

Botox. I bet she's had a lot of injections and filler treatments. Plus her lips look unnaturally full and there are no wrinkles on her forehead. The rest of her body looks fit. Maybe she's around sixty, but her face seems immobile, more like someone twenty years younger.

Extending her hand, Sasha said, "Hello. A friend of Flex?" She looked over at the man who watched. Olivia felt the hair rise on her neck.

"I'm Olivia Greer. I was there when they found your

father-in-law in the garden, and I'm very sorry for your loss. So much activity at the time, you may not remember me."

Sasha dropped her hand. "So you're not a friend of Flex's. I don't have time for pleasantries, if you'll excuse me." With a thrust of her shoulder, she turned away from Olivia, speaking to Flex again.

"I need help with the boxes that we talked about earlier. Bring them to Robert's room as soon as possible." She spun around again, heading back to the hallway. Her icy tone stuck in Olivia's head.

"Got my marching orders," Flex said dryly. "Maybe I'll see you at the funeral. It will be on Sunday, not sure what time exactly. You can call the front desk for details."

Olivia watched him leave through the entrance doors. Mayor Maguire did not follow, choosing to stay by her side.

CHAPTER EIGHT

"Young woman?" came a voice from the reception desk. Elsie gestured with her index finger for Olivia to come closer.

Olivia walked closer as Mayor Maguire peeled off, heading toward the outside exit.

Elsie explained, "I spoke to our manager and she told me to have you fill out a job application before you leave. She'll be in touch in a day or two." She slid a paper across the desk along with a pen.

Slightly faded with turned up corners, the form looked as if it had seen better days. "May I take this with me and bring it back later?" Olivia asked.

"It would be best to fill it out now. I'm not supposed to let these forms go all willy-nilly into the world—that's what Mrs. Curry, our manager, said."

"Okay then, I'll sit over there and get it done. Thanks." She walked back to the sofa, grabbing a thick magazine from the coffee table to use as a lap desk.

After Olivia filled out the first page, she was interrupted by a loud bark.

Olivia stood up and walked across the room. Looking

toward the parking lot through the back window in the lobby, she spotted M&M. As his barking grew more insistent, she shoved the application into her purse.

Mayor Maguire now lifted his paws on the passenger side window of her Ford. He tapped the window with one paw, his nose planted on the glass, tail wagging furiously.

"Bork, bork, bork!"

Olivia hurried past the reception desk through the front entrance. Once outside she sprinted around the corner of the building toward the sound of the barking dog. The closer she came, the more the mayor barked. She approached him, watching as he pawed incessantly at the window. A foot away from the dog she stopped to catch her breath.

"What's going on, M&M?" she hollered loudly to be heard over his barking.

He took a quick moment to look over his shoulder, then turned around to push his nose against the glass again. One bark, then two, then a cacophony of sound expressing his annoyance.

He began to growl in the back of his throat, wet nose making smears on the glass. *Has he found something in my car?* She inched closer, coming up alongside the dog. Reaching out, she touched his head. He stopped barking for a minute but kept staring in the window.

Olivia gasped. A hole the size of a basketball had been dug in her front upholstery. She inspected the back seat, hearing a loud chatter coming from inside. She put her hands on either side of her face to see past the window glare.

Stuffing scattered over the back seat, flung from more holes in the upholstery. From the floor she saw two beady eyes glowing, little front paws scratching. The bushy tail twitched as the animal crawled up the seat, diving into a hole. She took a deep breath. *A squirrel is trapped in my car.*

M&M's incessant barking began again. Olivia reached for the mayor's collar, giving it a tug. "I've got this," she told him, as she lowered him onto all four paws.

Mayor Maguire spun in a circle, forcing Olivia to drop her hold. He jumped up on the car again, balancing on his back legs and scratching at the window with his paws.

"Stop," she told him in a firm voice. "I've got this. Sit down."

This time Maguire sat on command. His nose quivered, his body trembled, as if aching to disobey.

I have to get that squirrel out of the car, but I can't do that as long as M&M is here. She took hold of his collar again, walking him away from the car. She gave a quick command. "Sit."

To her relief he sat down immediately.

"What's going on?" came a familiar voice. Flex Million stood in front of the mayor.

The dog growled.

Flex took two steps backward. He made a circle around Mayor Maguire to walk closer to Olivia's car. "You have a problem here. Yep, it's a squirrel, a vicious one too."

"It's tearing up my upholstery." Olivia looked at the dog. "Stay," she reminded him.

Flex turned to face her. "I've seen this before, an animal being trapped in a car. Causes lots of damage. Sometimes they get under the hood and start eating away at the wiring. Very expensive to repair."

"Once I settle Mayor Maguire I can call Brad at the Lily Rock garage."

"Oh, you don't have to do that. If you hold the wild beast," he pointed to Mayor Maguire with a smirk, "I can take care of this for you at no charge. I'll just open the door and let the critter out. Then I'll have a look underneath to see what's going on with the rest of the vehicle."

"I doubt if he's had time to chew into the undercarriage," said Olivia, feeling uncomfortable with his offer of help. *Does he like exaggerating to make a point?*

Olivia made a hand gesture toward Mayor Maguire. "Lie down," she told him.

He obediently lowered his body to the pavement but huffed his frustration.

Flex walked away from Olivia toward the other side of the car. She heard the door pop open. He waited and then opened the back door a bit wider. At first nothing happened.

Then a loud screech, followed by incessant chattering sounds.

The mayor stood back up on all fours.

"Sit," she told him. She walked closer to grab his collar, her fingers gripping the leather.

He sat back down.

Hand still on his collar, she caught sight of a squirrel scampering over the blacktop toward the woods.

With a swift move Mayor Maguire wrenched out of her grasp, racing after the squirrel. Olivia looked at the braided leather collar in her hand. Between his lunging and her tugging, the worn collar broke and the mayor escaped. *I guess I've been outdone by a squirrel.*

"Let him go. I can take care of this from here," Flex hollered.

"Not like I have a choice," she muttered, shoving the collar into her purse.

"You could come back inside and have a warm drink while I check your car for more damage. Won't take long. Give me your keys."

She reached inside of her purse. *What else can I do? He*

showed up and I need help. Olivia palmed her car keys, still reluctant to hand them over. She looked at Flex, who held out his hand. "You've got some scratches on your arm," she observed. Blood oozed from the skin on his right forearm. "I didn't see the squirrel do that."

"It's nothin'. The hazard of working in the old barn. Lots of places to get scratched on old boards and nails. Just give me the keys."

"I have to go. If the car starts I'll have Michael look when I get home." She smiled to ease her rejection.

As he lowered his arm, Olivia opened the driver's side door and slipped behind the wheel. The engine turned over on the first try. She slammed the door as Flex stood glaring at her. Before she could pull out, he walked to her side of the car.

She rolled down her window. "What I don't understand is how did that squirrel even get into my car? I made sure to shut all the windows."

A blank look came over his face. He shook his head. "That's really weird. Maybe the squirrel crawled up from underneath, like I said before—"

She cut off his explanation. "Gotta go. Thanks for your help." She rolled her window back up. After a quick glance into her rearview mirror, she pulled out of the parking space.

On her drive toward the main highway, she looked toward the woods. No sign of Mayor Maguire. As she accelerated onto the main road, she heard her phone ping. Keeping her eyes on the road, she felt around in her purse. Her fingers found the phone. Holding it up, she glanced quickly at the screen. Michael had sent a text.

Dropping the phone back in her purse, she accelerated out of a curve. Then she pulled over and safely parked her car to read the text.

Can't make it for dinner. Will be late tonight. See you tomorrow. xo

Olivia felt her chest tighten. *Maybe he's backing away.*

Her mind began to argue. *We've eaten dinner together every night for weeks. He's a grown man with things to do. Just because you've been inseparable, it doesn't mean he's cooling off. He probably needs some space to hang out at his own place.*

Olivia dropped her phone back on the passenger seat. She twisted the key in the ignition and the engine turned over. Back on the main road, she rolled down the window, the air blowing past her cheeks and lifting the hair on her neck.

I don't have a job and I have a boyfriend who wants space.

Her open hands bounced against the steering wheel in frustration.

I don't want to be this person, dependent on someone else to the point I lose who I am. I did the same thing with Don and look how that came out.

Olivia felt her chest tighten. *I'm overreacting. Stop it, Olivia. You need to focus on your independence. Anything can happen at any time. Just remember that.*

By the time she drove into her own driveway she felt better. *Maybe I'm just imagining that he's pulling away. I need something else to think about. I'll fill out that job application and see what happens.*

Olivia set the brake and then took a moment to look at the damage in the back seat. *Maybe Brad will have an idea about how to repair the fabric on these ancient seats. Or I could get a new car or maybe a truck. I can afford the down payment on a new vehicle. A new job would help with monthly payments.*

Her thoughts kept rambling. *I wonder how that squirrel got into my car in the first place? I remember closing the windows. I didn't lock the doors...*

Her cell phone rang. She reached into her purse. "Hello," she said to the unknown caller.

"Olivia?"

"Yes, who is this, please?"

"It's Raleigh. Remember we just talked the other day at Thyme Out?"

"Of course, hi, Raleigh. What's up?"

"I need to talk to you." Their voice quavered.

"Now?" asked Olivia.

"If that's okay, if it works for you, as soon as you can. I'm scared and I don't know who to trust."

The poor kid. Maybe I can help.

"I can come to you, or you could come to my house."

"Can I come to your house? I'm off of work and it would be more private."

"Of course you can. I'll text you the address and see you in a few minutes. And Raleigh? Don't worry, whatever is the matter, we'll work it out. Promise."

Raleigh ended the conversation with a click.

Olivia immediately texted her address. After pressing Send she went into the house and turned off the alarm. She left the front door ajar in case she didn't hear Raleigh arrive.

Crossing the great room, she pressed the button to open the wall of glass. She arranged two chairs facing each other, a small table in between.

Then she walked back inside to check the contents of the refrigerator. *Some cheese and crackers, I see celery and carrots. That should keep Raleigh happy. Do I offer an afternoon beer? Lots of kids their age drink beer in Lily Rock. Too bad Michael isn't here. He'd know how to handle Raleigh.*

She looked out the window over her sink toward Michael's house.

I bet we could rent that place to someone since we're

*together here most of the time anyway. Maybe I'll suggest that
to Michael. There's plenty of room. Unless he needs it so he can
have some space from me...*

The doorbell rang.

"Come in," she called out. Hurrying toward the front door,
Olivia called out again, "It's okay, Raleigh. Come on in."

The door opened the rest of the way. Raleigh stood on the
threshold, mouth hanging open. "Wow, I had no idea you lived
in such a cool place." They looked past Olivia to the interior of
the great room. "All those trees on the inside and that glass
wall. This is amazing."

"My boyfriend designed and built the house," Olivia said,
a sense of pride coming over her. "Of course, he wasn't my
boyfriend then but now we both live here."

Raleigh continued to look up and down, eyes widening.
"That's Michael, right? The one who's been hanging out with
Cookie this week?"

"That's him." Olivia heard the respect in Raleigh's voice.
Their red-rimmed eyes suggested recent crying.

Her heart twisted. "Would you like a drink, some
sparkling water or something?"

"Sure. Can I help out in the kitchen?"

"Don't worry about it, I've got this. Meet me outside. Have
a seat and look at Lily Rock and just breathe, that always
helps me when I'm feeling afraid or anxious."

Raleigh hung their head. "I guess I'm not hiding my feelings very well."

Olivia smiled compassionately. "Go ahead. I'll be there in
a minute."

She watched as Raleigh walked toward the deck outdoors.
Poor thing. I hope I can help.

CHAPTER NINE

When Olivia returned, she held snacks and two brimming tumblers of sparkling water on a tray. She set it down on the table in front of Raleigh. "Help yourself."

Raleigh continued to stare at Lily Rock in the distance. "Granddad would have liked to sit here."

Olivia sat down in the other available chair, turning it to face the same direction as Raleigh. "It sounds like you were pretty close to your granddad," she said, reaching for a glass of water. She handed it to Raleigh, who took it with a grateful smile. They drank all the liquid in a few short gulps.

"He was always on my side," Raleigh said. "Even when I changed my pronouns, he never blinked. Just picked up and ran with my decision, no questions asked. He made my dad pay attention. Granddad was the only one who could tell my father what to do."

"I don't think I met your dad or stepmom that parent weekend at the music academy," Olivia commented. She gestured to the empty glass. "Do you want a refill?"

"No thanks. They didn't come to parent weekend.

They've never cared about what I do, so long as I stay out of their way."

"How about your mom?"

"She died when I was five years old. Leukemia. I don't remember her much. Then dad married Sasha when I was in middle school. I tried to like her..."

"Just having to try makes me think it was difficult for you."

They put the glass back on the tray as the ice cubes clinked against each other. Then they reached for a carrot.

Olivia selected a piece of cheese and a cracker. She waited for Raleigh to speak again. *They sounded so urgent on the phone. I wonder what's going on?*

After munching on a carrot, Raleigh spoke again. "My stepmother came by Thyme Out this afternoon. She was all pissed off about Granddad and his will. I guess she couldn't find it when she was cleaning out all of his stuff."

"I imagine there's an electronic copy somewhere with his lawyer or estate planner," commented Olivia. "I just went through a similar situation with my friend Marla. She passed a couple of years ago and left me her estate. That's how I ended up with this beautiful house."

"Oh," Raleigh said with a grin. "I didn't think you made enough money for this place with your earnings from the band."

Olivia laughed. "You got that right. Sweet Four O'Clock will not be my retirement plan, at least as of now. So do you know where your granddad kept his will?"

"I have no idea." Raleigh's face clouded over. "But that didn't satisfy old Sasha. She's convinced I'm up to something. No matter what I do, she's suspicious."

"Why would she think that?"

"Simple. I was Granddad's favorite. Everyone knew that."

"Everyone being?"

"My dad and stepmother. I don't have siblings."

"Did you talk to your granddad about his will when he was alive?"

"Oh yeah. All the time. He loved telling me about his money and all of his accounts and the property he owned—several lots here in Lily Rock. He loved it here. I suppose that's why he ended up at Hello Age. Lily Rock brought back memories of his childhood. I think his godparents lived on Thomas Mountain."

"But no will?" Olivia asked quietly.

"He was going to tell me all that stuff—you know, how to deal with his estate—when I turned twenty-one. And he would have—"

Olivia looked at him sharply. "You were a high school senior only last fall. Most seniors are seventeen, so it would be a few years until you inherited the money."

"I was older than everyone else at school. Expelled from a few prep schools on the East Coast, which made dropping out of the Lily Rock Music Academy easier. I'd lost a lot of time. I'll be twenty-one soon, next December."

"But the academy let you in anyway? I'm surprised."

"It's my voice. Good a cappella tenors aren't that easy to find."

Olivia reached for a carrot, which she dipped into hummus. "Have some more to eat," she told Raleigh. "And tell me more about the missing will."

As they reached for another carrot, Olivia considered. *Raleigh's grandad must have been pretty savvy to accumulate so much wealth. Not the kind of guy to die without a will in place, especially with his Parkinson's diagnosis. He apparently loved his grandson enough to include Raleigh in his plans.*

Interrupting her thoughts, Raleigh said, "Even though no one can find it, I saw the will, the most recent one. Some

69

people witnessed it and it had an official stamp at the bottom. But the will thing, that's not even the really weird part."

Olivia stared at him. "Okay, I give up, what's the really weird part?"

"Sasha thought I was the last to see Granddad before he died. She accused me of killing him to get his money. She said I used cookies to make him choke."

Olivia's eyes grew wide. "I thought you told me your last communication with him was on the phone."

Raleigh ducked their head. "I actually saw him right before he passed away. I took him a cookie from the bakery. Sasha dropped by to tell me he was at Mother Earth. She figured I'd want to see him."

"But why would she think you had anything to do with his death?"

Raleigh shook their head. "I would never hurt my grand-dad, and she gives me the creeps." Rage rose in Raleigh's eyes. "Have you seen her face? She's a shoe-in for Mt. Rushmore, all stony like those presidents. Granddad and I would make jokes about her all the time."

"That couldn't have made your relationship with her or your dad any smoother. I'm surprised your granddad encour-aged you to make fun of her."

Raleigh recoiled, his arms folding across his gut. "You can say that, but you don't know Sasha. She's awful and my dad hasn't a clue. He just keeps going along with her—whatever she wants, Dad gives in. When he's had enough, he plays golf just to get away from her."

Olivia felt restless. She stood, walking toward the deck railing to look into the woods. Composing her thoughts, she turned around. "I'm sorry. You're right, I don't know Sasha. Sometimes making fun of people behind their backs is the only way to cope, especially when the person is unkind."

Raleigh nodded. "Sasha's always criticizing me. She's told me that I embarrass her so many times. She hates the way I dress and the way people look at me. That's why I called you today. Sasha wants me to leave Lily Rock and move away. I'm kinda freaked out and I don't know what to do."

I get it now.

Olivia returned to her chair. She placed her glass on the table.

"Now that Granddad is gone, I don't know what to do." Raleigh's shoulders slumped. Wiping tears with the back of their hand, they looked over the railing toward Lily Rock.

"Are you okay?" she asked.

"I feel better. Crying helped."

"I'm glad. I'll be right back, I'm going to get us a refill." She took Raleigh's glass, walking back into the house to give them a moment alone.

In the kitchen, Olivia reached for two more cans of sparkling water. *The stepmother wants Raleigh out of her sight. I can't believe she's that concerned about appearances. Raleigh needs someone to depend on, not someone who's embarrassed because they're different.*

When Olivia returned with the two glasses, she handed Raleigh theirs.

"Tell me more about Sasha and your father."

The words came with a rush of emotion. "Since they got married, we go out to dinner and she pays the bill. She sends me an allowance every month."

Olivia interjected, "You're twenty years old. Why does she send you any money at all?"

Raleigh looked puzzled. "Maybe because my job doesn't pay much, and she doesn't want to look bad to everyone else? I really don't know.

"Hello Age thinks she's perfect. All of Granddad's needs

71

were cycled through her. My dad never even visited Hello Age so far as I know. I barely get to talk to him alone. When Dad calls me, Sasha's always in the room on speakerphone. I can't even call him directly anymore. I mean, Dad and I have never been close, but now she's the only way I can get to him. I have to go through her."

Raleigh's fist clenched, their face contorted with anger.

"You said you spoke to your grandfather that last day?"

"I might have been the last one to see him alive. I think he knew he was dying. He was so sick. Some days he couldn't even talk to me. We'd just sit there, you know, and smile at each other. When I brought him the cookie, I was trying to make him happy. He liked thyme. I guess I told you before. He thanked me and grabbed my hand."

"So you think you were the last one to see him alive?"

"I guess I was," sighed Raleigh. "If I'd stayed with him instead of going back to work, I could have called the paramedics sooner and maybe they would have revived him." Tears pooled in their eyes again.

"So you weren't there when he stopped breathing?"

"No. I left Mother Earth the back way. He was fine then. A half hour later I heard Sasha come through the door asking for Cookie's help."

"Why didn't you rush out when you heard the commotion?"

"I was confused. I never know when I'm wanted, so instead of being rejected again, I ran away." Raleigh shook their head.

Raleigh doesn't know when to step up and when to retreat. Maybe because they have no confidence in themselves.

Olivia sat back in her chair, taking in Raleigh's story. She felt confused, especially about Robert Ulrich's cause of death. Giving herself a moment to think, she watched a crow swoop from a nearby pine carrying a stick in its mouth. Then another larger crow landed on the railing of the deck. He let out a loud caw before taking flight. Her thoughts cleared as she watched.

"I thought your granddad died as a result of Parkinson's. Sasha said as much that day we found him in the garden. She may blame you for your granddad's death, but she'd have to prove you did it. I'm not sure a thyme cookie is evidence, unless you knew he'd choke when he tried to eat the cookie."

"That's not the case. In fact, once Thyme Out opened, I had a place to bake, so when I visited Granddad I'd bring cookies." Raleigh's voice rose with indignation. "He could eat just fine. I'd have to feed him because his hands trembled, but he swallowed small bites okay. But Sasha always convinces people. She wants me to get out of their lives. That's why she's threatening me, because I'm a big inconvenience. I've always been too much trouble for my parents. They hate it when attention comes my way with my gender identity too." Raleigh crossed their arms over their chest, looking to Olivia like a frustrated child.

"You can't give in," Olivia said firmly. "This isn't another case of acting out and then getting expelled. You have to stand up to Sasha for your granddad, even if your father cannot. But you won't be alone. I'm going to help you figure all of this out."

Raleigh's eyes widened as if hearing something unusual. "I came for advice. You seemed to know stuff, even last year with the music academy murder. Does this mean you want to help, like, do an investigation or something?"

Olivia nodded. "This isn't my first rodeo with unexpected death. You might say I've become somewhat of an expert, even if I am an amateur. But first I have to consult with the constabulary. I'll tell Officer Jets about the missing will. She may have a few ideas about how to proceed."

"The cop is your friend? I remember that now."

73

Olivia chuckled. "She kind of is and she kind of isn't my friend. But I want to speak to her first. I'd suggest that you avoid Sasha if you can. If she wants to know about the will, just stall. Tell her you're innocent and thinking about your options."

Raleigh exhaled deeply, relief showing on their face. "Okay then, I'll wait until I hear from you." They stood. "Thanks, Olivia. Is there anything, you know, that I could do for you? You've been such a great help."

"As a matter of fact, I'd like your opinion," She stood and walked toward the open glass wall. "My car got trashed by a rambunctious squirrel. I wonder if you have any suggestions about what I can use to temporarily repair the upholstery."

Raleigh smiled. "I do know how to fix that. Duct tape. Plain and simple. Do you have any? I can tape it up before I leave."

"Why didn't I think of that? I'll get the duct tape. Meet me out front."

CHAPTER TEN

The next morning Olivia awoke alone in her bed. She reached over to Michael's side, her hand measuring the meaning of his absence.

He must have a new project. That's why he's keeping to himself. Stop overthinking.

After showering and dressing she walked downstairs, hearing the echo of her footsteps. Once in the kitchen she reached for the coffeepot, wondering, *Do I make coffee for two?*

Looking out her back window, her eyes rested on Michael's small house. No wood stacked by the front and none of the windows exposed. From the outside, the cabin looked unoccupied. *But that doesn't mean he's not still asleep.*

Realizing the downward spiral of her thoughts, she pulled herself up with a bit of positive self-talk. *Don't worry, be happy,* she told herself. Opening the top of the coffeepot reservoir, she poured water to the four-cup measuring line. *If he shows up, there will be coffee. If he doesn't, I'll drink the rest.*

She looked into the great room as she waited for the coffee

to brew. *You got this, Olivia. Keep on moving.* Cell phone in hand, she texted Janis Jets.

Got a question for you for a friend. Do you have time for lunch today? Plus I want to meet your new assistant.

Before Olivia could put her phone down, she heard it ping.

See you at noon. At the diner. Stay away from my new assistant.

Did she not just tell me that she wanted me to meet the new person?

Olivia walked back to the kitchen. After pouring a full mug of coffee, she looked out the kitchen window, taking her first sip. Crocuses bloomed in the far corner of her garden. *Maybe it's time to repair the fence and start planting seeds.* With coffee mug in hand, she unlocked the back door.

Once outside, she slowly walked the path to her garden. The back of her neck tingled. She felt apprehensive remembering Marla's lifeless body. *I feel uncertain every time I walk out here. Maybe I should plow the garden under and make something new...*

Olivia moved the wood fence aside to step inside the garden. Glancing over the overgrown herb beds, she sighed. Despite the weeds, some seeds had sent up fresh sprouts. *That's probably mint. I can harvest it and make some tea when it gets warmer. Michael and I agreed to share the garden this year. I wonder if he's still up for that, or if...*

She shook her head to clear her thoughts. Setting her empty mug on the fence, she walked on the path, stopping to pull a weed, then another. Before she knew it the sun had risen high overhead.

Realizing the time, she grabbed her coffee mug, stepping back through the gate toward the house. Once inside the kitchen, Olivia poured more coffee into her mug and considered her conversation with Raleigh.

Something isn't right about Robert's passing. I can feel it in my gut. Should I ask Janis if she has any reason to believe that his death was untimely? She's most likely read the autopsy report by now. Or maybe there wasn't an autopsy... If Janis figured, like everyone else, that Robert died from Parkinson's, she may not have made a request to investigate further.

Olivia looked at her cell phone. *Still no message from Michael.* She took her mug to the sink.

By the time Olivia finished tidying up the kitchen, the clock edged closer to noon. She picked up her phone to send two texts, the first to Janis.

On my way.

The second to Michael.

Missed you this morning. I hope everything is okay.

Neither Janis nor Michael responded.

* * *

The Lily Rock diner hummed with activity. Open from 8 a.m. to 2 p.m., local people filled the dining area, ordering a big breakfast or an excellent lunch. The smell of their signature dish, garlic fries, made Olivia's mouth water. Hungry people lined the walls waiting for tables, eyeing the plates full of food served to those already seated.

Most visitors to Lily Rock ate their meals at a trendier place on the other side of the park. Residents on the hill never recommended the diner to people who asked on the street. An unspoken agreement to keep one restaurant to themselves, locals in the diner felt free to call out to each other and speak what was on their minds. Today was no exception.

"I'm over here, Nancy Drew," called the familiar voice of Janis Jets. She sat at her usual place: at the counter with one other stool available.

Olivia smiled and crossed the room, but not unnoticed.

"Hey, Olivia, how ya doin'?" asked the guy from the drugstore.

"Olivia, dear, have you seen the mayor?" Meadow shouted out to her.

Olivia shook her head at Meadow, and then turned to sit next to Janis.

"What's the special?" she asked, tapping her fingers on the menu.

"Hot chili with lots of onions and cheese, and a side of garlic fries," said Janis. "Want me to order for you?"

"Since I don't like onions and I don't like cheddar, I'd just have a boring bowl of beans and some small chunks of meat. I'm sticking with my usual," said Olivia, closing the menu.

"One veggie sandwich on sourdough," she told the waitress, who didn't bother to write it down.

"That will be one chili with extra cheese and onions for Officer Jets and the usual for you, Olivia. Got it!" The waitress smiled, stepping to the side to get the next order.

"So what's on your mind?" asked Janis Jets. "No more dead bodies, I hope. At least I haven't heard of any, unless you're hiding one under your bed or something. Wouldn't put it past you, what with your record of interfering in my investigations." Jets grinned, enjoying herself.

"I do have a question for a friend," admitted Olivia, watching a plate filled with garlic fries pass by. When she looked back, she felt Janis's eyes drilling into her soul.

"You can have some of my fries if you want," Jets said. "And you know you're not asking for a friend, but for yourself. You're just saying that."

Olivia raised her voice in indignation. "I am asking for a friend," she insisted. Then she swallowed a sip of water. "But I understand why you might be skeptical, considering our previous...investigations."

"Not *our* investigations," Jets snapped. "*My* work; I'm the cop, you're a nosy person who gets herself into trouble. Two different things."

The waitress slid Olivia's plate across the counter and then placed a bowl of steaming chili in front of Janis. "I'll bring the rest in just a sec, hon," she said with a smile.

"Don't 'hon' me, Susie Q. I'm nobody's honey," muttered Jets under her breath. She picked up a large spoon.

Olivia looked over at her. "Speaking of honey, how are you and Cookie doing? Still a thing?"

"Yep," said Janis, taking a bite.

"Anything you want to add to that? You know, some detail?" prodded Olivia.

"What are we, girlfriends?" Jets stared into her bowl of chili. "Can't you see I'm eating here."

Olivia sighed. "I just wondered if Cookie and Michael hung out last night. He had important business and didn't show up this morning."

"You two lovebirds on the outs?" asked Janis.

"I'm not sure. Maybe we are, but I don't know why. You know how I tend to overthink things," Olivia explained.

"How about this? We don't talk boyfriends until we discuss what you texted me about. The friend..." Jets scooped a pile of onions and cheddar cheese into her bowl, giving it a stir.

"I guess you were right. They're not exactly a friend, more a former student."

"Oh no, we're not talking about they/them, are we? That Tone Ranger with the pretty voice?"

"That would be Raleigh Ulrich," Olivia said defensively. "I thought you finished your gender sensitivity training and passed the test."

"I did finish and got a big pass," chuckled Janis. "You can tell me what to say, but I don't always say what you tell me. Okay then, what's Raleigh's deal? Fill me in."

By the time Olivia finished explaining Raleigh and how Sasha wanted them out of the way, Jets had finished her bowl of chili. She offered Olivia a french fry, holding up the plate in front of her nose. "Here you go. I know you want some."

Olivia took three off the plate, stuffing them into her mouth. She spoke while chewing. "I get that Sasha may be uncomfortable with Raleigh. She's into appearances and wants to maintain her standing in the community."

Janis added, "I also get that Hello Age just loves that woman, especially if she's paying top dollar. Like the Mother Teresa of old people, only she's rich and well preserved." She pushed the empty plate of fries to the side. "I'm ahead of you, Girl Sleuth. You say Sasha Ulrich is using Robert's death as a tool to get rid of the awkward Raleigh. She's even got a cookie to blame, thinking the old guy choked on the crumbs. That may sound plausible in a mystery novel, but not to me. If the kid is all aflutter because the stepmother is threatening, maybe the kid should get out of town. Time to see the real world."

"So you're siding with Sasha?"

Jets glared at her. "I'm siding with parents who give kids a good shove out of the nest. Not like Raleigh isn't old enough." Her voice softened. "I'm just saying, maybe Sasha's basement isn't big enough for her husband's almost adult kid."

Olivia inhaled, holding back her defense of Raleigh. She looked longingly at the empty plate once layered with garlic fries.

"On the other hand," Jets's eyes narrowed, "I didn't even

consider a cause of death. I mean the whole scene looked like an open and shut case. Old dead sick guy ends his time in a small garden with a cookie in his lap. What's to worry about with that one? But if the Saint Teresa of Hello Age thinks it was suspicious, then maybe I missed something. I'll talk to Raleigh."

"But she threatened them!" Olivia said indignantly.

"They said, she said," commented Jets, "and I've never said that phrase ever before. Interesting, those pronouns."

"Raleigh is just months away from turning twenty-one," Olivia added, "not really a kid anymore."

"That old, huh? I'm surprised." Jets shook her head. "I double down on my original idea. The kid needs to grow up, tuck their sensitive teeny tiny feelings under their skirt, and get on with life's challenges, like earning a living."

Olivia sighed. "I'm not saying you're wrong."

"That would be a first," Jets said. "Are we done here?"

Olivia reached over to pick up the check. "I've got this," she said. "You paid last time." Olivia left the exact change plus tip under the edge of her plate. Both women slid off their counter stools, which were immediately leaped upon by two other people waiting next in line.

"I guess we're done then." Jets pulled her cell phone out of her back pocket. "Just a minute, I've got incoming..."

Olivia waited outside while Janis listened on her phone. "Yeah. Got it. South Circle Drive. Cabin with concrete wall in front. Open doors. Talk later." She turned to Olivia. "That was my very capable assistant. Unlike my previous assistant, no one has tried to strangle them for being too nosy. Anyway, a neighbor spotted a break-in on South Circle. I've gotta go."

"Can I come? I could use the distraction and I know I'll be helpful."

"I can't believe you'd ask to get involved in my work...

again." Jets shook her head. Then a small smile crept to the corner of her mouth. She chuckled. "On the one hand you are impossible, but on the other hand if you promise not to antagonize anyone, I could use the help. You have a way with interviews and you can knock on some doors to chat up the neighbors while I check out the house."

"Great," Olivia said. "I'd love to be your co-investigator. You driving?"

"I'm already regretting my offer," muttered Jets. Taking long strides, she walked through town toward the parking lot as Olivia followed behind.

"Do you have your weapon?" she called out to Jets.

The officer reached under her navy blazer, patting her back pocket. "I'm prepared for all situations. Just keep your eyes open and we'll talk afterward. It's probably nothing. I think I know the house. Used to belong to an older couple, but they rarely come up the hill anymore. It's been vacant for nearly a year. Probably a door blew open and the neighbor called it in. Get in the truck, why don't you? I haven't got all day."

Jets pointed to her vehicle, using her fob to unlock it.

Olivia slid into the seat, turning to grasp the seat belt. Jets shoved her key into the ignition. When she glanced over her shoulder to back out, Olivia asked, "Does your new assistant accompany you on calls?"

"My new assistant minds their own business and stays at the constabulary," muttered Jets.

"Bet your new assistant doesn't get to work undercover like when I was your assistant," added Olivia.

"Bet my new assistant isn't a pain in my behind either," added Jets. She shoved the gear shift into reverse to back out of the space. At the same time, Olivia's phone pinged. She looked at the screen.

Thanks for the text. Missed you too. I've got things to do down the hill today. xo

Her heart sank. *He is avoiding me. Sometimes my restless brain is right.*

CHAPTER ELEVEN

"This is it," said Jets, parking on the road above the cabin. "It's one of those late 1950s-style places, quite the real estate gem if you want to take on a renovation." She put the truck in park and then pulled her key from the ignition.

Olivia noted the A-frame style and shake roof of the cabin. Sitting in the middle of the lot, pines grew to the road. The woods could be seen behind the cabin toward the back. *No wonder the neighbor called the constabulary.* The open front door looked suspicious.

Jets came around to Olivia's side of the truck. She leaned in the window. "So here's the deal. I go in and figure out if the intruder is still around. You sit in the truck and twiddle your thumbs. When I decide—the emphasis on *I*, not *you*—that the cabin is safe, you can come and have a look for yourself. I'll text you. After that you can knock on a few doors and see if any of these neighbors were the ones who reported the break-in. Got it?" Jets glared at Olivia.

"Great," Olivia said with a smile. "I'll just mind my own business here in the truck while you go catch criminals. Have at it."

Jets's jaw tightened. "I don't trust you, but I do like having you around. Keep your eye out on the street. You may see something interesting, then you can report to me later. Understood?"

Olivia widened her smile. "Completely understood. And by the way, if you stop lecturing me and turn around, you'll see a bear leaving the cabin making a beeline toward the woods."

Jets spun on her heels. "Well I'll be damned," she muttered. "That old bear may be my intruder." Jets slid down the berm toward the cabin, her boots stirring up dust and pine needles.

Watching from the truck, Olivia chuckled as Jets walked cautiously toward the wide-open front door, her gun held at waist height. Pausing at the threshold, the officer inspected the open door first. Even from the road, Olivia could see scratch marks on the siding near the door. *The bear most likely made those scratches trying to get inside.*

Olivia watched as Jets disappeared through the open door.

She looked out the front windshield, feeling her pulse quicken. She waited a few minutes. Then her excitement got the best of her. *The bear could come back. What if Janis is his next meal? Maybe I'd better go down and close that door just in case.*

Ignoring Jets's previous admonitions, Olivia hopped out of the passenger seat, slamming the truck door behind her. Instead of sliding down the berm, she took the gravel driveway, noting ditches and scattered pine needles. Her boots slid out from underneath her, but she caught her balance before falling.

I wonder if this place has a caretaker...

She stuck her head in the door and stopped to listen.

When she heard nothing, she stepped into the mudroom, closing the door behind her. *Stay outside, silly old bear.*

Olivia walked from the mudroom into a hallway, where she found walls covered with paneling and matted olive shag carpeting. *What's next, a disco ball?*

She noted the floor plan: bathroom to the left, bedroom to the right, living room ahead, with a small kitchen tucked into the corner. "I closed the door behind me," she announced to the empty hallway, hoping Janis would hear.

A few short steps took Olivia to the center of the living room. She glanced toward the stairway leading to the loft and spotted Janis Jets facing the loft. "I'm here," she announced again.

Jets spun around, extending her weapon. When she saw Olivia, she dropped her arm and glared at her. "I told you to stay in the truck."

"And I thought you needed to close the front door. That bear may circle back, you know. Find you messing with his cabin."

"Who made you the queen of the forest?" muttered Jets. Glancing over Olivia's shoulder toward the kitchen, she shrugged her shoulders. "That stuff on the counter looks familiar. Why don't you turn around and see what's over there?" she directed.

Olivia turned slowly. From the middle of the living room she could clearly see the kitchen counter. Sure enough, there were lots of crumbs and an array of half-eaten bagels, cookies, and other bakery items strewn across the tile. She moved closer. *The floor is a mess. I presume this is Mr. Bear's lunch.* Then a paper sack caught her attention. She picked it up.

"Looks like our bear has a sweet tooth," she said, holding the bag for Janis to see.

"Put that down!" commanded Jets. "Don't you know it's evidence?"

Olivia let go of the bag, watching it float to the floor. It landed label side up. "Like I was about to say, this bag should look familiar to you."

Janis came closer. She leaned over. "The bag's from Thyme Out, Cookie's bakery. I helped him pick out the logo a couple of months ago." She inspected the counter more closely. "And I'm pretty sure the bagel, croissants, and the chocolate chip and thyme cookie are his signature bakes."

Olivia nodded in agreement. "So did Yogi Bear go shopping and bring back the bakes in a sack, or did Boo Boo smell the goods and break in to have a private feast?"

Jets snorted. "Cartoon bears aside, I warn you, don't touch anything. We may still have a human intruder. I'm going to check out the bedroom and the loft. You stand here while I do that. I'll call you when I've determined an all clear."

Jets backed out of the kitchen. Once she stood in the middle of the living room she turned around and raised' her gun. Holding it aloft in one hand, she used her other hand to steady her grip. Olivia watched Jets's head turn side to side, taking in the living room before she took cautious steps toward the stairway to the loft.

Olivia resisted the urge to follow Janis. She felt fairly certain that the bear would not return. *I'm not an expert, but I think we're alone in the cabin. Gut instinct,* she told herself, adding, *my inner detective.*

A few minutes later Olivia heard Jets call from the loft, "Hey, Nancy Drew. Get up here. I want you to see something."

Like a dog practicing obedience moves, Olivia felt released from the kitchen. She hurried through the living room, up the stairway. When she reached the top step, she found Janis Jets staring at an old leather sofa.

A sleeping bag had been spread across the seat cushions, with a pillow stuffed in the corner. One empty glass with fingerprint smudges sat on the shag carpet next to the sofa.

"Someone's been sleeping here," Olivia commented dryly.

"Maybe Goldilocks," Janis chuckled. "I don't think the cabin owners would sleep in a bag on the sofa. Both of them are in their eighties. I'm an old friend. Maybe one of their grandchildren came by?"

"Wouldn't a grandchild sleep in the bedroom, not on the sofa?"

"When I looked in the bedroom all I saw was an old mattress, not even sheets or pillows. But the bed would have been the obvious choice for a family member," commented Jets.

Olivia looked up. A skylight had been installed in the A-frame. Despite cobwebs it had been opened to let in a cool breeze. She looked toward the far wall where the roof slanted. Braced between the raised beams, she saw a shower curtain rod that held a few empty hangers and an old shirt next to a familiar patterned skirt. Jets followed Olivia's gaze. She walked closer to inspect the clothing.

"I think we have a woman who likes to wear prairie-style skirts and plaid shirts," mused Jets. She didn't touch the garments. "Not exactly the best fashion choice."

Olivia's stomach clenched. She moved closer, standing next to Janis. "I have news for you. I know the skirt and I know who wears it most of the time."

Jets put her weapon behind her jacket, snugging it into her belt. Then she gave Olivia a shove. "You do not. How could you pick out a piece of clothing and know it belongs to a particular person?" Jets shook her head.

"If you identify as they/them and wear that skirt all the time and call yourself a Tone Ranger, then that's your skirt," Olivia responded dryly. "It belongs to Raleigh Ulrich. I would bet on it."

Jets's face looked grim. She pulled out a pad of paper from her front pocket. "That Ulrich kid is getting a lot of attention today. First they come to you for help and now they may be a suspect for breaking and entering. Unlike television cops, I do believe in coincidences. They happen all the time," Jets muttered. "Maybe this is nothing, but then again...I'm going to find that kid and figure out what they're up to."

Olivia's stomach clenched.

Jets continued, "Okay, I'd like to know who called this in. My assistant says they disconnected before giving a name. They didn't even use a cell. Some of the cabins have landlines up here. I suppose I could trace the call, but it may not be necessary. Let's check on the Ulrich kid first. Where can I find Raleigh?"

I could give her Raleigh's cell number. But I don't think they'd pick up.

Olivia pushed that thought aside. "I bet we can find them at your boyfriend's bakery. If we hurry we can beat the afternoon scone crush. Back into town then?" Olivia headed toward the stairway, not waiting for Jets to answer.

On the short drive back, Olivia spoke first. "Raleigh never told me where they lived in town."

"Looks like they had the whole cabin to themselves," said Jets. "Rent free."

"So you think they broke into a vacant cabin and stayed, thinking no one would notice?"

"Could be." Jets's mouth tightened. "Kind of lonely for a kid that age to be staying in an abandoned old cabin. I guess the electric and water were turned on, so it wasn't too bad."

As they approached the center of town, Janis drove down the alley, parking her truck on the curb behind Thyme Out. The back gate stood partially open. "Are you thinking Raleigh will run?" asked Olivia.

"Kids that age who live rough are always a bit jumpy. Let's stay in the truck and discuss our plans. Then we'll look really organized when we get out. Not like we did in the cabin, when you disobeyed my direct orders yet again."

Olivia tried not to laugh. "That was pretty funny, the bear running away and you waving your weapon in the air."

"Police work is never funny," Janis insisted, discrediting her words with a smirk. "How about this? Why don't you go find Raleigh, engage them in conversation? Text me and I'll come in to join you. You get his guard down and I'll haul him in for questioning. Trespassing is no joke."

"Good cop, bad cop," commented Olivia.

"Sneaky cop, organized cop... I can't believe I just called you a cop."

Still laughing, Olivia slipped out of the passenger seat, closing the truck door. Walking around, she stepped through the back gate into the outdoor patio.

Much to her surprise, she saw Cookie and Michael chatting at the corner table.

"Hey, Olivia," Michael called to her, beckoning with a huge smile. "Come on over and talk to us." He pulled out a chair at a nearby table.

"I can't right now," she told him, feeling her heart twist.

I thought he was going to be down the hill for business.

Olivia kept moving through the bakery door. From over her shoulder, she heard Cookie talking to Michael, then both men chuckling together.

As her eyes adjusted from the bright sunshine, she noted Raleigh behind the counter. But not the Raleigh she'd seen just a day before. This Raleigh wore faded jeans and athletic shoes, plus a Thyme Out T-shirt tucked in.

They feel like a boy today. That's why the skirt was hanging in the cabin's loft.

She stood behind a man who peered into the glass bakery display case. He pointed to an empty tray. "Do you have any more of those thyme cookies?" he asked in a dry voice.

"No, sir," answered Raleigh. "I do have our lemon with a hint of rosemary. We'll have thyme scones tomorrow though, if you want to come back."

Raleigh looked over the man's bent back to nod at Olivia.

Once the customer selected two rosemary shortbread cookies, Raleigh rang him up. Olivia stepped forward, lifting her phone out of her purse.

"Hey, Raleigh. Just a sec. I have to finish this text." She typed Time for organized cop, and then hit send.

"What will you have today?" Raleigh asked, then added in a whisper, "Did you get a chance to talk to your friend at the constabulary?"

Before she could answer, Janis Jets came through the back door, striding toward the bakery counter. She stood beside Olivia. In a firm voice she said, "Raleigh Ulrich, you will accompany me to the constabulary for questioning. Come out from behind that counter. Don't make me come and get you."

Raleigh's face turned angry. They looked at Olivia. "I trusted you," they said in an accusing voice.

Olivia's heart sank. *I'm sorry*, she mouthed.

Once they came from behind the counter, Jets took Raleigh's elbow firmly in hand. "Right this way," she directed, her voice lowering. "We'll go out the back. My truck is there and I'll be your escort."

"Do I need a lawyer?" asked Raleigh.

"I haven't charged you with anything yet," Jets said, walking toward the doorway.

Olivia followed them, watching Jets half drag and half march Raleigh across the patio. Michael and Cookie looked up.

"What's going on?" Cookie called out.

"None of your business," yelled Janis Jets. "Except you have a crowd of hungry customers at your counter."

As Cookie walked inside the bakery, she heard him ask, "How can I help the next customer?"

Michael looked at Olivia. "What was that all about?"

"I can't talk now. I want to be there when Janis interviews Raleigh." She brushed past him, feeling his eyes following her.

Walking through the park, she stopped to look at the constabulary before crossing the street. To her surprise a woman dressed in knee-high boots and tight-fitting jeans, topped by a black leather jacket, stood in the doorway.

How did Sasha Ulrich find out about Raleigh?

CHAPTER TWELVE

Olivia sprinted across the street. She opened the constabulary door and stepped inside. A voice called out, "Hey, Olivia. What's happening?"

Olivia blinked, realizing who Janis's new assistant was. She looked around the office, trying not to appear surprised. "You're the new administrative assistant."

"That's me." Brad May nodded. He moved a stapler across the tidy desk. Then he moved it back. Olivia looked him over carefully. Compared to his usual attire, Brad had cleaned up his act. His hair had been trimmed and he wore a shirt that she was pretty certain had been...ironed.

"You look great," Olivia said.

"I am the public face of the constabulary," he announced, as if he'd learned the phrase from a brochure somewhere and memorized it for just such an occasion. "Officer Jets is in the back. Do you want me to tell her you're here?"

Brad reached for his cell phone before Olivia could object. She watched him text. The phone pinged as Brad read aloud, "'Tell Olivia to go away. I've got this.' I guess she doesn't want to see you right now. Come back later, okay?"

Olivia shrugged. "So how long have you been working here?" she asked, making an effort to sound casual.

"Since you got fired after the parent weekend. Officer Jets says I'm a perfect fit for this job." He sat up straighter.

Olivia bit back her words. *Since when is the town weed dealer and part-time car mechanic the perfect fit for the constabulary?* She made an effort to sound encouraging. "You look like you know what you're doing."

Okay, Olivia, change the subject fast. She cleared her throat. "Actually I have a car question. I was going to bring my car in for some maintenance and an estimate for reupholstery. Are you still working as a mechanic or did they hire the town's dog walker to do that job?"

You don't sound objective. That might have been considered kind of snarky even.

"Oh, the dog walker still has her job," Brad said, unfazed by Olivia's sarcasm. "And I am still a mechanic. I work here from nine to two and then get lunch. Afternoons and evenings I'm at the garage. Bring your car in today. I'll have a look." He turned to face the computer.

Look at you, Brad May. Growing up before my eyes. Like every other Lily Rock resident, you have at least two jobs.

Olivia felt her irritation dissolve. She sighed deeply. "I'm happy for you, Brad."

"See you later," he said, eyes still focused on the computer.

Exiting the constabulary, she made her way down the boardwalk toward the library. *I can hang out with Meadow and use her window to see who comes and goes. Maybe I'll see Raleigh when Janis is done with them and try to explain.* She walked through the library doors, looking immediately to her right. Meadow stood behind the counter stamping books.

"Hey, Meadow."

"Hello, dear. How is your day going?"

"I've had better ones," she admitted. "Would you mind if I stood behind your counter and watched out the window that faces the street? I'm waiting for somebody to come out of the constabulary."

"Of course, dear. Just walk around. I'll put you right here at the edge so that you can get the best view."

She doesn't even care if I'm being nosy. In fact, she assumes it's normal and helps me out. Olivia walked behind the librarian to stand facing the window. Meadow kept stamping books.

The steady thumping sound caused her to turn around and ask, "Don't you check things out on a computer?"

"I do both. The computer keeps track, but I stamp the date the book was checked out on the card in the front. A stamp is so much more satisfying than a computer notation."

Olivia nodded. "I see." She turned to look through the window. *Still no sign of Raleigh or his stepmother.* She turned back to Meadow.

"Just out of curiosity, do you know Sasha Ulrich?"

Meadow's lips pursed. She stopped stamping, her eyes narrowing. "I have spoken to her. She wanted computer access. Since she's not a Lily Rock resident, I told her she had to wait in line until the next public computer became available. She fussed, of course. I tried to explain that we have to keep all but one of our computers available for those who live here in town."

"I didn't know that was the policy," Olivia mused.

"Now that you are a resident, it would be a good thing to attend more council meetings to keep up on what's what," commented Meadow.

"You mean rules and regulations?"

"'That's right, dear. Every well-run town has a few...rules and regulations."

Olivia smirked. *I wonder if there's a rule about spying on people's browsing history?* In the past Meadow had made no secret of looking over Olivia's shoulder and even into her library account after she'd finished. That experience prompted her to ask, "Do you know what Mrs. Ulrich was trying to research on the computer? I'm just curious."

"Something about probate laws in the state of California," said Meadow without hesitation.

"Really?"

"She was here two weeks ago—spent an hour or so."

So Sasha was looking up probate law before her father-in-law's death. Did she think he didn't have a will?

Finished with her stamping, Meadow kept talking. "I also know Raleigh Ulrich. They spend a lot of time in the library, sitting over there." She pointed to an overstuffed chair in the corner, next to a small window.

"Raleigh also works at Thyme Out," Olivia said.

"And they rent a room in town, or so they say," added Meadow.

Maybe Meadow doesn't know about Raleigh and the cabin.

Meadow continued, "I asked Raleigh for an address when they applied for a library card. They gave me Charles Kravitz's information on Main Street, where they work, not where they live. I don't know the exact location of the room they rent." Meadow stared at Olivia. She shut an open book with a thud. "Being curious is in my nature too. We are alike in that way." A quizzical smile came to the librarian's lips. "For want of another subject, I'd love to have you, Michael, and Sage for dinner sometime this week. We could catch up then."

"I'll talk to Sage, but I don't know about Michael. It seems he's ditched me for another project."

"I doubt that, dear. You do seem more nervous than usual. I can create an herbal tea that will restore your confidence and adjust that sensitive empathic nature. I'll work out my blend and send it over."

Olivia shrugged. "That would be great." She didn't have the heart to tell Meadow that since the first time, she never drank any of her tea.

Meadow continued, "The council and I were surprised to see Michael at our meeting without you. He seems like a man on a mission."

Olivia sighed. "He's been, shall we say, individuating as of late. Meetings down the hill, sleeping at his place, showing up unexpectedly at Thyme Out."

Meadow's eyes widened. "I'd ask him, if I were you. He probably has a very reasonable explanation."

Olivia sighed again. She stepped to the window to check the area. *About time.* Raleigh and Sasha Ulrich stood outside the constabulary. Sasha looked calm while Raleigh argued, their fists clenched as if angry.

"Gotta go," Olivia told Meadow, rushing around the library counter. Once outside, she slowed her pace, stepping next to the building into a shadow to overhear the conversation.

Raleigh yelled at Sasha. "That cop shouldn't have called you. I don't need a parent. I'm over eighteen, and for your information, I'm not moving out of Lily Rock."

"Of course she called us. You've made a nuisance of your-self in this town and you can't stay now that your grandfather has passed," Sasha said calmly. "We've packed up his belong-ings and moved everything out of Hello Age. There's no reason for you to be living in an abandoned cabin, getting arrested for trespassing. I'll give you some money for first and last months' rent on an apartment by a community college up north. Try San Francisco." Sasha looked around. "There are more people like you there. You'll fit in. But if you stay here, not a dime!"

"I don't need your money," Raleigh shouted. "Granddad left me plenty for college. He told me that. It's in his will."

"You must have misunderstood your grandfather's intentions. He wasn't making any sense the last few weeks. Of course he left his estate to your father, the next of kin. As soon as we find the will, I'll let you know." Olivia felt the hair rise on her neck. *Is Sasha acting deliberately calm to infuriate Raleigh further?*

"That's not what Granddad told me," Raleigh yelled.

"Who would believe you?" Sasha smiled, the condescending words rolling off her tongue easily. "You don't even know what gender you are from one day to the next. Leave it alone, Raleigh. I'm warning you." Olivia felt a chill down her spine.

"I don't want to live up north. I love Lily Rock and my job. I may want to be a professional baker, you know, like Cookie. You can control Dad, but you don't get to control me!" Raleigh took a step backward, as if ready to end the conversation.

Sasha, holding her ground, scowled.

Now's my chance. Olivia moved from the shadow. She hurried forward, stopping next to Sasha and Raleigh. "Hello," she said calmly.

Raleigh looked over and then scowled. "Get away from me!" Instead of waiting, they ran across the street. Olivia watched Raleigh disappear into the park.

Sasha spoke. "Don't mind them. Raleigh's always been in a mood or disagreeable, like his father. Both require handling and boundaries." Sasha pulled her leather jacket close to her slim body. "I have to drive home now. Better get going before I hit rush hour traffic."

"What happened in the constabulary?" Olivia asked.

"None of your business," she snapped.

"Will I see you at the funeral for Robert?" Olivia tried.

"You're coming? I suppose anyone can attend. Yes, I'll be there. Open casket." She walked briskly toward her car. Olivia watched as she slid into her black Mercedes convertible.

Sasha takes good care of herself. Expensive clothing, physically fit, and treats herself to a high-end automobile. Yet Raleigh works for an hourly wage at Thyme Out, alternating between one worn prairie skirt and a pair of jeans. She's withholding support to get him to move away.

Olivia walked toward the constabulary and reached for the doorknob. It did not turn in her hand. The sign in the window read closed. She pulled out her phone and texted Janis Jets.

How did the interview go?

Janis immediately texted back. None of your business.

You released your suspect?

Again...not your business.

Brad's your new assistant?

He's the one. Go away. I have work to do.

Olivia clicked off her phone in frustration.

Meadow's right. I do feel more nervous than usual. What do I do now? I know, I can buy a new plant. That will be more helpful to my mood than one of Meadow's teas.

She glanced across the park toward Mother Earth. A familiar truck caught her eye. Walking briskly across the street, she stopped to look inside the truck. Three camera bags and a tripod lay on the back seat.

Thomas Seeker, you sly devil. Are you visiting Mother Earth?

Olivia had not spoken to Seeker for a couple of months. At the time, he'd shown her his new business card.

"See, Olivia? I no longer take pictures of people without getting consent," he'd assured her. "Meadow's helped me be my authentic self without compromising other people."

The card read: Thomas Seeker, Lily Rock's finest photographer. On the back in bold letters it said: Do I have permission to take your photo? *A good gimmick and a great way to keep Thomas out of jail*, she'd thought at the time.

Once inside the garden, she found Echo staring at Thomas Seeker with a disarming smile. "I'll pay you by the hour if you show me photos at the end of each day. Just keep following him. I'll pay more if you find him in a compromising situation."

Thomas did not look pleased. He handed Echo what looked like a business card. "You're asking me to photograph Cookie without his permission..."

Olivia watched, fascinated by how Echo might respond.

Echo threw the card at Thomas's feet. "I'm not hiring you to take pretty pictures for a gallery. I want to know his daily routine and to satisfy my curiosity about his new girlfriend."

Thomas bent over to pick up his card. He dusted it against his pants and slipped it back into his pocket. "I don't do that kind of work," he said quietly. "I'm legit now. You'll need to hire a private detective instead."

Good for you, Thomas.

Thomas shrugged a camera bag over his shoulder and walked toward the front entrance. Olivia stepped in his path. "Hey, Thomas."

"Oh hi, Olivia." He looked down at his shoes.

"I overheard you talking to Echo."

"You must know I didn't take her job offer then."

"Good for you," she said with a smile.

"I'm learning," he admitted. She wanted to question him

more but then thought better of it. *It's not fair to quiz him about a habit he's working so hard to change.*

"See you later."

Thomas and I have something in common. I'm a recovering alcoholic and he's a recovering peeping Tom.

CHAPTER THIRTEEN

Lying awake in her bed the next morning, Olivia felt quite alone. *Two nights without Michael and no real explanation.*

She glanced to the corner of the room where she'd placed her newly purchased maidenhair fern in a metal plant stand. It stood two feet from the floor, delicate fronds springing from the center. Light green and graceful, the sun rays danced through the leaves. She sighed. *Better than tea, I feel calm when I look at living things.*

Sitting up in bed, she swung her legs over the side, her feet touching the floor, remembering Echo's words from the day before.

"Wait until the fern is nearly dry and then take it to a tub or sink. Water it from the top then leave it for an hour. The roots will soak up what they need. Shake the plant over the sink to remove any dead leaves. Then place it near a window with indirect light."

Olivia stepped closer to the plant. She tested the dirt with the tip of her finger. *Still feels moist. There's no need to water today.*

By the time Olivia had showered and dressed, her

thoughts drifted to Michael. *Maybe I'll treat him like a tropical fern. Lots of indirect light. Touch base occasionally. Water when necessary. And shake off the dry excess in the sink to encourage new growth.*

She felt perplexed. *How can the same woman who wants to hire a photographer to stalk her ex-husband and punish him be the same woman who nurtures and loves her plants...*

In the kitchen she didn't bother to make extra coffee. She popped bread into the toaster and then sat down with her coffee at the table. A note with Sage's scribble caught her eye.

Sorry I missed breakfast with you and Mike. Have an early meeting at the academy. Would have texted. I forgot to charge my phone last night. See you both for dinner if you're around.

Sighing, Olivia finished her toast and coffee. After rinsing the dishes in the sink, she put them in the dishwasher. Then she grabbed car keys. *I'll stop in at Thyme Out for my second cup of coffee. Maybe I can find Raleigh to explain.*

Once at Thyme Out, Olivia entered through the front door and looked for Raleigh, who stood in the usual place behind the counter. Resisting the urge to walk right up to them, she stood behind the last person in line. As those at the front of the line ordered pastries and coffee, everyone still waiting looked at their cell phones until it was their turn.

Olivia glanced over the heads of the people in line. *I don't see Cookie.* Behind the counter, the doorway into the kitchen revealed a well-lit kitchen but no chef. *I guess the boss trusts Raleigh to run everything smoothly.* Inhaling the smell of freshly baked bread, Olivia looked back at her phone. Still no messages from Michael.

Finally she was the first person in the line. The glass case displayed thyme muffins, cookies, and bagels. When Raleigh didn't speak to her, she started the conversation. "Hey, good to see you this morning."

They did not return her greeting. Instead of waiting for her to place an order, Raleigh looked around Olivia and then up at the ceiling. When she failed to decide right away, Raleigh looked past Olivia to the next person in line. "You're next," they said to the man.

So that's the way it's gonna be.

Olivia broke in before the man behind her spoke. "I'd like two thyme shortbread cookies and a cup of the daily blend."

When Raleigh didn't respond she spoke louder. "Two thyme cookies and a cup of the daily blend."

Raleigh shrugged, picking up the cookies with tongs, then pouring a mug of coffee. Facing Olivia, there was no eye contact, just the sound of the mug and plate being slid toward her on the counter.

"How much?" she asked.

Raleigh pointed to the sign.

A sigh of exasperation escaped her lips. "Okay then, here's the money, keep the change. And if you want to talk, I'll be on the back patio. I didn't turn you in to Janis Jets, by the way. Please let me tell you my side of the story."

Olivia took her mug and the small plate of cookies, walking outside and sitting down on the patio in the far corner. Before taking a bite, she looked up at a nearby oak tree. Buds showed early signs of spring. A bird sat in a nest, feathers fluffed up as if covering eggs.

She considered Raleigh's behavior behind the counter before taking a bite. *That was a lot more stressful than I antici-pated. Sasha was right. Raleigh is a pain and kind of moody.*

She shook her head, reaching out to grasp the coffee mug by the handle.

So Raleigh isn't speaking to me. Janis Jets replaced me with

Brad of all people, and my boyfriend has some kind of work down the hill that keeps him away. My comparing Michael to a plant will only go so far. Do I take this personally?

Olivia took another sip of coffee. *A hint of blueberry, if I'm not mistaken. Just like Michael's solstice blend.*

"Hey, Olivia," Cookie called from the kitchen doorway. "Good to see you this morning. I'm done baking. Do you have time for a chat?" He pointed to the empty chair at her table.

"Sure, come on over," she said. *Might as well, since no one else is speaking to me.*

Cookie disappeared into the kitchen. Then she saw him walk through the bakery door, still wearing his apron. "How's the coffee this morning?" he asked, sitting in the empty chair.

"It tastes familiar," she said.

"A Bellemare blend," Cookie said, smiling. "Did he tell you? We've made it official, going into business together. My bakes and his seasonal coffees."

She leaned forward. "I haven't spoken to him in a couple of days. He's been working with you?"

"On the cell mostly," Cookie admitted. "I've been busy keeping track of my newest employee. It seems they ran into trouble with Officer Jets yesterday and ended up getting arrested for breaking and entering. Sasha, the kid's step-mother, showed up to bail them out."

"I saw her," Olivia commented dryly.

Cookie eyed Olivia's empty plate. "Want some more cookies? They're on the house."

"Thanks, but I'm not very hungry." Olivia's voice dropped.

"Why so down this morning?" he asked, leaning back in his chair.

"I came over to talk to Raleigh, but they're giving me the silent treatment. I suppose they blame me for Janis and the constabulary. She didn't take them in for questioning on my account. She had every reason to believe Raleigh broke into a cabin and was sleeping there." Olivia told him about the anonymous phone call and the bear who was partial to Thyme Out baked goods.

Cookie smiled. "Raleigh explained the situation. I felt bad. I had no idea they were living in an abandoned cabin. I thought they rented a room."

"Raleigh kind of implied they were renting," Olivia said.

Cookie glanced at his watch. "Speaking of Raleigh, it's time for their break. They've been standing behind the counter since six o'clock. I'll see you later. If you want, I'll try to make Raleigh listen to your side and open up the conversation between you two."

"I'd like to talk it through," Olivia admitted. "See what you can do."

When Cookie slid his chair back under the table, she glanced up at the tree just in time to see the bird fly away from the nest. She waited to see if Raleigh would appear, but finally she gave up and took her plate and mug back to the counter. From inside the bakery, she spotted Raleigh standing outside the front entrance.

The bell over the door jingled as she stepped outside. When Raleigh didn't say anything, she spoke. "If you need any help with the funeral tomorrow, let me know. I can set up chairs or do whatever's necessary. I'm sorry you're still mad at me. I'm willing to talk, but I don't like it when people give me the silent treatment. I won't beg you either. I'll just let it go. If that's what you want..."

Olivia left Raleigh staring at the pavement. *I guess I have to accept their silence.* On the way back to her car she came to a conclusion. *I don't deserve to be treated this way, by Michael or Raleigh. I'm going to ask for clarification.* She stepped to the side to text Michael.

Missed you this morning. Is everything okay?

When he didn't respond, she opened her car door and sat behind the wheel, her heart beating rapidly. *Why am I being so needy? The next thing I know, I'll be crying for no reason. People get busy and mad, that's okay. I wish I weren't so sensitive.*

Instead of starting the engine, Olivia looked out the front windshield to the Sequoia trees rising high above the park. Her eyes stopped when she discovered Mayor Maguire sitting on the pavement in front of a wooden bench. He held his head up to watch people pass by. His ear lifted, then his head swiveled, his shiny eyes looking directly at her.

Look at you, silly doggo. In an instant her mood shifted. Mayor Maguire had that effect on her. One sight of his bright eyes and her irritation melted away. She rolled down her window and called out, "Hey, M&M, want a ride?"

The dog leaped to all fours and bounded past a couple, bumping against a golden retriever who walked with them. He came to a halt on the passenger side of Olivia's car. She rolled down the window, flipping the handle to open the door wide enough for the mayor to jump in.

Once on the seat, he leaned his furry head over and licked her arm. "I'll get your door," she said. She jumped out of the car and walked around to shut the passenger door, reaching in to pat the mayor's head.

It only took a minute for her to sit back down on the driver's side. As she inserted the key in the ignition, a voice called through M&M's open window. "Looks like you fixed your seats," Flex Million said loudly.

Mayor Maguire turned to consider Flex, issuing a low growl.

"I've got this, Mayor," she told him. "I used some duct tape.

A friend helped me," she told Flex over the mayor's objection. "Not a permanent solution, but it works for now."

Million's lips drew down. "Like I said, I'd be happy to call my guy and set up an upholstery appointment. He'll come to your house. I can be the middle man and negotiate for you. It's the least I could do considering you were at Hello Age when it happened."

Olivia ignored her misgivings and reconsidered. *Maybe I need to give Flex another chance. A new guy might be better. Then I don't have to deal with Brad.*

"Sure," she told Flex. "Why don't you give your guy a call? Put your number in my phone and then I'll text you so you have mine. Let me know what your guy says." Before she could hand him her phone through the mayor's window, the dog growled.

Flex grinned. "I'll put my number in your contacts if you think doggie won't mind me using your phone. He's pretty protective." Flex glared at Mayor Maguire.

"Come around to my side. That way he'll be less defensive," she suggested.

Flex walked around the front of her car. At her open window, he held out his hand for her phone.

He watched Olivia as she quickly input her phone password. When she handed him the phone, he turned around as he entered his information. Once he'd finished he faced her again and handed her back the phone. "Any chance you want to meet up for dinner later? I'll be in town and could use the company. I may have my guy's information by then, you know, to set up an appointment."

Olivia felt herself flush. She sensed his interest. Normally she'd say no, but since Michael was so busy, she wasn't sure what to do. Taking a minute to scroll through her texts, she saw that Michael had not responded. "Sure," she said. "Or you could come by my place and meet my sister. We'll grill something for dinner."

Flex grinned. "I'd love that. Text me your address. What time should I show up?"

"Around six o'clock." As soon as she'd said yes, she knew it was a mistake. Her stomach jumped in protest, and her hands got clammy.

Backing out of the parking spot, Olivia shifted into drive. Out of the corner of her eye she saw Flex Million wave. She didn't wave back.

Oh come on, Olivia. Lighten up. Sage will be there. It's a grilled burger, not a date.

CHAPTER FOURTEEN

"So who is this Flex Million guy?" Sage asked as she handed Olivia three dinner plates.

"We met the day Robert Ulrich died. He drives the bus for Hello Age, and he helped me when that squirrel tried to make a nest in my car."

"Oh, that guy." Sage smiled. "I'll get the knives and forks. Where's Mike, by the way? I haven't seen him for a couple of days."

Unsure how much to tell Sage, she walked to the kitchen, eyeing the breakfast table. *It feels like weeks since the three of us sat together drinking coffee.* She selected cloth napkins. Walking past the dining room table, she considered her words carefully. "I haven't seen nor heard from Michael since Tuesday. He dropped out of sight and isn't answering my texts."

Sage placed a fork on top of a napkin. "Is he camping with Wanda again? I thought they only got together once a year."

"I don't think so, unless they've gotten back together."

Sage looked up, surprise on her face. "I don't think Michael and his ex would ever get back together. That couple is done, especially after what they've been through, their child dying and all. Plus he loves you. It's so obvious." Hands on hips, Sage stopped to consider. "Have you looked at your phone this evening? Maybe he's on his way and texted."

"That's what I'm trying to tell you," Olivia said. "I haven't gotten a text for hours. He usually sends several when we're not together. This isn't like him."

"Do you think he's in some kind of trouble? Maybe somebody will contact you with a ransom request very soon." Sage giggled.

"I don't think so. Abduction isn't that common. No one wants an architect in their trunk. That only happens in movies." Olivia stepped back to look at the table. "Looks pretty good, for an impromptu dinner party. Why don't you let me do the grilling so that you can chat with Flex? Maybe it's just me. I'm curious if he makes you uncomfortable."

"What do you mean?"

"His eyes focus on things for a long time and they get kind of narrow and intense, like a squirrel looking at a peanut."

Sage laughed. "You describe stuff so specifically. Now when I meet him I'll see a squirrel."

The doorbell rang, accompanied by a sharp bark from Mayor Maguire. He rushed to the front door, adding more barks to his greeting. Olivia hurried after him.

"It's okay, M&M," she assured him. "We have a guest for dinner. Sit and be polite. No jumping or sniffing, at least not until I say it's okay."

She opened the door.

Flex Million stood outside, a six-pack of beer in each hand. "Am I late?" he asked, holding out the offering.

"Right on time." She waved a hand to welcome him inside.

Gone was the muscle shirt, replaced by a chambray long-sleeve button-up that he'd tucked into faded jeans. Hair, slicked back from his face and over the ears, covered the back of his collar. She saw wet marks on his shoulders as if he'd just gotten out of the shower.

"You drink beer, I hope." He walked toward the center of the room. "I assume the kitchen is through there?"

Mayor Maguire growled. Olivia bent over to give his collar a tug. He pulled away playfully, wagging his tail. "Okay, Mayor, you can say hello."

The dog bounded across the room, pushing his nose against the back of Flex's knee.

"Hey, doggie." When Flex didn't offer a pat, the mayor turned away, his eyes on Olivia.

"Come here," she called out. The mayor complied, sitting at her feet.

Flex raised one hand with a six-pack. "I'll put these in your refrigerator." He stared into the other room. "Nice kitchen, by the way, looks state of the art with those appliances."

"You must be our dinner guest." Sage came from her bedroom. She walked past Olivia, raising her eyebrows. Olivia bent over to pet Mayor Maguire.

From the kitchen she heard, "I'm Sage, Olivia's sister." Olivia didn't hear Flex respond. She left the mayor, moving closer to the conversation. Watching from the doorway, she saw Flex open the refrigerator, yanking with his index finger. He leaned in to inspect the contents.

"You can tell a lot about people from what they keep in their refrigerator." Flex slid the six-packs on a shelf, pulling one bottle out. "I'll drink this one. You girls want a beer now?" When no one answered, he turned the bottle in his hand.

"I'll get you an opener," Sage said, stepping closer to the bank of drawers. Before she could reach inside, Flex placed the bottle top under the counter, popping the bottle with his palm.

"Not necessary." He took a long gulp. "The counter edge

works fine. Nice quartz. Must have cost a lot." He eyed Olivia as he took another gulp. Then he let his gaze drop, sweeping her body with a slight twist at the corner of his lips.

She felt his challenge, angry at herself. "Don't do that again," she told him. "Use the opener, not the counter."

And stop looking me over while you're at it.

"Sure," he responded with a sly grin. Then he took another sip.

Behind Flex's back Sage's eyes opened wide as she stared at Olivia.

Olivia grimaced in response. "Sage, honey, would you get the burgers from the top shelf? Let's go out on the deck while Flex finishes his beer."

Sage reached for the burgers in the refrigerator. "Do you want the usual drink?" she asked Olivia.

"That would be great," Olivia said, her previous exasperation sliding from her voice. "Meet us outside."

Meeting Flex in the great room, Olivia opened the glass wall. "Let's sit on the deck," she suggested, consciously sounding as neutral as possible.

Flex stepped onto the deck. His eyes searched the woods and the view of Lily Rock beyond. "I heard you had a really stunning view." He sat down in the closest chair. "But I never expected this. Modern architecture comes to Lily Rock. Makes me want to move right in and stay awhile." He winked at Olivia.

"I inherited the land and the home, but we have a full house," she hastily said.

"You and your sister..." He shifted his gaze back to the woods. "Just you two with no man around."

"Michael, my boyfriend, lives here too. And he also has the place right past the garden. He's always here," she lied. Well, it had been true just a few days ago.

A smug grin came over Flex's lips. Then he took another sip from his bottle. "That's funny, I heard different." Before Olivia could ask what he meant, Sage came from the house with two glasses.

"Here's your drink," she told Olivia. "I got the same for me."

When Flex turned his head around, he frowned. "No beer for you girls? Did I catch you on an off night?"

"Olivia doesn't drink," Sage said firmly. She raised her glass. "To new friends and a good meal." Olivia raised her glass, watching Flex over the rim.

He took another gulp without a comment, then finished the rest of his beer. "I'll go in and get another bottle if you don't mind," he said. Rising from the chair he walked into the great room. Olivia watched him glance at the dining room table as he headed to the kitchen.

"I don't trust him," she told Sage in a low voice.

"Me neither." Her sister nodded. "Follow him into the house, would you? I'll start the grill. Let's get him fed and out of here as soon as we can."

Olivia set down her drink and walked through the open glass wall toward the kitchen. To her surprise she found Mayor Maguire observing Flex as he pulled another beer from the refrigerator.

When Flex reached to place the bottle cap under the counter, Maguire barked sharply, adding a low growl at the back of his throat.

Flex glared at the dog. "You ain't the boss of me," he muttered. Holding the bottle against the quartz counter he brought his hand down, the cap spinning across the floor.

"I asked you not to do that." Olivia spoke crisply from the door.

This time Flex ducked his head with a sheepish grin. "Ah

sorry, Olivia. I just forgot," he said.

Before she could disagree, the doorbell rang.

Mayor Maguire spun away from the kitchen, racing to the entryway.

Sage beat him to the door and opened it.

Olivia felt a wave of anxiety. *Is it Michael?* She met Sage at the door, placing
her hand on the mayor's head for moral support.

"I'm here on an emergency," explained Jets. She held up her phone. "Apparently I'm now the intermediary for people who don't know how to use their damned cell phones." Jets stepped into the house, looking straight at Olivia. "Your dearly beloved wants to know why you're not answering his texts. He told me to check up on you."

Olivia's eyes grew wide. "I've been texting him most of the day. He's the one who hasn't responded."

Jets shook her head. She handed Olivia her cell phone. "Just talk to him, would you? He's on the line."

Olivia reached for the phone. "Hello," she said into the speaker.

"Olivia, where have you been?" came Michael's worried voice. "I've been sending you texts and you keep asking me what's wrong as if you haven't received them. So now it's my turn. What's wrong?"

At the sound of his concerned voice, she felt relief. "I don't know," she said quickly. "I've been worried about you but thought you needed space so—"

Jets pulled the phone from Olivia's hand, holding it up to her ear. "Enough of this lovey-dovey stuff on my phone. Would you two just get together and work this out, preferably not on my time?" She clicked the phone off and shoved it into her back pocket. And then she lifted her chin to sniff the air. "Do I smell a hot grill?"

"We can set another place," Olivia told Jets. *And then we won't be alone with Flex Million.*

"Do you know our visitor, by the way?" Sage asked, pointing toward the fireplace where Flex stood. Before Jets could answer, Sage handed Olivia her cell phone. "Why don't you use my phone to call Mike back? I'll make the introductions and get Janis a beer." Olivia took the phone with a smile, leaning in to plant a quick kiss on Sage's cheek.

"Thank you so much. I wonder what's the matter with my phone?"

As she headed down the stairs to the lower level, she stopped to grab her cell phone sitting by the table. Tapping in her password, she looked at her screen. *No texts from Michael.*

She sat on the edge of her bed, a cell phone in each hand. A quick memory brought up a new concern. *I gave Flex my phone to put in his contact information.* Olivia put down Sage's phone to look more carefully at the settings on hers. It only took a few clicks for her to find the issue. *Michael's phone number and all of his texts were blocked.*

She touched the block toggle to green. Within moments her text alert pinged, showing a number of communications from Michael just in the past several hours.

With a deep sigh, Olivia called him. He picked up in one ring.

"It's you, thank God," he said. "I didn't know what to think."

"Me neither," admitted Olivia. "Even Sage was puzzled. We did briefly consider the possibility that you had been abducted and were sitting with tape over your mouth in someone's trunk."

Michael laughed. "I think I can put up a better fight than that. Plus I've got no connections to the Mafia. Do you think I'm living a movie lifestyle of the rich and famous?"

"That's pretty much what I said to Sage." She cradled the phone in her hand, smiling. "Your number was blocked on my phone. As soon as I released the block your messages came right up."

"Did you block me on purpose?"

"Of course not. I was really concerned when I didn't hear from you." *I'm not going to tell him how insecure I felt.* "So where are you?" Olivia asked, still wondering.

"I'm on speaker driving up the hill. Should be at the house in under an hour. Have you had dinner yet?"

"Burgers are on the grill. We'll save one for you for when you get here," she said instantly. "Just so you know, we won't be alone. There's Janis, the mayor, and Flex Million, probably on his third beer by now. I needed company since you weren't around."

"That's quite a crowd," he said. "Did you miss me?"

"I was bereft. That's how much I missed you. I thought you'd ghosted me. So I got Flex to come over for dinner. He weaseled his way into an invitation and then he showed up with two six-packs and an attitude."

"I should know better than to leave you alone for a minute. You have a gift for attracting the odd ones. As your bodyguard I suggest you get Flex fed and on the road. Ask Jets to escort him out if necessary. It sounds like he was trying to get it on with you in my absence, plying you with alcohol. Did he know Sage would be there?"

Olivia hastily explained. "I invited him over and told him about Sage after he asked me out for dinner. Don't worry, I'll have him out before you get here. Since he's drinking, maybe Janis will give him a lift."

She clicked off her phone to the sound of Michael's laughter.

CHAPTER FIFTEEN

Saturday rolled around to a beautiful spring day. Olivia and Michael decided to stay home and get a few chores done. He inspected the upholstery damage to her car first, leaving a message at Brad's garage.

"We don't need Flex Million's advice," he told Olivia at breakfast. He put his mug down and added, "We've got perfectly good resources in Lily Rock."

Afterward Olivia cleared the dishes. Then she sat down at the kitchen table to finish her application for the temp job at Hello Age.

"I'm heading out for a couple of hours," he told her, kissing the top of her head.

"See you later," she said, absorbed with her application. *I'm not going to ask where he's going.*

By mid-afternoon they reunited on the back deck. Michael and Olivia looked out at Lily Rock, partially covered with gray clouds. Feet placed on the railing, both chairs close enough so that their elbows touched. "Things are falling into place for my new project," Michael commented as he patted Olivia's knee.

"I noticed how happy you were," she said nonchalantly, "especially last night."

"Last night was the best," he nodded. "Do you think absence makes the heart grow fonder?"

She shook her head. "I don't think I can be any fonder of you. When we had that texting problem, I felt out of sorts."

His hand left her knee as he grasped her fingers in his. "We're back now, so all is well. Take a look at Lily Rock. She's only barely visible. Maybe we need to go inside? Looks like we might get some rain."

"The sky felt full," she admitted. Lifting her face, she inhaled deeply. "I love the smell of rain in the pines."

Michael stood, pulling her up from the chair. "How about this? We go inside for some afternoon delight, followed up with dinner at the pub? It would be good to catch up with Cayenne and Arlo."

"So many good ideas. Dessert before the pub makes sense to me."

Michael dropped her hand. One push on the button and the glass wall opened. She joined him on the threshold, between inside and out, resting her hands on his chest. Raindrops began bouncing off the deck.

He looked into her eyes. In one motion he swept his shirt over his head, exposing his bare chest. Thunder cracked in the distance. The rain intensified, pelting them. Olivia laughed, "It's a flood." She sheltered her head with both hands.

He pulled her inside and then touched the button for the glass wall to close.

Olivia followed him as he led the way downstairs. "Good thing Sage has other things to do this Saturday," he said, looking around. "We could just hang out here by the fireplace instead of our room."

"Better not. Let's go downstairs. That way if she comes home we won't be interrupted."

"Okay," he said quietly.

I love living with Sage, but it does have its disadvantages.

"Lock the front door," she called out, heading downstairs toward their room.

She heard the click and then his footsteps coming after her.

* * *

By five o'clock the pub hummed with activity. Cayenne stood behind the bar handling drink orders by herself. When she caught sight of Michael and Olivia, she pointed to a table for two in the far corner. Olivia grinned and waved at her while Michael claimed their table.

The open dining room was filled with high-top tables and space heaters. Plastic sheets, rolled down from an overhead covering, had been secured to the railing to keep everyone warm and dry.

"I'm really hungry," Michael said, helping her with her chair.

"Me too," she answered with a smile.

"Busy afternoon," he grinned.

"Very busy," she admitted, beginning to chuckle.

Cayenne swept past. "Be right back," she said over her shoulder. "Arlo's got a night off and our help is short. Do you need a menu?"

"Nope," they said together.

Olivia watched Cay clear the table next to them. She walked a few steps to take an order from another table, and then she dropped off a bill on the way to the bar. Cay left the dirty dishes in a tub of sudsy water. *She's really busy.*

"So is the memorial service for Robert Ulrich tomorrow?" Michael asked.

"Yes, the funeral is tomorrow," Olivia agreed. "Will you come with me?"

"You couldn't keep me away," he said, reaching to hold her hand across the table. "Do you know where it's being held?"

"There's a small worship space across the lobby at Hello Age. It's being held there."

"I suppose an upscale place like Hello Age has their own pastor..."

"They call her the chaplain. I haven't met her but people say good things. By the way—"

A young man came to their table with two glasses of water, his iPad shoved under one arm. He placed the water glasses on the table and reached for his iPad. "Cay sent me over," he explained.

"I'll have the beer of the day." Michael didn't look up. "And the lady will have a sparkling water with a slice of lemon."

The waiter paused. "Do you want food?"

"A chicken sandwich on sourdough with garlic fries," Olivia said.

"Make that two," added Michael.

The waiter tapped their order on his iPad. "I'll be right back with the beer and water," he said before scurrying away.

"So, on the topic of Hello Age, they're looking for a part-time person. I inquired about the position on the day of the squirrel incident but was unable to fill out an application."

His eyebrows raised. "Do you still want to work there with Flex Million?"

"I don't like him," admitted Olivia. "But I'd like a part-time job, you know, for my own independence. Plus I can make it with dividing the inheritance between Sage and me, but it's pretty tight. Sweet Four O'Clock won't have their first concert of the season for another month, so I'm not very busy. And don't say you can keep me busy," she hastily added with a laugh. "That's not the same."

His face looked thoughtful. "I get it. I don't exactly have to work for the money. But I do because I need to express myself and be useful."

When he didn't elaborate further, she asked, "And how's that new project?"

"I do have one. I'm not talking about specifics yet because if I do, I'll lose the energy and vision. My creative process is like making a stew in a pressure cooker. I have to add all the ingredients and let things simmer. I don't want to take the lid off too soon. Does that ever happen to you with the music?"

"It does happen to me. If I talk too much about my process I disconnect from the muse and I get bored with my ideas. Better to wait for just the right moment and then produce the music for a rapt audience. At least that's how I handled our band. When I first thought of Sweet Four O'Clock I didn't envision Sage as a part of the mix. I only had an idea. But then when I found out she's my half-sister, well the whole vision came into focus, almost effortlessly. So don't tell me about your project until you're ready. Just know I support you."

Before Michael could respond, they were interrupted.

"So how are things?" Cayenne asked. She looked very tall, dressed in slim-fitting jeans and a gray button-up shirt. Her braid hung over her shoulder. "You ordered, right?"

"We did," Olivia said with a grin. "I haven't seen you in ages. It's no wonder, this place is hopping."

"Been busy with my staff and helping out here at the pub. All is well," Cay added.

"For me too," Olivia said.

Michael spoke up. "I called Arlo last week. Did he tell you?"

"He did not," Cayenne said.

"I wanted advice about how to approach the Lily Rock town council. I thought Arlo would know the ins and outs better than anyone else."

"He's a bit of an expert on small-town politics, especially after getting his weed dispensary off the ground."

Before Olivia could respond, a loud voice came from across the crowded bar. "I need a refill!"

All three looked over, as did the rest of the pub. Olivia saw Flex Million waving his empty beer glass in the air.

"That's the guy who works at Hello Age," Cayenne commented dryly. "He comes in nearly every night. Good for business, but he's kind of obnoxious."

"He's the bus driver," Olivia said. "I'm applying for a temp job at Hello Age."

Cayenne looked down at Olivia, her face immobile.

"I just filled out an application, but I haven't sent it along," she admitted.

"Any chance you will change your mind?" asked Cayenne.

Olivia felt a tingle up her spine. "Have you heard something?"

"Just a rumor," Cayenne said. "Not necessarily true."

"What's that?"

Cayenne flipped her braid off her shoulder and shrugged. "I'll explain more later. For now I have to take orders and refill beers. Keep your eyes open at Hello Age, that's all I'm saying. A lot of people being carried out of that place feet first."

When Cayenne left, Olivia let out a large sigh. "People die at retirement facilities, right? I'm not even driving the bus or doing nursing. Just the average run-of-the-mill administrative assistant, working in the back office, probably billing insurance companies—that kind of thing."

"Just stay away from our pal Flex," Michael muttered.

At the mention of Flex's name, Olivia's eyes narrowed. "Do you think he had something to do with blocking your name on my cell?"

"At first I didn't think he was smart enough, but now I think that's the impression he gives deliberately," Michael admitted.

"He doesn't seem like the sharpest tool in the box."

"But it could be a big act. Maybe Flex Million isn't what he seems to be, hiding his cunning behind the aw-shucks facade."

By then the waiter had arrived with their plates. "Two chickens on sourdough with garlic fries. Here's another beer on the house." He shoved the pint glass toward Michael and plopped the plates on the table. "Anything else?"

"Not for me," Olivia said.

"Me neither." Michael lifted the sandwich to take a bite.

They ate in silence. Olivia finished her own fries and then reached for one from Michael's plate. A voice made her hand freeze above the plate.

"Hey, Olivia," Flex Million said, turning his back to Michael. "Will I see you at Robert Ulrich's funeral tomorrow?"

"Michael and I will be there." She moved her head to the right to catch Michael's eye.

Michael shoved himself back to stand up. Towering inches above Flex, he said calmly, "I believe we've met."

Flex shrugged, turning to Michael with a sheepish grin. "I'm just admiring a beautiful woman. Who could blame me, right?"

Olivia felt her jaw tighten. "My beauty isn't a topic for

conversation with me sitting right here. So, Flex, see you tomorrow. And Michael, let's get out of here." She rose to her feet, sidestepping tables and chairs, making her way toward the pub exit.

By the time Michael caught up with her in the parking lot, he was laughing. "Man, sometimes I underestimate you. It must have been all those drunk people at concerts, but you certainly know how to handle yourself with creeps like Flex."

Olivia grinned. "Glad you saw me in action."

"So I'm not going to worry about you applying for that temp job at Hello Age. You got this."

"Once I call over and find out the timing of the funeral, I'll sign my application. Then I can drop it at the front desk tomorrow when we're there for the funeral."

Darkness fell over the parking lot as they made their way to Michael's truck. Instead of opening her door, Michael leaned against the passenger side, pulling Olivia close to his chest. "I want to kiss you for a while. Then you can tell me about how you learned to stay so cool and collected when confronted with the Flex Millions of the world."

She felt a shiver as his mouth touched her neck. He worked his way to her chin and then her lips. She wrapped her arms around his neck, opening her mouth slightly to touch his tongue with hers.

"My cool attitude comes from a song, 'The Gambler'," she said, her mouth moving against his ear. "Know when to walk away and know when to run." His mouth covered hers again.

She felt Michael's hand reach into his pocket. Without removing his lips from hers, he pulled out the key fob to unlock the truck. "Know when to hold them," he sang. "Let's go home." With one last kiss, he opened her door, helping her slide into the passenger seat.

On the drive she reached out to rest her hand on his thigh. "The moon is beautiful tonight," she said, looking out the windshield into the inky sky. "Stars shining. Maybe we should try the jacuzzi, since it's still warm."

"That's an excellent idea." He smiled. "And if Sage isn't home, we can forget our swimsuits."

CHAPTER SIXTEEN

"I'm heading over to Hello Age a few minutes early, before the funeral starts," Olivia told both Sage and Michael the next day. They sat together at the kitchen table, the remains of lunch between them.

"Why don't I drive with you?" Michael offered as he collected the empty plates.

Sage checked her cell phone. "I know it's Sunday, but I'd like to spend a couple of hours in the office getting ready for tomorrow. Spring exams are coming up and I'm proctoring for a few teachers. So I'll meet you there."

"I'll rinse the dishes," Michael offered.

"You go ahead and get ready," Olivia said. "Leave the dishes on the counter. I'll put everything in the dishwasher."

He handed her a towel with a smile. "Then I'm going to take a closer look at your car if you don't mind. Want to make sure there's no damage to the wiring underneath."

When Michael and Sage left the kitchen, Olivia reached for the empty coffeepot. As she scrubbed the bottom with her sponge, she looked out the window.

After loading the dishwasher, she scoured the sink.

Finished cleaning up, she sat down at the table and opened her laptop to do some research. Hello Age came up quickly, faces of happy people on the home page, along with a few quotes.

"I've made so many new friends at Hello Age," Don Jones, a new resident, was quoted as saying.

I wonder if Don Jones is a real person?

"So many opportunities for rejuvenation and well-being," said Amanda Smith, also a new resident. Olivia looked more closely at the woman in the photo. *No lines on her face...a good camera lens or maybe frequent visits to the dermatologist?*

At the top of the website was a drop-down menu. Olivia clicked on employment opportunities and found a part-time administrative position. *Better get moving. There's the funeral to think of.*

Grabbing her phone, Olivia walked into her office where her paper application sat on her desk. She slid it into a manila envelope. *I'll take this with me and drop it off before the service begins.*

"Better hurry up," Michael called from the other room.

"I have my clothes set out." She headed out of the office.

Dressed in a black short skirt and blouse, Olivia hurried to meet Michael, who waited by the front door. He wore a black button-up shirt, open at the collar. He'd tucked the shirt into black slacks, finished off with a leather belt.

"You look good in black," he commented to Olivia, his eyes drifting to take in her bare legs and high heels.

"You too," she said with a smile.

Michael opened the door, stepping back for Olivia to go first.

A few minutes later Olivia looked out the car window at the woods beyond while Michael negotiated the curving road.

"I haven't been to a memorial in a long time," Michael said.

"I haven't been to a funeral for decades," Olivia added. "We had a memorial service for my mom and a cocktail party for Marla a year after her death."

"Is there a difference between a memorial and a funeral?"

"Funerals have bodies in caskets, memorials do not."

"So Robert Ulrich will be there, all dressed up for his own service." Michael's voice sounded uneasy.

"Does that creep you out a bit?"

"More than a bit," he grimaced. "I'm used to people being cremated. Maybe their ashes are at the service, but that's not always the case.

"They haven't cremated him so far as I know."

Once they reached Hello Age, Michael turned onto the circular driveway. Cars had already parked along each side, making the driving space more narrow than usual. He slowed the truck. "There are more parking spaces around back," Olivia suggested.

Michael drove carefully down the center and then turned right, heading toward the back lot. Once he found a place to park, he hopped out of the truck to get her door. "If this crowd of vehicles proves anything, the funeral will be well attended," he commented. "Was Ulrich a Lily Rock resident?"

"According to Raleigh he lived here part time. I think Robert Sr. has been coming to Lily Rock since he was a child." Once out of the truck, Olivia smoothed her skirt with her hands.

Michael stared at her feet. "I'm not used to seeing you without boots."

She grinned. "I can dress up now and then."

He locked the truck and took her by the arm. "Let's do this."

"Don't forget I need to turn in my application at the reception desk first." She reached into her black tote, pulling out the manila envelope.

Once inside Hello Age, Olivia nodded to Michael, heading toward the reception desk. Elsie Meyer stood behind the counter. "I see you've come for the funeral," she commented.

"And to turn in this application for the temp job." Olivia handed her the envelope.

She watched the older woman's eyes grow vague. *Does she remember me from the other day?* Elsie opened the top to slide the form out. Glasses tipped on her nose, she read to herself.

"Oh, I remember now. I told you not to take the form home but it seems you did anyway." She placed the form back into the envelope.

"That's right." Olivia smiled brightly. "Do you have any idea when I might hear about the job, if I have an interview?"

"It's Sunday, so Agnes, our head supervisor, won't be back to her office until tomorrow morning. She'll look at the form then. Just so you know, she has things to catch up on from the weekend. But I'll call. You can be sure of that."

"Thank you so much." When Olivia stepped back, she bumped into someone standing right behind her. Turning to apologize, she found Flex Million too close to her.

"Is that what I think it is?" He pointed to the envelope that Elsie held.

"If you mean a job application, then yes it is. I planned on filling it out sooner, but the squirrel incident got in the way." She looked for Michael, making her way around Flex.

"I never called my guy about your upholstery."

"We're working on getting it fixed." She looked closely at him. His eyes wandered to the left, then the right as he waited for her to say more. She glanced toward the crowded room one more time. To her relief she caught sight of Michael. He walked rapidly toward her.

Flex took a step closer to Olivia, close enough for her to feel his breath on her face.

Michael arrived at her side before Flex could ask another question.

"Flex wants to know if he can help with the car's uphol-stery?" Olivia said.

Michael looked down at Flex. "We've got the car handled," Michael said calmly.

Off balance, Flex tottered to the left then right. Michael took Olivia's elbow, moving away from him.

"Good to hear about the car. I can't chat anymore, the Ulrich family needs me to carry the casket." Flex turned to go. Then he turned back around. The next question he directed toward Michael. "Do you want to help us with the casket?"

"I didn't know the deceased. So I think I'll pass this time," Michael said. "Plus I want to sit with Olivia." Hand still on her elbow, he directed her toward the chapel entrance.

People had already gathered at the door, waiting to be admitted for the service. Residents in wheelchairs were at the front of the line, as ushers stood with their backs to the closed doors.

"You turned in the application?" Michael asked her quietly.

"I did," she answered.

"Million wasted no time sidling up to you. I watched him from across the room. When you looked like a deer in head-lights, I stepped in."

Olivia sighed and took his hand. "I appreciated your help this time."

Michael scanned the large reception area. "Flex got to you pretty quick. He came in the front doors when you were talking to the woman behind the counter. So I wonder if he has access to surveillance cameras? I suppose they've installed them all over the place, you know, to keep an eye on the memory care folks. How else would he have seen you so quickly?"

"He seems to be everywhere and anywhere," Olivia agreed.

At that moment the ushers turned around and pulled on the doors, giving people admittance to the chapel. When the ushers stepped aside, a woman pushed the first wheelchair through the entry, and others followed.

Olivia took a program from a resident who stood in the aisle handing them out. She watched an usher place programs on the laps of the residents in wheelchairs. Most did not have the strength to pick up the paper, let alone read the contents.

Olivia and Michael sat on the right-hand side near the aisle. The casket had been placed front and center on the chancel. Rolls of satin fabric spilled over the sides, draping to the floor. The lid, propped open, provided the perfect backdrop for the body of Robert Ulrich. Lying on his back, hands folded over his suit coat, he appeared at rest.

Olivia blinked. *Do I see a program in his hands?* Before she could decide, her eyes drifted past the casket to the pulpit. And then past the pulpit to a large wooden cross that dominated the back wall.

She leaned over to whisper in Michael's ear. "I guess everyone here is Christian?"

Michael leaned into her. "That would be a surprise to the Jewish families."

"And the 'nones,'" Olivia nodded. "I like the church up the hill. No crosses, but a labyrinth outside."

"So you like religions to keep their symbols to themselves?"

"I'm a Christian, at least I think I am," Olivia admitted. "But I say live and let live."

"And I have no idea who runs the show, but I'm willing to tell you it's above my pay grade," Michael said with a smile.

"Good thing we had this discussion," she patted his knee.

He took her hand and squeezed it gently, keeping it in his lap.

The four rows in front of Olivia and Michael had been filled. She took her time to assess the assembled with quick glances. She found Sage sitting in the back. Olivia caught her eye and smiled. Then she saw Janis Jets sitting with Cookie. She elbowed Michael. "Look who's here. I don't think either of them knew Mr. Ulrich."

Michael looked over his shoulder, his eyes settling on the bank of stained-glass windows. "You mean over by the good shepherd window?"

"That's them, right?"

"Look, Janis just saw us." Olivia nodded in Jets's direction.

Janis's eyes stopped when she saw Olivia. She lifted her chin in recognition and then turned away.

"Maybe Cookie came because of Raleigh and Janis came because of Cookie," Olivia said. "That's how these things go. No one wants to face death alone, so best to bring a friend."

"Very insightful of you." Michael nodded.

The crowd grew quieter as a man stepped to the front of the chapel. He wore a long black robe, with three red stripes adorning each sleeve. A small black book lay between his outstretched palms.

"Looks like Pastor Jim will lead the service," Michael said. "The Ulrichs must have arranged for him to be there. I've met him before."

"Pastor Jim is all dressed up," noted Olivia. "Or is that a converted bathrobe that's he dyed black for special occasions?"

Michael held back a laugh.

Pastor Jim spoke. "I'd like to welcome everyone to the funeral service of Robert Bartholomew Ulrich, Sr. His family appreciates seeing all of you, especially during this time of grieving. And now please turn off cell phones while we center our hearts and minds on God." He opened his small black book.

A piano began to play a melody unfamiliar to Olivia. She opened her program. "Time for the family to start the procession," she read in a whisper.

The congregation stood, so she stood too. As the family walked down the center aisle, Olivia felt a twinge in her stomach. Raleigh was the last in line. Their head hung down. She could see Raleigh's fingers inside their pants pocket, working against the fabric. Raleigh sat in the last chair of the front row.

Michael leaned closer to Olivia. "Raleigh looks agitated," he whispered.

She nodded.

It only took fifteen minutes for the chaplain to finish the eulogy. After a short prayer, he invited people to walk forward to pay their respects to the deceased.

An usher pointed to the row behind the family. People made their way forward, maintaining a certain distance for others to pay their respects. Olivia watched each person step up to the casket. Some spoke, some prayed before they moved on. She and Michael stayed seated as people moved past them toward the casket.

Olivia leaned into Michael. "I don't have to walk up front, do you?"

He shook his head. "We're here for the family. Since we didn't know him until after his death, I think it would be odd for us to pretend otherwise."

Only after everyone else made the journey did the family rise from their seats in the front row.

Robert Ulrich Jr. stood next to his son, openly weeping. Sasha Ulrich stood on the other side of her husband, dabbing at her eyes with a tissue. The family filed past the casket, each pausing and then moving on.

On the way back to their seats, Robert tried to slip an arm around Raleigh's shoulders. Wild-eyed, they shrugged him off. Instead of sitting back down with the family, Raleigh exited through a side door with their father following right behind.

As the chaplain stood to lead the final prayer, one clear voice could be heard from the hallway.

"I didn't kill him. Why are you blaming it all on me!"

CHAPTER SEVENTEEN

"The family invites you to a reception in the dining room following the benediction," Pastor Jim announced in a booming voice. He looked straight ahead, as if oblivious to the commotion from the hallway.

He's trying to distract us from Raleigh's outburst.

Following his own instruction, Pastor Jim nearly sprinted down the aisle after blessing the congregation, his face looking more frightened than sad. The piano picked up the pace with a hymn, as the rest of the congregation stood to follow the pastor out the door.

Olivia's shoulders tightened. Finally the usher nodded, the cue to move forward into the recessional. She and Michael joined the others.

"Raleigh may be at the reception," she told Michael under her breath. "I wish they were speaking to me. After that outburst, I want to have a word."

"I can try to chat with him. Then you can come over as if by chance. It might work. Worth a try." Michael took her hand as they waited for the people ahead. Once outside the chapel, they kept moving with the crowd toward the dining room.

The line moved ahead in short bursts. Michael and Olivia came to a stop in front of the reception desk. Olivia looked around, seeing Elsie with a plate of food. The older woman demurely lifted a fork to her lips and then dabbed them with a cloth napkin.

Olivia looked behind the desk and something caught her eye. A metal trash can, located at the end of the counter, had been filled to overflowing. A familiar envelope was placed on top.

She dropped Michael's hand. "Wait a minute. I have to get something," she told him. He remained in line as she walked the few short steps closer to the reception counter. Reaching around it, she brought up the manila envelope. Undoing the clasp, she confirmed her suspicion. *My application didn't even make it to the director's desk.*

"May I help you?" asked a voice from behind.

Olivia swung around. Elsie Meyer stared at her.

"I see you've accidentally tossed my paperwork," Olivia said hurriedly, embarrassed that she'd been caught picking things out of the trash.

Elsie's eyebrows shot up. "I didn't put it there, if that's what you're thinking. The last time I saw the envelope was on the director's desk in her office."

Olivia stuffed the envelope in her tote bag. "Not to worry. I'll send in an electronic copy instead, more reliable." She didn't wait for a response, making her way back to stand in line with Michael.

"Get what you needed?" he asked.

"Yep, got everything. There was a clerical error," she said, her cheeks feeling hot from annoyance. *I'm going to apply online as soon as I get home.*

In a few more minutes, they made it to the dining room. Olivia looked over the area from the doorway. People sat in every available chair, plates of food from the buffet line balanced in their hands. The round tables, decorated with white cloths and napkins, looked formal and inviting. The early birds filled every seat.

Michael scanned the room and then took her to one side. "Looks like the residents got here first. Are you hungry?"

"Not really," Olivia said. "I don't see Raleigh either, but I am interested in what's going on over there."

A familiar person held a microphone in her hand. Janis Jets stood in front of the food tables as if she had an announcement. "May I have your attention?" she called out with a voice of authority.

The voices quieted down, so Janis continued.

"Will Robert Ulrich Jr. please meet with me right over there." She pointed to the corner where two uniformed police stood. The Ulrich family table looked around at each other. Robert Jr. was nowhere in sight. Janis waited for someone to get up. When no one took the initiative, she pointed at Michael. "Bellemare, would you step into the men's room for me? I need to see Ulrich Jr. now. No time to waste."

"Will do, Officer Jets," he shouted for all to hear.

Knives and forks hit plates as everyone stopped eating, eager to see what might happen next. Within minutes Michael returned with Robert Ulrich's elbow firmly clasped in his hand. All at once, people began to talk.

"What's going on?" asked a woman who stood next to Olivia, wearing a black hat with a veil draped over her eyes.

"I have no idea," she answered. "Enjoy the reception." Olivia walked quickly toward the side door where the officers and Janis Jets stood. Sidling up to Jets, she leaned closer, speaking quietly into her ear. "What's going on?" she asked.

Jets shrugged. "Can't tell you now. Meet me at the constabulary in an hour. We've got to transport the body to the coroner, talk to Robert Jr., and then I'll answer any of your questions." Jets continued to look out at the crowd.

Olivia felt surprise. *She wants me to meet with her... I expected her to say none of your business. Wait a minute, did she just say coroner?*

Janis turned back to Olivia. "Since you were on the scene when Robert Ulrich Sr. was found dead, I need to take your testimony."

"Why do you need a testimony? From what I heard he died of Parkinson's disease." She felt a tingle of surprise run up her spine.

"On the one hand, we were led to believe that Parkinson's got him," answered Jets. "But on the other hand? I've just learned that four Hello Age residents have passed away just last month. Statistically that alerts certain health officials, so the health department alerted me. I can't do much with the cremated bodies, but since I have Ulrich's body, I'm starting with him. A full autopsy has been ordered."

Olivia gulped. "What's going to happen to Raleigh's dad?"

"Since he wasn't there on the day Robert Sr. died, we're gonna question him to find out what he knows about his father's health issues. I also want to know who stood to benefit from Robert Sr.'s untimely death."

Back from his assignment, Michael listened to the last part of their conversation. Then he directed a question to Janis. "Do you need me to stay here and bring in other people?"

"You're done for the day," she smirked. "Nice work by the way, very masterful. Remind me to put you on my payroll."

Olivia rolled her eyes. *Oh sure, you can employ Michael, he doesn't even need a job. But you fired me. Thanks a lot, Janis.*

She swallowed back her irritation, forcing a smile. "So

we'll hang out a bit and then meet you at the constabulary." She gestured with her head toward the door, moving away from Janis.

Weaving and sidestepping through the crowd, Michael followed Olivia as she eavesdropped on the conversations around her. A clear voice came through.

"That Raleigh, they're such a problem for their dad and me. Always has been. What with the gender issues, doesn't know who they are from one day to the next. Then for no apparent reason, they drop out of high school. Imagine, no one does that in our family. We are riddled with university gradu- ates. Raleigh is the first one to show absolutely no promise. And now this!"

Olivia glanced through the crowd, looking for a person to match the voice.

"I don't even know where they're staying, *if* they have anywhere at all to stay. They can't have enough money to rent an apartment, even with the trivial job they try to hold on to."

"Let's walk over there," she told Michael. He leaned down to hear her voice over the crowd. "I think I hear Sasha Ulrich talking about Raleigh," Olivia explained.

Sasha stood near the exit door, a group of four women surrounding her.

"She's over there with her fan club." Olivia inched closer to hear more of the conversation.

"I hope my husband tells the police everything he knows about Raleigh. Even a father must see the psychological instability."

The small crowd nodded in agreement. Olivia watched as each one leaned forward to give Sasha a peck on the cheek, as a way of saying goodbye.

Michael whispered to Olivia, "If Sasha had a ring, I'm pretty sure those women would have kissed it."

"If it weren't so serious, I'd be making more jokes right now. But Michael, she's digging a hole for Raleigh and I'm not sure they won't fall in and get buried."

"What do you mean?"

"Without a will, Raleigh may not inherit Robert Sr.'s estate. Sasha sounds prepared to discredit Raleigh in court. She's painting Raleigh as a barely employed, emotionally unstable person who has nowhere to call home.

"To make things worse, Janis caught Raleigh trespassing. From what everyone heard after the funeral, even Raleigh's father accused them of killing their granddad."

A look of admiration came up in Michael's eyes. "You're good at this, assessing the potential for trouble ahead. I had not put all that together. Okay, I came here today to have a conversation with Raleigh, and so far I've not followed through."

"I don't think Raleigh came to the reception." Olivia glanced around one more time. "Why don't we look inside the chapel? And then if all else fails—"

"We can find Raleigh at Thyme Out," Michael finished her sentence. He reached in his pocket to hand her his set of keys. "Wait for me in the truck while I have one last look around. The kid might bolt if they see you." He kissed her forehead. "Unlike me, Raleigh doesn't know you're the best advocate a person can have."

They parted company as Michael headed back to the chapel and Olivia made her way to the front entrance. She noticed an older couple lingering in the entryway, heads huddled together as they spoke.

Olivia smiled as she approached. "Excuse me," she said, trying to get past them to the exit.

"We were just talking about you," the woman exclaimed. "Weren't we, Walter?"

The bald man nodded.

"Did I just see you talking to the police in the dining room?" the woman asked.

Olivia explained, "I used to work for Officer Jets as her administrative assistant."

"Then I might as well tell you," the woman said, her voice rising with emotion. "I was just explaining to my friend Walter here, there's something odd going on at Hello Age that I can't quite put my finger on."

Olivia felt her curiosity aroused. "What do you mean?"

"My neighbor across the hall, Robert, it was his funeral today. He was such a nice man, and that grandson or maybe granddaughter—not that there's anything wrong with that—couldn't have been more attentive. I always heard them laughing when I walked past and when I dropped in, they'd be playing checkers together, chatting up a storm.

"I remember now, the grandkid's name was Raleigh, but anyway that young person was so unusual. Most other family members who visit, you can tell they can't wait to leave. Raleigh was different. Those two really got along."

The older man leaned forward as if he wanted to speak. He cleared his throat. "Robert was gay, you know. He told me he'd spent most of his life as a family man, but he was gay and he worried about Raleigh."

The woman's lips drew a thin line. "Just because Raleigh looks like a girl one day and a boy the next, it doesn't mean they are gay. You know that, right?"

"I do," Walter said. "But that doesn't mean life is easy. Robert felt compassion for his grandchild, both of them being different and all."

Olivia wondered what to say. "Actually I know Raleigh fairly well. I was his singing coach at the Lily Rock Music

Academy. I hope to help them out, so thank you for telling me your concerns."

"You seem like such a nice young woman," commented the older lady. "My name is Sheila, by the way."

"Nice to meet you both." Olivia dangled the keys in her hand. "I do have to go, but I want to make certain I heard you clearly." She inhaled deeply. "Sheila, did you say something is going on at Hello Age that you can't put your finger on?"

"Oh yes, I did say that." A light came up in her eyes. "What I wanted to tell you, what with your close proximity to the police, is that Robert Ulrich wasn't that sick. It wasn't time for him to die. I know about that kind of thing because I volunteer for hospice. People have a way about them when they're ready to go.

"Robert wasn't vague, nor did he start packing a suitcase and talking about going home. He knew everyone in his family by name and every resident too. Very intelligent man, regardless of his Parkinson's. He couldn't walk alone and his hands shook, but his mind was sharp as a tack."

"And he talked a great deal," Walter added. "He'd get quiet when his medication wore off or when he wanted to ignore his nurses, but otherwise he spoke just fine."

Olivia took in the information. "So you're both surprised that Robert passed away when he did?"

"Now listen to me closely, young woman. I may be ninety-one years old and have a bit of hearing loss, but I know one thing for certain." Sheila lifted her cane and thumped it onto the carpet.

"And that is..." Olivia asked, moving her foot away from the cane.

"I'm no doctor, but residents here get a feeling about things. Lots of people come and go."

"What she's trying to say," butted in Walter, "is that Robert Ulrich did not die of Parkinson's. It wasn't his time to go."

CHAPTER EIGHTEEN

An hour later Michael and Olivia made their way down the hallway of the constabulary toward the break room in the back. "So Janis hired Brad to replace you?" Michael asked, once the glass doors shut behind them.

"Janis can hire anyone she wants," Olivia muttered. "But more importantly, there was no sign of Raleigh at Thyme Out."

"They might have discovered another cabin to squat in; probably holed up without cell phone reception..."

"That would not be a good choice, considering they already have been charged with trespassing."

"We're the first ones here." Michael nodded toward the round table in the center of the room. "Might as well sit down and wait." He pulled out two chairs.

"You can text Janis," Olivia suggested.

He looked at her closely. "You seem edgy since finding that file at Hello Age."

"My application for the job was trashed," she said. "I saw it by accident and spoke to Elsie. She acted like she knew nothing about it. As soon as we get home, I'm going to fill out a form online."

"I think that's peculiar," Michael admitted. "But I admire your tenaciousness." He shook his head. "Are you sure you want a job at that place? Flex Million is enough to put anyone off. Do you think he trashed your application?"

Olivia shrugged. "I need a day job, even if it's part-time. This one seems perfect for me. I can do the work and then move on to touring with Sweet Four O'Clock this summer."

"Flex Million was standing behind me at the desk when I handed over my application. He may have snagged my file. But why would he trash it? Makes no sense."

Michael's brow wrinkled. "I'd think Flex would want you to work at Hello Age. It would give him an opportunity for a workplace romance with me out of the way."

"That's just not happening." Olivia scowled. Before she could say more, she felt her phone vibrate in her tote. She pulled out her cell to read the text.

My assistant told me you're in the break room. Meet me in interview room one.

"We're being summoned," she told Michael. They both stood and pushed their chairs under the table, heading to the doorway.

The interview room door stood partially open. Jets stood in the corner closest to the door, eyeing Raleigh's father behind the interview table. She had one hand on her cell phone. "Push the button to close the door," she told them. Michael did as Jets suggested.

Robert Bartholomew Ulrich Jr. looked like any other fifty-year-old businessman. He was still dressed in an unremarkable black suit, black tie, and white button-down shirt from the funeral. If it weren't for the glare he sent Michael, Olivia might have found him as unremarkable as his clothes. *There's something about his eyes, not the color but the shape, that reminds me of Raleigh.*

Olivia gave him a slight smile, taking note of his well-manicured nails resting on the table.

Jets motioned for Olivia and Michael to stand aside as she sat at the table.

We're supposed to listen but not interrupt.

Janis cleared her throat. "Now as you know, Mr. Ulrich, you are not under arrest. I'm just gathering information here. That's why I invited Olivia and Michael to listen and observe. They were at the garden when Echo Kravitz, the owner of Mother Earth, called for help after discovering your father unconscious."

"Olivia and Michael both watched the paramedics try to revive your father. And they waited as he was taken away in the ambulance. Since neither are family members, they provide a certain perspective. If you have any questions about that afternoon, now's the time to bring them up."

Robert Jr. nodded at Olivia and Michael. "I don't have any questions."

"I have a paper for you to sign so that we can do an autopsy on your father's corpse."

Robert's eyes widened.

Jets continued to explain. "I know it's a bit late, an entire week, but something has come to our attention to make us wonder if your father did not die from complications of Parkinson's, like it says on his death certificate."

Robert looked downward as if he were deeply considering Jets's words. After she waited a few long seconds, he finally spoke. "My dad was pretty sick. I think you're barking up the wrong tree. But then," he paused to swallow, "I didn't see much of Dad those last months. Not for the last few years, if I were to be completely honest. After I married

Sasha, she took over all the family care. She handled all of his needs."

Olivia's jaw set. She blurted out, "What about Raleigh? They hung out with your father a lot. They were quite close."

Surprise showed on Robert Jr.'s face. "I know Raleigh and Dad got along, but I didn't know they visited Dad at Hello Age."

Jets turned toward Olivia, giving her a glare. She pointed to the closed door. When Jets stood up, her chair scraped on the floor. Olivia understood and followed her into the hallway. Jets closed the door behind them, placing hands on hips.

"Did I ask you to butt your way into my interview? No, I did not. Did I not imply that you were supposed to listen? Yes, I did. Shape up, Nancy Drew. Go back in the room and keep quiet."

Olivia nodded, keeping the smirk from her face. Jets shook her head, opening the interview door, waiting for Olivia to go first.

Once the door closed, Janis sat down and continued the interview. "Since your father was a resident at Hello Age, I can tell you that there have been a number of deaths in the past weeks that the county health department asked me to look into. Unlike those other dead people, your dad was not cremated. So we can find out if there was any hanky-panky in the autopsy. That's why I want," Janis slid a paper and pen across the desk, "you to sign this paper, so we can get going on the process. Can you do that for me?"

Ulrich took the paper. He glanced over it but did not pick up the pen.

"Come on, Robert, what's stopping you on this? You want to know if your father died from his disease or was killed, don't you?" Jets's voice held impatience.

He reached up to scratch his head. "Have you spoken to

Raleigh yet? They might have some information for you about Dad's health in the final weeks. People decline from Parkinson's at different rates, some very quickly." He tapped his fingers on the table. "Plus it's over now. You can't bring Dad back and frankly, his care was very expensive. I don't think Dad *wanted* to live anymore. Maybe all of this is a blessing, isn't that what people say when old sick people finally die?"

Olivia stared at Robert Ulrich, doing her best not to look shocked. She glanced out of the corner of her eye at Michael. His usual smile had turned into a straight line. Her eyes went to Jets. Even she seemed flummoxed.

The longer the silence grew, the more Robert fidgeted in his chair.

He as much as confessed to a police officer that if an inconvenient old man was killed, it was the right thing to do.

Jets cleared her throat. "We will speak to Raleigh...and your wife. But now I need you to sign that form, and frankly, Mr. Ulrich, even though you weren't at the scene, your hesitancy to sign could be construed as guilt. Have you ever thought of that?"

Ulrich's head jerked back. Olivia watched him carefully, noting that his right eye began to twitch. He reached up to smooth the lid with his forefinger. After a moment he picked up the pen, scrawling his signature at the bottom of the form.

In one motion Janis swiped the paper, leaving the pen on the table. "I'll take this to my assistant," she said. "You three can chat. When I get back, we'll finish this up. Families need time to grieve, especially after the funeral service."

Once she left the room, Michael spoke. "It's good to meet you officially," he told Ulrich in a friendly voice. "I know Raleigh from the music academy. Olivia here," he nodded his head toward her, "coached Raleigh's a cappella group."

"I wasn't aware of that." Ulrich looked over at Olivia. "Raleigh is, as they say, an acquired taste."

Olivia shook her head. "Oh no. I love Raleigh and did from the beginning, a good student and an excellent tenor."

Before Robert could disagree, Jets burst back into the room. She spoke directly to Ulrich. "You can go now, but I want you to know that Raleigh will be picked up for questioning as soon as we get the paperwork in order."

Standing up from the table, Ulrich Jr. pulled at his suit coat and then buttoned the jacket. "According to my wife, Raleigh may have wanted my father's money. That's for you to look into. I washed my hands of them when they turned eighteen." Ulrich walked around the table, past Jets, through the open door.

"Just follow the exit signs," Janis called after him. Then she turned to Olivia and Michael. "You heard that, right? He thought it didn't matter how his dad died."

"I got the impression that old man Ulrich had outlived his usefulness and that his son wanted him out of the way," muttered Michael.

"What do you think?" Jets asked Olivia.

"I think we need to talk to Raleigh. Sasha's claiming Granddad did not leave a will and Raleigh knows differently. Raleigh saw the will, one that had been witnessed and stamped by the court."

"Witnessed and stamped, you say?" Jets looked curious. "Did Raleigh know who was the beneficiary of the estate?"

"They never said, but I got the impression Raleigh thought money was coming their way."

"A lot of money?" Jets's eyebrows raised.

"Enough so that Raleigh could settle down without having to use other people's cabins for shelter. Sounds like someone took a hike with the will," Olivia said hastily. "If it isn't found, then Raleigh may not inherit. And if it is found, as the beneficiary, Raleigh may be accused of killing his granddad."

"That's exactly what I am thinking," Jets agreed.

"And I can add more to that theory," Olivia said. "Raleigh told me Sasha wanted them to move to San Francisco and attend a community college. She wants to get them out of the way, the sooner the better."

"If Raleigh flees, they will only look more guilty," Jets commented dryly.

"Except don't forget, Raleigh loved his granddad." Olivia spoke firmly. "They were in no hurry for Granddad to die. I even heard that from two other residents, that Raleigh and Robert Sr. spent lots of time together."

Jets held up her hand. "Let me think a minute." She shifted from one foot to the other. "So I have to get Raleigh back to the constabulary to talk about the inheritance and what they know about the will. Either of you know where I can find the kid?"

Olivia sighed. "Raleigh hasn't spoken to me since you pulled them in last time."

"Okay, so I did react pretty quick on that one. I had to arrest Raleigh for breaking and entering. But I didn't know the rest of the circumstances."

"I tried to tell you." Olivia's eyes penetrated Jets's glare.

Michael came between them. "Okay, water under the bridge. Let's see if we can locate our ex-Tone Ranger, the sooner the better. I say we make ourselves available at Thyme Out. Raleigh will show up eventually."

Jets looked at Michael, then back to Olivia. "While you two find Raleigh, I'll make up some excuse to bring Sasha back in for a little chat. I was suspicious when she showed up the first time I interviewed the kid. I didn't invite her. She paid

Raleigh's bail, but that wasn't what she was most interested in. It's like she wanted to control the narrative."

"So we all three have our marching orders," Olivia commented dryly. "What about Brad in the office? Does he help out with the investigations?" Olivia aimed her question to needle Jets.

Instead of pushing back, Janis said, "A little animosity between you and the new assistant?"

Olivia ducked her head. "I'm fine. See you outside." She raised an eyebrow at Michael on her way past.

Hurrying through the doors toward the front entrance, Olivia paused. *I don't want to see Brad again.* Taking the back exit, she waited for the door to close before stopping to pull herself together. *You're acting like a child. Janis can hire and fire anyone she wants.*

Michael joined her outside and they walked to his car. Needing a moment, Olivia reached into her pocket to check her texts and calls. "Give me a minute, would you?"

Michael smiled as he opened her car door. She sat down and opened the browser on her phone.

Finding the Hello Age website and employee information was easy. Since she'd already filled out the paper form, it only took a few minutes for her to complete the form online and press Send. "Thanks for letting me do that," she told him.

By the time they got home, Michael made his way toward the kitchen while Olivia stopped to put down her purse. Her phone pinged. *Someone left a voice message.* Still standing in the entryway, she held the phone to her ear to listen.

"Ms. Greer, this is Agnes Curry, director of Hello Age. We'd like to schedule an interview for Monday morning. You sound like the perfect temp candidate and it would help us if you're available sooner rather than later. Please arrive by 9:30 a.m. I'll meet you at the reception desk. And if possible, could you bring the autoharp you mentioned on your application? We encourage all of our employees to share their gifts and talents. I'd like you to work with some of our residents, sing with them, as part of your interview. None of our other applicants had a music skill that could be used. I think the autoharp would be a big hit."

Olivia listened to the message one more time, a smile coming over her face.

Well, there you go. My autoharp has finally become an asset for temp employment. Now that's a first!

CHAPTER NINETEEN

The next morning Olivia stood at the Hello Age reception desk, her autoharp under her arm. "Hello again, Elsie. I'm here for an interview with Agnes Curry."

Olivia had dressed in black jeans, a T-shirt, and a black blazer. Her hair, swept back into a ponytail, made her neck feel exposed. She smiled when she remembered Michael's remark that morning: "If it weren't for the T-shirt, I'd say you're going corporate on me."

Elsie Meyer stood at her usual place behind the desk. When Olivia spoke she looked up, a blank expression on her face. *Does she recognize me from before?*

"I'm Olivia, Olivia Greer, the one who applied for the temporary administrative assistant job yesterday. I left you my application in a manila folder..."

Olivia watched Elsie's expression. Her mouth creased at the corner as if she was concentrating. "I don't remember where I put that file." Nervously glancing to her left and to her right, she looked agitated. Rather than remind her about finding her application in the trash, Olivia took stock. *Elsie may be forgetful. Not surprising. This is a place for older adults, most of whom have cognitive issues.*

"It's no big deal," she assured the woman. "I filed online and Ms. Curry already called me back. She expects to see me this morning."

Relief flooded Elsie's face. "I'll tell her you're here." She made an about-face, walking toward the narrow doorway to the offices beyond. When she returned, a tall white-haired woman followed. Wearing dark slacks with a matching jacket, the woman exuded confidence. The aqua blue of her silk blouse matched her eyes. She blinked behind square-framed glasses, a big smile exposing large white teeth.

"I'm Agnes Curry." She stepped from behind the counter to shake Olivia's hand. "You've arrived right on time." Her voice had a slight Southern twang, softening her vowels in a pleasant speech pattern.

"Is that the autoharp?" she asked, pointing.

Olivia held up the autoharp for inspection. "This is it, my instrument of choice," she said with a smile. "I know it's not a conventional one."

"Oh, I think it's marvelous," exclaimed the director. "And perfect for our residents. When I was a girl my grandmother played the autoharp. Brings back such delightful memories. Let's move quickly so that you can sing and play for everyone this morning."

Agnes walked past Olivia toward the chapel. She stopped to call over her shoulder. "Move along now, we don't want your audience to get restless."

Olivia tucked the autoharp more snugly under her arm, hurrying to catch up.

Through a side door from the hallway, Agnes led the way to the front of the chapel. Instinctively Olivia observed her audience, testing the mood, taking in details. The room had changed dramatically since the funeral the day before.

The cross and cloths were no longer visible. The casket was gone, the folding chairs rearranged in a semicircle. Men and women sat in the chairs, a line of walkers parked against both walls. People in wheelchairs formed their own semicircle in the back row behind the chairs.

The podium remained where it had been the day before, front and center. When Agnes walked forward, a quiet fell over the room. Olivia stood behind Agnes. Since the day before, the communion table had been changed with a new cloth. It was now covered with a bright quilt to match the one on the podium.

Agnes Curry turned to explain, "You're not hired to play music, but I like that this is a talent you can share with our community. As you know by the application, the job is temporary. Your main job is to input data from our facility to the corporate system."

Sounds like I already have the job. Are they moving past customary hiring practices due to desperation?

Agnes Curry stepped toward the microphone, ducking her head slightly to speak. "Good morning, everyone," she called in a hearty voice. "I'm here to introduce Olivia Greer. She'll be entertaining you on her autoharp this morning. Please welcome her with a round of applause." Loud clapping came from the back of the room, followed by scattered applause. Olivia glanced toward the back of the room, looking for the source of the loud clapping. She shuddered.

Flex Million, my number one fan. He stopped clapping to wave at her with one hand.

Deliberately changing her expression into a smile, she walked closer to the microphone. "Good morning, everyone.

You must be the earliest crowd I've ever sung for. How are you today?"

Heads bobbed. One man on the end of the row lifted his hand to adjust the hearing aid behind his ear.

"I know it's hard for everyone to hear without my autoharp being amplified, but I'll do my best with the sound. Please nod if you can hear me."

Heads bobbed forward and back, except for a woman in the wheelchair row, who looked as if she was asleep. As Olivia ran her fingers over the strings, she thought about what to sing. When she looked up, her throat unexpectedly constricted with emotion. She sniffed and turned her back, pretending to tune the autoharp, but mostly to regain her composure. *I'm not sure I can handle all of these old people. They're so vulnerable. What can I give them to make everything better?*

She inhaled and then turned back to her audience.

In her loudest voice Olivia called out, "Let's sing 'This Land Is Your Land'. You know that one, right?"

Again the heads bobbed. Some people even smiled.

"Join me on the chorus and I'll sing the verses." Olivia jumped right in with three chords, singing the first verse. Soon she heard humming, and then tentative singing from the audience. By the end of the first verse, nearly everyone joined in on the chorus.

As she began the second verse, she felt her shoulders relax. To her surprise, the residents kept singing the words to the verse. Only a couple had dropped out to just listen. By the time the chorus rolled around again, full-throated appreciation came from the small assembled crowd as they sang the familiar sixties protest song.

"Wow, that would have made Woody Guthrie proud,"

Olivia said after the song ended. "I could take all of you on a road trip," she teased.

She stepped forward to duck her head as the audience offered a loud round of applause, glancing at the director, who gave her a questioning smile. Agnes Curry stepped up to the microphone.

"Wasn't that splendid? Let's have two more songs and then," she turned to Olivia, "you can meet me in my office while the residents head to the dining room."

Olivia stepped up to the microphone again. "I don't think we're ever too old to sing about that guy named MacDonald and his farm. What do you say?"

"I'll be the cow," chimed a small bent-over gentleman in the front row.

"You were the cow the last time," interrupted a large woman sitting beside him. "You get to be the chicken. I am the cow."

Olivia pointed to a few other residents, whose hands were raised. She assigned animals as she went. When they ran out of the barnyard regulars, the last woman said, "I'll be a lion." Everyone in the audience laughed.

They're just like children. It doesn't matter if lions are not kept on farms. It really isn't important.

She finished the last verse of the last song and then stood up to more applause. As soon as she bowed, people began to stand. Some hurried to their walkers as wheelchairs were rolled closer by volunteer attendants. Everyone headed to the exit.

Olivia glanced at the clock over the back door, then her eyes drifted to a woman pushing a wheelchair. *What is Sasha Ulrich still doing here?* Sasha, a smile pasted on her full lips, pushed the resident forward.

Olivia tucked her autoharp under her arm just before an

older man grabbed her elbow. "You were wonderful, honey. Please come back and sing for us again," he said, his eyes gleaming with tears.

When the man continued to speak, she leaned down to hear him better. "You remind me of my granddaughter," he added. "I haven't seen her in so long."

She patted the man's shoulder. "Kids just get so busy. I'm sure your granddaughter thinks about you all the time. What's her name?"

Before he could answer, a cold voice interrupted. "It's time for Mr. Adams to go back to his room." A walker had been rolled toward the old man. Olivia recognized the woman instantly.

"Hello, Echo. You work here too?"

"I volunteer at Hello Age," she corrected Olivia. "It's good for the soul to help out others less fortunate, don't you think?"

Less fortunate must mean in worse health, since everyone here is rich.

Olivia nodded. "That sounds right." *But it doesn't feel right coming from you. Maybe volunteering is good for the soul, but I wonder if you have another motivation?*

Elsie Meyer stood behind Echo, waiting to speak to Olivia. When Echo walked away, Elsie said, "Agnes had to leave."

"I'm so sorry," Olivia said. "I didn't realize she was in a..."

Elsie's eyes grew wide. "Tell me your name again."

"Olivia Greer," she said.

"Working with the elderly requires a lot of patience," Elsie said as if Olivia had posed a question. Then she looked at her own hand, where she held an envelope. "Here, Agnes left this note for you."

Odd that she calls other people elderly but doesn't include herself.

"You're a volunteer resident?" Olivia asked.

"I live here," Elsie proclaimed. "Though I know I look a lot younger than most. I volunteer to help out at the front desk. They keep me busy."

Olivia looked more closely at Elsie's face. Her blue eyes, large and wide, were devoid of crow's feet at the corners. Her smile, wide and cheerful, showed no visible wrinkles next to her mouth.

Why am I all of a sudden counting everyone's wrinkles?

"I appreciate your help this morning," she told Elsie with a smile. "I better be going." Olivia moved slowly toward the exit with the envelope in her hand. *I need to adjust my pace when I'm here. I don't want to run over a resident.* Once out the door she ducked around the corner to read the contents.

Congratulations. We've checked your references with your temp agency. They recommended you highly and forwarded us a recent background clearance. Please bring your social security card and other pertinent details tomorrow. After you sign our customary paperwork, we can begin your training.

By the time you finish the first week, your more formal background check will be completed and the probationary period will begin. Clock in by 9 in the downstairs work room. You will have a half hour for lunch and then leave at 2. Regards, Agnes Curry, Director, Hello Age

Folding the paper back into the envelope, she walked toward her car. Once in the driver's seat she took a minute to read her letter again. *I thought they'd ask for another interview and then go through corporate. But then Lily Rock is such a small town, maybe they needed to hire me right off the bat. My official job is to input data. The autoharp thing feels off, but then entertaining the residents must be a high priority. I'll text Michael the good news.*

I have a new job at Hello Age. Going to look for Raleigh at Thyme Out. Let's celebrate tonight and have dinner at the pub.

Before she could put her phone down, she heard the ping of a new text.

Great news. I'm with Cookie. No sign of Raleigh. Come join us for coffee.

She texted back.

Be there in 10.

She thrust her car into drive, heading back to the circular driveway. The benches along the grassy areas were occupied by residents. A few, basking in the sun, had their eyes closed. Olivia waved to a couple who waved at her. The last bench held two familiar women. Sasha and Echo huddled together, laughing like old friends.

It looks like those two know each other pretty well.

With sunshine streaming through the driver's side window, Olivia drove into town. She parked in front of Thyme Out, feeling a sense of accomplishment. *I've got a job!*

Inside the bakery, the warmth and aroma of yeasted bread made her stomach growl. Cookie stood behind the counter serving a customer. He gestured with his thumb toward the corner where Michael sat, a coffee mug on the table in front of him.

Olivia walked closer, bending to give Michael a quick kiss on the cheek. She glanced into his coffee mug. "For a guy who used to doctor his coffee with all sorts of sugar and milk, you've certainly changed your mind."

"Oh, that was the old Michael, before he discovered flavored coffee. Now I'm a caffeine convert. Can I get you a coffee?"

Olivia sat down in the chair opposite. "Yes, you can," she said with a deep sigh. "I'm feeling right with my world today."

When Michael returned, he had two mugs, steam drifting up from each. He placed them carefully on the table. "Look out, they're really hot," he warned. "Now tell me about the job interview." He sat across from her, leaning his arms on the table. His eyes lit up, encouraging her to speak.

Olivia told him the details of her morning. "By the time we sang another Woody Guthrie and the last moo, moo, moo of 'Old MacDonald,' the residents looked so alert and happy. I loved singing with them. Kind of surprised me," she admitted.

"Where have you been?" Cookie's loud voice brought silence over the bakery. Michael's brow wrinkled and Olivia stopped talking.

"I told you I had things to look into," came a familiar voice.

Olivia leaped to her feet, her chair scraping against the floor. *That's Raleigh.* Without explaining to Michael, she moved quickly to the counter. She found Cookie glaring at his employee.

"I want to talk to Raleigh," Olivia said.

"I have nothing to say to you," Raleigh growled.

Olivia felt Michael behind her. He stepped around, clearing his throat. "You may have nothing to say to her, but you'll listen to me. You got arrested because you were trespassing. Olivia had nothing to do with that, it's on you. Now take some responsibility and stop shifting the blame, because Janis Jets? She wants to have another chat."

CHAPTER TWENTY

Olivia woke up early the next morning, excited about her first day at the new job. Since Michael had taken a phone call, she was the first in the kitchen. He burst in a few minutes later, hair slicked back from his morning shower, speaking in an urgent voice. "Cookie just called. He'd like us to drop into Thyme Out this morning. The bakery's been vandalized."

"What do you mean?" Olivia turned from the sink, the dish towel in her hands.

"Somebody broke into the bakery last night and spray-painted a bunch of slogans on the inside."

Her heart began to race. "Did they catch the culprit?"

"No, but Cookie says he has someone on closed circuit. Maybe he wants to ask us to help with the painting and repairs. Let's go down there right now. We can have our coffee at Thyme Out and talk to him, figure out how we can help."

Olivia nodded. "I'm ready. Just have to grab my purse and lock up. Don't forget, this is my first day at Hello Age."

Michael looked down at his bare feet. "We'll hurry. Give me five minutes and I'll meet you at the truck."

By the time she turned to lock the front door, he'd already

started the engine. He reached over to give the passenger door a shove open.

Olivia hoisted herself into the seat and slammed the door behind her.

On the short drive to town, Michael was the first to speak. "Are you thinking what I'm thinking?"

She pulled her hair back into a ponytail. "Maybe our reluctant teen has taken revenge on their employer?"

"Right. That's exactly what I was thinking. Raleigh was in such a mood and so defensive yesterday. Once Janis picked them up and hauled them to the constabulary, I don't suppose the mood improved."

Olivia sighed. "You tried to talk sense to Raleigh. I hope Janis was able to listen and make some headway. I'm still wondering where Raleigh hangs out when they're not working."

"Maybe Janis put them in a cell overnight." Michael smiled.

Sighing, Olivia said, "Did we make things worse by confronting Raleigh and turning them over to Janis?"

Michael shrugged as the truck rumbled into town. "It's so early there's a spot in front of the bakery." Michael circled back to pull into a parking space. They both hopped out of the truck, Michael stopping to close her door.

"Everything looks okay from the outside," Olivia remarked, eyeing the bakery window.

"Except for one thing." Michael pulled up his sleeve to look at his watch. "By seven o'clock there's usually a line out the door."

Olivia's stomach growled. "I know two customers who are ready for coffee and a thyme muffin," she said.

Inside Thyme Out, Cookie stood behind the counter, arranging pastries in the glass display case. He looked up and smiled, though Olivia immediately noticed a wary look around his eyes.

One glance around the room made her realize why. Everywhere she looked, slogans had been sprayed on the walls with black paint. "Trans people won't be erased," the main wall stated in big letters. Scribbles and arrows pointed to the next message: "Protect Trans Kids". This one was printed in block letters on the wall beside the entrance.

Flowers sketched in black paint seemed to mock the words, as Olivia noted more and more messages. The one over the restroom surprised her. "All gender restroom," it boldly stated.

Olivia shook her head. "But that restroom was already for anyone who wanted to use it. Since Raleigh worked here, they wouldn't have painted that message."

Ignoring Olivia's remark, Cookie said, "Thanks for coming right over, guys." He looked at the walls and back to them. "What a mess." Then he swept his hand over the pastries. "By this time of the day we're usually out of cinnamon and pecan rolls. I'd try one of those."

Michael looked around at the empty tables. "People are staying away. I wonder why?"

"I'd love a pecan roll and one to go," Olivia said, stepping closer to the counter. "You just painted and now this. How exasperating!"

Cookie threw his hands into the air. "I gave them the job. I did my best to support their unusual appearance, and now this?"

Stepping away from the counter, Michael took a closer look at the damage. He inspected each wall and even two tables that were spray-painted over the top. "I don't think we should jump to conclusions," he said. "This may not be Raleigh. That's who we're all thinking about, right?"

The door jangled. Olivia spun around. Janis Jets, looking grim, stepped inside.

"Officer Jets, what a surprise," Olivia said, sarcasm dripping from her voice.

"He called me," she pointed to Cookie as she looked around the room. "Love what you've done with the place," Jets said, stepping between the tables, her hands behind her back as if she were admiring artwork in a gallery. Then she pointed at one of the messages. "This one about trans rights are human rights? I can't argue with that."

Cookie threw his hands in the air again, exasperation written on his face. "Always the cop. I want to talk to my girl-friend, do you suppose you could conjure her up for a minute?"

Jets grinned. She swayed back and forth and then crossed her arms in front of her body. With the flip of one hand she untied the bun at the back of her neck, her curls falling around her shoulders in a soft array. "You mean like this, big boy?" She sauntered over, slipping around the end of the display case.

"You poor, poor man. You've been attacked and maligned by one kid and a spray can. I'm so sorry for your loss." Jets batted her eyelashes, keeping her cheeky grin.

To Olivia's amazement Cookie roared with laughter. "Come here, you sexy goddess. Give me a kiss." He reached for Janis, enveloping her in a bear hug.

Janis inched her fingers up his chest to his face to stroke Cookie's goatee.

"Happy I could be of assistance, but that's enough of that," she said, stepping back from the embrace. "I'd like a large mug of black coffee, ten thyme shortbread cookies, and a table to take notes."

"Say please," warned Cookie.

"You're not getting a please from me," Janis said firmly. "At least not this morning. Maybe later. I'll think about it."

Once Cookie brought everyone coffee and pastries, he flipped the sign on his door to Closed. "Not like anyone wants to come in, but at least now it's on my terms."

Janis, her hair tucked back into a tight bun, opened her iPad. "So I'll take some photos and write down the details. Did you get a chance to look at the closed-circuit camera?"

Cookie slid his chair closer to Janis, looking over her shoulder. "I looked at the tape right away. I'll send you what I have. But let's just say it was a thin person, average height, with a black hoodie and black sneakers. I couldn't see the face, they'd pulled up the hoodie. The hands were covered by gloves."

Jets sighed. "I know it seems like Raleigh did this."

"I knew you'd blame Raleigh!" accused Olivia.

"As I was saying, it looks like Raleigh, but I don't think so."

Olivia took a deep breath. *Where's she going with this?*

"I say that because Raleigh and I had a good talk yesterday, and I'm convinced they're not responsible for Robert Ulrich Sr.'s death. Like Olivia has been saying, there was genuine love between grandfather and grandson. We ended our conversation on good terms, so I let them go."

"That's what the Hello Age residents told me about their relationship," Olivia admitted. "But then who did all of this?" She looked around the room.

"We'll call in the crew to look for fingerprints and clues, but I don't think they'll find much. If what you say is true and the person had gloves, chances are they were too careful to leave incriminating evidence."

"What I want to know," Michael said, "is how the person got into the bakery. I mean, Cookie has a camera and he locks the place. Plus I can see there's an alarm. The intruder must have known the code."

Cookie shook his head. "Someone might have looked over my shoulder to get the code. You know, an early coffee drinker. Sometimes they wait for me and I let them in. I come in two hours before I officially open, around four o'clock. That's my baking time."

"Anyone in particular?" asked Janis.

"Echo next door is always up early. She stops by. Then another man who lives up the hill, the retired insurance sales-man, he waits very early. Sometimes other people, even tourists. Oh, and the bus driver from Hello Age. He comes by himself really early on some mornings." Cookie scrunched his face and then relaxed as the other three stared at him. "That's my muscle relaxing technique," he explained. "Eases my anxiety."

Jets leaned over the table to whisper in his ear.

Cookie laughed. "That would work too," he told her with a wink.

It was Olivia's turn. "I'm worried about Raleigh. Even if they didn't do this, where are they staying?"

"They've found somewhere to sleep," Janis said. "They told me yesterday. They assured me they weren't breaking into any more cabins, so I let it go."

Cookie looked at Janis. "So when can I clean up this mess? Customers don't like to be told how to think when they're nibbling on a bran muffin."

Jets reached into her pocket. "I'll call the team and get them in here to gather the evidence. You can probably start painting over the slogans late this afternoon. I'll come and help," she said with a smile.

"We'll come too," added Michael.

Olivia's eyes flew open. "Oh no, I almost forgot. I have to

get to work." She looked at the time on her phone. "I only have half an hour to stop by the house to change clothes and then head over to Hello Age."

Michael reached into his pocket and handed her the keys. "We rode together so I'll catch a ride back home and pick you up. When do you punch out?"

"Two o'clock," she said.

"You're working at Hello Age?" Janis asked.

Olivia nodded. "Got the job yesterday. They liked my autoharp playing."

"You've got to be kidding me," Jets snorted. "I thought you were a temp typist, not a temp entertainer."

Olivia stood up, hiding her irritation behind a smile. "You know me. I can't help myself. Just a sing-along kind of gal."

Before anyone could object, she left the table, walking toward the door. Out on the street, she eyed the truck. To her surprise the Hello Age bus was parked in the next space in front of the bakery. "Hey, Olivia," called a familiar voice. Flex Million stood on the bottom step of the bus, a smile of greeting on his lips.

"You're here with residents?" she asked.

"Nope. Too early. They're all eating breakfast." He scratched behind his ear. "Between us, now that we're working for the same place, the old people get on my nerves. I need morning space so that I don't strangle an old person before lunch. So I'm here to put in an order with Kravitz. We're having a fancy reception next Friday."

"I thought you were the bus driver..."

"I do a lot of odd jobs for Hello Age." Flex glanced over her shoulder at the sign hanging in the door. "Looks like the place is closed."

"There's been a problem—vandalism inside the bakery. Cookie had to shut down so the police can investigate."

"Really? I didn't think Lily Rock had that kind of thing, you know, vandals."

"Oh, we have our share of crime," Olivia said. "Why don't you knock on the door? Cookie will let you in."

"Nah, I don't want to disturb him." Flex looked through the bakery window and then back at Olivia. "Looks like he's drinking coffee with that cop and your boyfriend. I'll come back later."

Olivia took a step toward the truck and then stopped. "You could have called."

"What do you mean?"

"Why didn't you place the order with Cookie over the phone?"

"I tried, but no one answered. I gave up and drove over. Everything's so close here and like I said, I need a break from the old people."

Olivia shrugged. "I'm off to my first day of work. See you later."

Once behind the wheel, she backed out from the space and then headed home. She rolled her window open, appreciating the breeze on her face, taking a moment to breathe and let her thoughts wander.

She remembered how good it felt to sing with the residents, and then her mind slipped further back to another time.

"Why are you always with your mother?" Don had accused. *"She's on her way out, dying from cancer. She looks terrible. It must be so depressing for you."*

"I love my mother. I only have a little time left to spend with her."

"I was just asking," he said defensively, with a slight smirk on his lips. *"Let the dead bury the dead, that's my motto."*

"Jesus said that. But I'm pretty sure he didn't mean ignore people who are sick."

"Jesus is your guy, not mine." Don shrugged.

Olivia shook her head, releasing the memory as quickly as it came. She pulled the truck onto the gravel road in front of her house. *I had to fight Don just to be with my mother. I should have known then.*

After parking the truck, Olivia walked toward her front door. She reached for her key and then caught sight of Mayor Maguire standing next to a potted geranium. His tail brushed back and forth, knocking dirt from the container.

"Hey, buddy. Last time I saw you, you were chasing a squirrel. Did ya catch him?"

The mayor's tongue hung out the side of his mouth. He stepped forward to lick her hand.

She bent over, wrapping her arms around his neck. "You're the best doggo ever," she told him. "Come on in. I can't play catch this morning, but I can give you a dog treat. I haven't told you yet—I have a new job!"

CHAPTER TWENTY-ONE

With fifteen minutes to spare, Olivia parked Michael's truck in the back lot of Hello Age. *I don't want to be late on my first day.* She grabbed her keys from the ignition, stepping from the driver's seat to the pavement, and hurried across the lot.

Unlike the upscale main entrance, the lower-level entrance reminded Olivia of a hospital. The red curb marked ambulance parking. Benches had been placed on the sidewalk, convenient for people to sit down to wait and to gather their strength. Olivia noted the two automatic glass doors and the accessible ramp leading from the building to the curb.

Durable bushes delineated distinct grassy areas. Green metal containers with signs reading "Please clean up after your dog" made proper dog waste disposal a priority.

A woman standing in the middle of a grass patch waited for her Corgi. She wore a straw hat and sensible shoes, and her powder-blue tracksuit was not a recent purchase.

"Sheila?" Olivia called out in greeting.

The woman extended the Corgi's lead before turning toward her. "Oh, I see you got the job. I was surprised to see you again at the concert. What a voice! You should be a professional."

Probably not the time to point out I actually am a professional.

"I'm glad you liked the singing. I have to clock in, but I'd love to talk to you later."

"You can come right up to my room," she said without a pause. "Room 1 1 7. Just knock. On your break, of course."

"I don't know where my office will be, but I'll find you," she promised.

"You can text me. I'll give you my number." The woman pulled a cell out of her pocket, putting in her code and handing it to Olivia. "Put your number under contacts and I'll text you and you can text me back. That's how it works."

Is there such a thing as woman-splaining? Olivia did as she was told. She handed back the phone. "See you soon." Once inside the building she stopped at the admittance desk. "I'm a new employee. Where can I punch in?"

"Break room, first door past the elevator," a man told her. Unlike the volunteers in upstairs reception, he spoke briskly as if he had much better things to do than give directions. She hurried away. *He's not a volunteer resident, he's an employee. That's the difference.*

Once she slid her time card through the digital time clock, she took a deep breath. *I made it with a minute to spare.* She hurried down the hall, stepping into the empty elevator.

When the door slid open on the second floor, she walked out into a completely different atmosphere. Gone were the clearly marked signs and people in hospital scrubs. Even the paint colors came from a different palette. No more bright white, the reception area was painted in shades of calming blue, carefully coordinated with the selection of chintz fabrics on sofas and occasional chairs.

She made her way to the reception desk. "Hello, Elsie," she said, waiting to see if she'd be recognized today.

"You're here right on time. I have the keys to your office," Elsie responded. She gestured for Olivia to follow. Olivia noted an inner atrium on her left as they passed closed office doors.

"How are you today?" Olivia asked.

"I'm well, though a bit groggy. Sometimes I sleep like the dead." She smiled. "Gallows humor, in case you wondered."

Olivia's eyebrow raised. "I suppose you get used to talking about death here at Hello Age."

Elsie frowned and then stopped. "We do our best to avoid the topic. Here's your office," she said, pointing to the first door on the right. Once unlocked, she handed Olivia the key, taking a quick glance over the room. "There's not much to show. The employee before you only stayed three months, but she kept the place tidy."

More like a spartan cell. So I have a desk, a chair, and a computer. No window. And there's a desk phone.

Elsie watched Olivia take in the space. Then as if she'd read her mind, she said, "You don't need a window to do the computer work. By the way, Agnes will be here in a minute to explain about your security code. I have to go now."

Elsie closed the door behind her.

Olivia walked around the desk, pulling open the bottom drawer and shoving her purse inside. Before she could adjust the chair, a knock came at the door. It opened a crack as Agnes poked her head inside. "Good, you're here," she said in her no-nonsense voice.

This morning Agnes looked the height of efficiency. Hair neatly coiffed in a '60s style, it reminded Olivia of a bouffant helmet. Glasses on her nose, her instructions were brief. "You'll have to set up a password and connect with our computer department. Dial one on the phone and they'll help you. They'll also send you a video tutorial about corporate rules and regulations."

Olivia scratched her head. "Could you explain the nature of my work?"

"Necrology. That's what you do."

Her stomach dropped. "Dead people?"

"The most important task of your job is to keep the records up to date when a resident dies. Once you've input the data, you send the completed form to corporate and then you clear the field."

"Clear the field," Olivia repeated faintly. "And what does that mean exactly?"

"I'll explain more later, after you finish the tutorials and get connected. Don't forget you take one fifteen-minute break and then a half hour for lunch. Those are the regulations for all part-time employees." Agnes turned on her heel and left the room, the slight smell of lacquer hairspray lingering in her wake.

Olivia sat down and spun her chair toward the computer screen. When she picked up the receiver and dialed one, a familiar voice answered.

"Flex Million," came the response.

He's also the tech guy?

"This is Olivia Greer."

"You must be in your office. I'll be right up to get you logged in." The phone clicked off.

If he comes in this small room and closes the door, I'll feel trapped. She leaned over to open the bottom drawer, nervously digging into her purse. Cell phone in hand, she shoved the drawer closed with her foot and walked out of her office. *At least I won't be trapped alone with Flex Million. He can tell me what I need to know here.*

Blue doors lined the right-hand side of the hallway. Through the glass windows surrounding the atrium, she could see more blue doors across the way. In front of her, against the glass, orchids bloomed.

The sign to her left read "Residents Welcome". Seeing an empty bench along the wall, Olivia walked closer and sat down.

"Need help?" A woman stuck her head out the door. She wore blue scrubs with her hair pulled back in a net.

"I'm Olivia Greer, the new temporary administrative assistant."

The woman nodded. "That bench is usually reserved for residents. We're the drop-in clinic. Since you're new here, I'll make an exception." The woman disappeared into the room, where Olivia could see an eye chart on the wall and a white coat hanging from a hook. At that moment Flex Million rounded the corner.

"I told you I'd come to your office," he said, standing in front of her.

"I'm still getting used to the building. Maybe we could walk and talk. You could show me around since I didn't get a tour last time."

"I don't have time for a tour," he said impatiently. "Let's go into your office and we can talk. Can't have one of the old geezers listening in."

"You can tell me everything I need to know right here," she insisted.

He shrugged, flopping down on the bench, sitting so close that his thigh touched hers. She immediately slid away.

Unfazed, he removed a paper from his front pocket. "Here's your access code. You can go in and get a password." He handed her the note and rose from the bench.

She glanced at the paper. "You could have told me this on the phone."

"Naw, that wouldn't have been as much fun. I wanted to chat with you without the boyfriend."

Olivia ignored his leer. "You know what I do, right? Something about necrology?"

"Oh yeah, I know. You'll last about three months. No one goes longer than that. Too depressing." Flex walked away, disappearing around the corner.

The writing on the paper looked childlike. *Handwriting says a lot about people.* She folded the paper and walked back to her office.

Behind her desk once again, Olivia logged into the computer, creating a new password. Then she logged into her account where she found an employee training video. While it loaded she thought about her new job.

So I'm supposed to input all the information from a resident's medical record. Then I send that to the corporate office. When all of that is completed, I click "clear the field". Someone's entire life erased in one click. She shuddered.

Later that morning, cell phone in hand, she decided to use her fifteen-minute break by walking around the Hello Age campus. She stepped outside the glass door around the corner marked Exit.

This side of the building had been carefully landscaped with grassy patches for residents to take their dogs. Everything looked well-manicured and flat. A man with a walker strolled past. He stopped to stare at Olivia.

"Who are you?" he demanded in a gruff voice. "Somebody's granddaughter?"

"I'm Olivia Greer, a new employee," she explained.

"I remember you now. I heard you play autoharp. I used to play that thing in grade school."

Olivia laughed. "We autoharp players have to stick together."

He shook his head. "You're too nice for this place. You won't last long. None of them do." He shrugged and rolled his walker toward the door.

Olivia's cell phone pinged. She lifted her phone. Sheila's name popped up.

Come up on your lunch break. Room 117.

She texted back. See you around noon.

Make it one. I'll be back from the dining room by then.

Okay.

After a few deep breaths, her break was over. Olivia returned to her office. She logged into her computer again, double-clicking on the first report. To her surprise it was Robert Bartholomew Ulrich. *He must have been the last person to die.*

She glanced over the statistics, scrolling down the page to his cause of death. The doctor's report read: "Patient died of asphyxiation resulting from complications of Parkinson's disease."

Olivia took a quick breath, feeling herself recoil. *I'm going to set aside Mr. Ulrich's report and work on another one. This feels too close to me right now.* She checked the larger file, making note of the recent deaths. *Four people died at Hello Age in the past month, just like Janis said.*

None of the other names looked familiar.

By 12:45 she'd finished her first report. The data entry had been routine. Unable to push the Clear the Field button, she closed down the computer. *Maybe I'll be ready tomorrow.* She found a granola bar at the bottom of her purse. After she wolfed it down, her cell phone read 12:55.

She found Sheila's room on the other side of the first floor and knocked. "Hello," she called out. "It's me, Olivia."

"Come in," came a faint reply.

The doorknob turned easily in her hand, and Olivia walked inside. She inhaled, smelling a combination of muscle ointment and chlorine disinfectant. "I'm right here," called the old woman.

Sheila sat facing the sliding glass door, which looked out on the Hello Age back parking lot. She turned the chair to face Olivia. "You can sit there." She pointed to a matching chair only a foot away. "We'll watch the parking lot together. Very entertaining."

Olivia sat as directed. "Thanks for inviting me," she began the conversation.

"It's my pleasure. How was your first day at work?"

Olivia folded her hands in her lap. "It's been interesting," she said.

"You don't have to hide anything from me, dear. I know what you do. I was friends with the girl before the last girl who had your job. She told me everything. As soon as Agnes discovered we were friends, she got the girl fired." Sheila's eyes darted around the room. "I wish I could remember her name, such a nice young woman."

"I signed a paper that said I wasn't supposed to make friends with the residents." Olivia watched Sheila's reaction.

Sheila chuckled. "It's so much more complicated than that. You are supposed to pretend to make friends with the residents, call them by name, especially when family members visit. Like a Disney character at a theme park, you're supposed to play a role, which makes the home-away-from-home atmosphere more authentic. But the truth? You'll get yourself fired if you get too close to anyone who lives here."

"So you invited me over so that I'll get fired?"

"I wanted to talk to you since you fill out all the forms for the dead people," she said matter-of-factly. "I want you to know something odd is going on here."

Olivia nodded.

"People just disappear. They get sick, go to the hospital care wing, and then *swoosh*, out the back door to the morgue. We won't hear until the funeral or memorial service that our neighbor, or even friend, has passed."

"Why the secrecy?"

"Corporate can't hide the deaths, but they don't want to draw attention to them either. Families may be concerned and take their loved ones away from Hello Age. The retirement community business is competitive. Overall, dead people are kept quiet because death isn't good for business."

"Empty beds don't bring in the cash," Olivia commented.

"That's sad but true," Sheila explained. "Once someone passes they make the bed ready for the next resident. There's a line of people wanting their elderly parents to live here." Sheila reached over to pick up a plate of cookies. "Care for one?" she asked.

"I ate five of those for breakfast, so not today. Thanks anyway."

"I do love Thyme Out. When the bus takes us into town, I ask Flex to stop at the bakery first thing." She munched a cookie, crumbs falling to her lap.

"How often do you go into town?" Olivia asked.

"Once a week, sometimes twice. We've been taking a cooking class, and then I like to walk in the garden next door. The woman who runs the place showed us how to pot herbs for our outdoor patios. It was fun."

"Were you on the bus when they discovered Robert Ulrich?" Olivia asked.

"I was, but I'm not surprised it was Robert."

"Why not?"

"We predicted he'd be the next to go."

"We?"

"My friend Walter and I. We keep an eye on everyone. It's getting so we can predict who will drop off next. It's become sort of a game between us, a competition actually."

"What do you look for?"

"First people take to their wheelchairs. Volunteers and nurses push them around publicly for a few days, so that everyone notices how they're well cared for. And then they're gone. Just like that. One week later someone new moves into the room."

CHAPTER TWENTY-TWO

Later that evening after they went to bed, Michael rolled over to take Olivia in his warm embrace. "You seem a bit distracted tonight," he said, nuzzling her ear. "Something you're not telling me..."

She burrowed her face deeper into the curve of his shoulder, closing her eyes.

"I'm finding my way." *I hate to tell him every time I'm preoccupied with my own teeny tiny feelings.*

"I'm glad," his drowsy voice answered. She felt his chest rise and fall, followed by a gentle snore. Michael's soft, steady breathing made her smile. She really didn't mind avoiding a deeper conversation with so much on her mind.

"First people take to their wheelchairs," Sheila had said.

The older woman's words had looped in her mind all evening.

Sheila and Walter can predict who will die next. Were those people going naturally...or were they pushed to an inevitable conclusion for other reasons? She rolled away from Michael's sleeping body to lie on her side. *And then what about Mr. Ulrich's death certificate? It says he died from*

Parkinson's disease. Maybe he tried to swallow a bite of cookie and a crumb got caught in his throat. Surely the coroner would have found evidence... Maybe not. People make mistakes. I only know that my gut tells me that Raleigh wasn't necessarily to blame...

Olivia closed her eyes to concentrate.

People die at retirement facilities, that's not new. But do so many people die in just a month?

Olivia's eyes opened. She curled her body so that her knees touched her chest.

In a fetal position, she remembered a conversation with her mother.

"Would you rather live in a care facility?" Olivia had asked that day. *"Professionals will be on call 24/7. You might feel more comfortable."*

"Olivia, I'd rather you had a little money left when I'm gone, to pay bills and get on with your life."

"You are more than money to me, you're my mom and I don't want you to go."

Olivia remembered sobbing as her mother held her hand. *She was so patient with me those last months.*

The months of treatments and the fear of loss had washed away during the weeks of outbursts. Olivia realized finally that she'd care for her mom at home. She got the courage to tell Don and went ahead. Not because of the money, but because she wanted to spend all the time she had left with Mona.

Olivia punched her pillow into a ball and then rolled over on her back. Head sinking into the softness, she closed her eyes. Finally her breath softened, becoming more regular. Aware that sleep approached, she sighed and then fell asleep.

* * *

When she awoke the next morning, Michael was sitting on the side of the bed. "I brought you coffee." His lips grazed her cheek. "You have to get to work and I have to drive down the hill."

She opened one eye, seeing steam rise from the mug. "Hot," she said, closing her eye.

He placed the mug on the nightstand. "I feel bad. Since I was tied up all day and then I fell asleep last night, you didn't have chance to tell me more about your new job."

"Yes, you did fall asleep." She opened her eyes, raising her head, and thumped her pillow. Shoving it against the head-board, she leaned back to smile at him. "While you were asleep, I processed my first day of work."

"Are you going to like Hello Age?"

"I can tell you more tonight." She touched the outside of the coffee mug. "Still hot."

"Give it one more minute to cool down. Do you mind if I shower and get going? I have a lot to do today."

A ping went off inside her head. Her eyes opened wider. "Are you okay? Anything you want to tell me?" She tossed out the question just to see if he'd duck or volley.

"I'm great," he said. "Just perfect. Going to see my lawyer about business. I'll be back for dinner, let's say around six?"

Olivia swung her legs over the side of the bed. She lifted the coffee mug to her lips and took a sip. "Lovely, just right."

Michael tousled her hair, making his way toward the bath-room. She heard the shower start, then smelled the sweet scent of lavender-musk body wash.

When he emerged from the bathroom, she'd left the bed to look out the window toward the woods. He had a thick towel wrapped around his waist. "How about I bring dinner home? I can stop at the Thai restaurant on the way up the hill."

"Satay chicken?"

"And two entrees," he added, "with pineapple rice for you."

* * *

This time Olivia circled the driveway at Hello Age fifteen minutes earlier than the day before. Steering toward a parking spot, she noticed a barn at the very back of the lot. *I wonder what that's used for.*

She parked the Ford in the shade. But instead of heading to the nursing care and employee entrance, she walked in the opposite direction toward the outbuilding.

Drawing closer, Olivia smelled a distinctive odor. *Smells like fresh paint.* A five-gallon can with three brushes and a metal lid opener stood by the front entrance. The door was closed, but an open lock hung on the hasp as if waiting for someone to return.

I don't want to knock because of the wet paint. So instead she removed the lock, hanging it on the metal hasp as she tugged to pull the door open.

"Anybody here?" When no one answered, Olivia stepped inside. As her eyes adjusted to the dim light, she looked around.

"Not what I expected," she said aloud.

Old furniture, rolled-up rugs, and boxes filled the room. Against every wall, chairs and tables had been stacked. At least six dining tables had been turned over, with boxes crammed between the upside-down wood legs. A narrow stairway rose up behind the furniture, heading to a loft. The opposite wall provided a backdrop for several china cupboards and two six-foot-tall bookcases. *This place looks like a used furniture store.*

185

She inhaled, smelling the familiar scent of lemon oil furniture polish, along with a touch of mildew. *Probably from the old fabric on the sofas.* Walking closer to a china cabinet, Olivia reached out to pull open a drawer. Inside she found silver cutlery, knives, forks, and spoons.

She lifted one knife, feeling its heft in her hand. *Not silver plate, more like the expensive kind. Must be worth a fortune if it's a service for twelve.* She slid the drawer closed. A scraping sound from the loft above made her look up.

"Anybody here?" she called again, feeling her heart flutter. The rickety stairway, dusty and worn, did not look safe. Walking closer, she put out her foot, tentatively testing the bottom step. *Probably just a cat or maybe a mouse...*

As Olivia drew her foot back, she heard her name.

"Olivia Greer. What the hell?"

Spinning around, she saw Flex Million. He glared at her from the doorway.

"This is private property," he announced, his eyes narrowing. He looked her up and down before adding, "Unless of course you came to visit me."

Olivia shrugged. "I called out, but no one answered. Since the door was unlocked, I thought I'd have a look. Part of my Hello Age campus tour."

He shrugged. "Oh yeah, I remember, the campus tour. This is your second day of work and you're already snooping around."

"Not snooping. I'm learning about my new job location. You must know that's important." She felt embarrassed. She also felt agitated, as if he had an advantage. *He's standing in front of the door. This is just the situation I wanted to avoid.*

"If you didn't come to find me, then get back to your own job. Temporary assistants belong in their office, not in the maintenance area."

Olivia ignored his threat. She turned to look over the room. "What is all of this, if you don't mind me asking? Looks like a used furniture store."

When he didn't move away from the door, Olivia pointed to the wood hutch. "That looks expensive. My mom had one like that, filled with all of her treasures, ones she collected over the years. I looked in the drawer—"

"You what?" He walked closer to pull open the drawer and look inside. "You can't do that, this isn't your stuff." He shoved the drawer closed. "It belongs to the residents."

"Just curious." Olivia's voice sounded calmer than she felt.

"You better leave that silver alone," he warned.

Since he no longer blocked the exit, she edged closer to the door. Before he could stop her, she shoved the door with her foot and stepped outside. Moving a few feet away, she pulled her phone from her pocket. *If I pretend to take a call, I'll look less scared. Boy, he gives me the creeps, but I don't want him to know. It would give him power over me that I don't need.*

When he stuck his head out, she announced, "Gotta go clock in. Thanks for the tour."

He sputtered and disappeared inside, closing the door behind him with a yank.

She began to sprint across the parking lot.

Approaching the entrance, she took shorter strides, and as she drew closer she came to a walk. By the time she stepped inside, she was no longer out of breath. On the elevator she thought about what she'd learned. *So Hello Age has a storage area for lots of antique furniture and valuables. Maybe residents keep their extra belongings there instead of foisting them on family members. Not everyone appreciates old stuff, even if it was Granny's from a bygone era.*

The elevator door slid open. She looked toward the reception desk. *No Elsie this morning.* Olivia walked toward her office when a familiar man appeared behind the desk, whistling softly.

Walter rested his gnarled hands on the counter and looked at her. "What can I do for you?"

"I wanted to say hi to Elsie."

"Out sick. How can I help you?"

"I met you last week at the Ulrich funeral. I've been hired as the new part-time administrative assistant." Remembering how residents could forget names and faces, she added, "My name's Olivia Greer."

"Yep. I remember you. Sheila told me they hired you. What brings you to the front desk?"

"I have an aunt who's looking for a retirement community. I wondered if you had any brochures I could share with her?"

"Oh, we got brochures." He reached under the counter, coming back with three glossy folios, all showing happy residents on the front cover. "We've got one brochure for every group," he added. "Is your aunt a woman of color? I have this one with Asians on the front, this one with blacks, and this one with other tones of brown skin."

Olivia looked at him sharply. *Does he realize how he sounds?* She decided to ask, "Are you being sarcastic?"

Walter's eyes suddenly softened. "Nice catch, young lady. I thought you'd just come for the job, but I see you are a keen observer and aren't afraid to ask good questions."

Olivia returned a smile as he continued to talk. "Sheila said you spent your lunch break with her yesterday. I was pretty sure I liked you when she told me that, but now I know I like you. Here's the info you want." He shoved the glossy brochures across the counter toward Olivia.

Olivia pushed them back. "I don't need these and I don't have an aunt."

"And so you lied to me." His bushy eyebrows wiggled up and down.

"I did lie, but I'm feeling very peculiar about this place and I want to talk to someone. I have an innate curiosity. I call it my inner detective." She smiled engagingly.

When he stared at her, she continued, "I feel like something's being hidden right in plain sight. I was up last night trying to sort out what was keeping me off balance, besides your bus driver, Flex Million."

"Oh, he's a creep. Let's make that clear. Even the old ladies have figured him out." He leaned on the counter. "So say more about what's bothering you exactly."

Olivia sighed. *I am confiding in residents when I've been strictly ordered to keep my mouth shut as a member of staff. I've gotten involved with these people. Only two days on the job and I'm already worried about them.*

"For one thing," she leaned over to whisper in his ear, "how much does this place cost?"

He stood up straight, a serious look on his face. Gesturing with his index finger, he nodded to invite her to his side of the desk. When she walked around, he pointed to a small black box on the counter.

Her eyes flew open. "Someone listening?" she mouthed.

His head bobbed up and down.

She returned to her side of the counter before speaking. "I have to get to work," she said in a loud voice. "Nice chatting with you." Olivia waved and winked.

Okay, so now I'm really uncomfortable. Why would management need to eavesdrop on an old man volunteer at the reception desk?

A tingle of apprehension raced down her spine.

CHAPTER TWENTY-THREE

A few minutes before two o'clock Olivia shut down her computer. With only a light to turn off, she was ready to go home.

She had to admit the solitude of her office affected her mood and spirit. *Sitting by myself, inputting data about the dead makes me feel jumpy and out of sorts.* She made a hasty exit through the building and into the parking lot. She ignored the outbuilding and unlocked her car. *I'm not going to think about Flex Million or that crazy outbuilding for the rest of the day.*

Once out of the parking lot, she turned onto the mountain road. The sense of relief felt immediate. *It's only two fifteen, I'm going to stop at Mother Earth and buy myself a new plant. Maybe that will help settle my nerves.* As she drove into town, the sun made her blink as it lowered behind the trees. Scattered bits of light bounced off her windshield. She lowered her visor, keeping her eyes on the road.

After she found a parking place, she walked toward Mother Earth. The wood gate stood slightly ajar. Olivia opened it slowly, anticipating the serenity of the garden.

Someone had recently watered; drops of water still clung to leaves. She took a moment to appreciate the smell of fresh loamy soil.

"In the back," called a voice, "be with you in a minute."

Olivia took note of the greenhouse a few feet away. *I bet that's where the houseplants are.* She entered the glass door, inhaling the humid earthy aroma. Varieties of fern attracted her instantly. She stood in front of a lacy maidenhair fern, resisting the urge to touch the tender leaves. *I want them all, but only one today.* Her eyes shifted to a larger fern in the back.

"Are you in the greenhouse?" came the voice.

"I'm right here," she answered.

"Let me know when you're ready to check out."

Olivia picked up a Boston fern and looked under the plastic pot for the price. *I could transplant you into a bigger clay pot; I bet you'd like it in our bedroom in that sunny corner next to Maidenhair. Ferns like to hang out together. That's what I've heard.* Decision made, she left the greenhouse, making her way to the cash register. She heard a strong voice speaking angrily. Instead of interrupting, she ducked to the side.

Echo's voice, sounding harsh, spoke out. "I moved here to open a nursery and plant shop. It has nothing to do with you. I didn't even know you lived in Lily Rock."

She held her breath.

"You don't even know your own mind. You may think it's a coincidence, but I mail you a check every month, and you knew where I lived by my return address. Stop kidding yourself."

That's Cookie.

"I keep telling you to use direct deposit like everyone else. Then we wouldn't be having this discussion," Echo retorted.

"And you are changing the subject yet again. Are you here to stalk me? Do I need a court order?"

Olivia's stomach clenched. She stared at the plant in her hand. *Maybe it's okay to interrupt this fight. They aren't getting anywhere.* She called ahead to give them notice. "Is anyone at the register?"

Cookie looked up. "Hey, Olivia." His eyes darted at Echo and then back. "I think I already told you we used to be married."

"Only for a few years," Echo said dryly. "Then he left me for another woman. No warning. Just goodbye."

Cookie rocked back on his heels, biting his lower lip.

He doesn't dare disagree. She'll only ramp up the anger. Olivia looked at the plant in her hands. "Glad to see you remained friends." She held back a grin, raising her eyebrows at Cookie.

For a minute she thought he'd explode, but then he took a breath. He nodded at her.

"How much is the plant?" Olivia asked, leaving no room for more squabbling.

Echo took the pot. "Ten dollars with tax," she said, slipping the fern into a paper bag.

Before she could pay, Cookie said, "See you later."

"Later," Olivia called. She turned to Echo. "Thanks so much," she said, lifting her plant from the counter.

"Oh, you're welcome. Now that you've heard us arguing, I might as well ask, have you known my was-band very long? I mean, you're single and he's single and I just thought you may have met, you know, in a Lily Rock bar or something. He used to work at the academy."

"I did meet him at the academy," Olivia admitted. "He's dating a friend of mine." As soon as she said it, she felt regret. *Oh man, I blew it. She doesn't need to know that her ex is dating. Not if she's the type to move her business right next door. What are you thinking, Olivia?* "Nothing serious though," she added quickly. "They're mostly friends, at least colleagues, that's what it seemed like, weeks ago, months really, not even important after he left the academy and started his bakery in town."

Stop babbling, Olivia. You sound like an idiot.

"Is that so..." Echo looked thoughtful. "He didn't mention anyone to me. What's her name again, your friend?"

Olivia ignored her question. "I have to go now. Thanks for the plant. Love your nursery and garden." She walked briskly away, holding her purchase to the side to protect the delicate fronds.

Once on the boardwalk, Olivia looked next door toward Thyme Out. *I want to check on Raleigh, but I'd better put the plant in the car first.*

Fern on the back seat, she rolled down the window an inch for air before locking the car and walking back across the street. She entered the bakery. "Where is everyone?" she asked Cookie, who stood behind the counter.

"We cleaned and painted, but the usual crowd hasn't returned. Business has been slow since the break-in. I don't know what else to do." He used a towel to wipe the already clean counter.

"So this one incident keeps the coffee drinkers of Lily Rock away?"

"Honestly, I'm wondering if my only employee may be the reason. People can be uncomfortable with the gender thing, and the walls were filled with gender references."

Olivia looked around the room. "I don't get that, but I can't argue with the evidence. No one is here." She glanced into Cookie's eyes. He shook his head.

"So another topic? You and your ex really don't get along."

"You can say that again. Want a muffin or a cookie?"

She came closer to inspect the freshly baked items. "What do you do with all the extras at the end of day?"

"I can sell some as day-old, but mostly I send them to Hello Age. The residents aren't picky."

Olivia laughed. "A resident offered me one of your thyme shortbreads just a few days ago. And then Flex said he came to pick up trays of cookies for some event. I think they keep dozens of cookies frozen at Hello Age, just in case they need them."

"That Flex guy was the first one here after the vandalism. He looked around and commented on every slogan. Kept asking me how I felt about it. Anyway, Hello Age keeps me in business, at least until the break-in becomes yesterday's news. So what will you have?"

"I'll take a thyme muffin and an herbal tea. I'm feeding my spirit with a new plant and some time at my favorite bakery. My new job feels depleting, so I'm doing my best this afternoon to improve my mood."

He handed her a plate with a muffin. "I'll start the hot water. Have a seat and I'll bring you the tea."

Sitting at a table for two, Olivia admired the freshly painted walls. Only one slogan remained, and that one had been refreshed. A new sign over the restroom door read Gender Neutral.

I bet Raleigh inspired that choice.

A few minutes later, Cookie placed the mug of tea on her table.

"Is Raleigh still working here?"

"I may not be able to pay them for much longer if business doesn't pick up." Cookie shrugged, watching Olivia admire the oversized lemon and thyme muffin.

After a bite she said, "These are delicious. The best muffin

I've ever tasted."

The bell over the door rang a few minutes later as Olivia licked the last crumb from her finger. "Hey, Raleigh," Cookie called out. "Come on over and say hi."

They came toward the table, the familiar prairie skirt dragging against worn running shoes. "Hey, Olivia," Raleigh said shyly, eyes downcast.

"Hi, Raleigh," she said brightly. "Good to see you. What's new?"

Raleigh looked at Cookie, a slight blush rising up their neck. "I came in to ask the boss a question. Echo wants me to help out with the plants while she's at the dermatologist. Would you mind, since it's not that busy this afternoon?"

"Are you working for her now? That's the third time this week you've ditched me for Mother Earth."

"I like it here, but Echo's paying me more and I need the money." Raleigh's head hung down.

"What's she paying you?" asked Cookie.

"She asked what you paid and she offered me two dollars more an hour. Like I said, I need the cash."

"I get it. Go on and help her out. We're only boxing up the day-old stuff. I can handle it."

"Thanks," Raleigh said, heading to the back exit.

"That was hard for Raleigh to ask," Olivia observed after he'd left.

"I know. We've been over and over the job and what I expect. It's just that Echo keeps coming in here and asking for Raleigh's help, interrupting the work with me. I get the feeling she's ready to steal my one employee."

The bell over the door jingled again. "Looks like you have another customer."

Janis Jets rolled in, all business in her police uniform and dour expression. "Need a coffee," she said, plopping herself down in the extra chair at Olivia's table. "How are you, Nancy Drew? New job must be keeping you busy."

"It's kind of weird, but I get a bad vibe from the place and all I do is input information about the dead. Pretty depressing."

"Not like solving crime, is it?" Jets smirked. "Now that's the life. Everyone wants to be me, kicking butt on a daily basis, interviewing suspects, hearing complaints from Brad every morning, pretending I care."

Olivia laughed. "Okay, so I'm not the only one disenchanted with her employment."

"Here's your coffee," Cookie said, putting the mug on the table. "Want a muffin, muffin?"

"I'm in uniform. Keep your sweet talk for later," mumbled Jets, eyeing Olivia's empty plate. "I'll take a muffin though. Make it one of those giant chocolate chip ones. Heat it while you're at it."

"Oh yes, ma'am," Cookie answered, stepping away smartly to comply.

"Just saw Raleigh walk in," Jets commented, taking a sip of coffee.

"I'm happy to announce the silent treatment is over. Did Raleigh tell you about their stepmom wanting them out of town?"

"They spilled their guts, if that's what you're asking. My problem is now that we've ousted them from the empty cabin, I don't know where the kid is living."

"I kind of wondered that myself. But I'm afraid to ask for fear I'll get the door slam again."

"It's not our business. But I don't want the kid to get into any more trouble. I can help with this first offense, but if they do it again, my hands are tied. I have to write them up."

Cookie stood by the table, a plate with an enormous

muffin in his hand. "And if you arrest Raleigh, you will not darken the door of my bakery again."

"Give me the damned muffin and stop talking nonsense. No one has arrested the kid yet." Janis lifted the muffin from the plate. She smiled at him and took a bite. "Yum," she said, licking her lips.

He burst out laughing.

Jets leaned back in her chair. "So, you and Mike want to go out for dinner sometime?"

"We'd love to have dinner with you guys. Let me talk to Michael when I get home." Olivia felt herself flush. "I thought since you fired me that maybe we weren't going to, you know, hang out."

"You thought wrong. Plus Cookie likes your company. She leered at Cookie, who stood next to the table with another enormous muffin. He grinned back.

A few moments later, the bell over the door tinkled again.

Raleigh walked inside, eyes wide. "Your car!" They pointed toward the outdoor patio. "Someone damaged your car. Come and see."

"Not my baby!" Cookie knocked over a chair as he hurried toward the back door. Olivia and Janis followed him outside.

Cookie stood, arms over his head, fists punching the air. A quick look at the Porsche explained why. The paint had been scratched from the front to the back on the driver's side. Long gashes, cut into the shiny red finish, made Olivia wince.

Cookie ran his finger along the gashes on the car. He followed one wide scratch that disappeared around the trunk. "They got over here too," he yelled. "The paint job is ruined."

His pride and joy.

Janis Jets's jaw clenched. "We will get whoever did this," she said calmly. "Someone will pay." Yanking her phone out of her pocket, she made a call.

"Get a fingerprint guy over here at once. Another act of vandalism at Thyme Out. And this time I want the evidence I need to arrest."

CHAPTER TWENTY-FOUR

By Thursday, Olivia finished entering the information for the residents who had passed away. The process of listing the information and sending it to corporate felt painfully slow. But the part where she cleared the field was insurmountable. All four residents' information still remained on her desktop.

How can one human being just sit back without a pang of conscience and click Return, effectively erasing another person?

After avoiding the process for days, she knew she had to make the move. *They've hired me to do this job.* She pressed the button for the first resident reluctantly, adding a silent prayer. *Be at peace.* Then she followed the process until she reached the last resident. *I can't clear the field for Raleigh's granddad. I just can't.*

She reviewed the information of Robert Sr.'s file once again. *I wonder if there's an answer on this form that could help Raleigh come to peace with their granddad's death?*

Hands posed over the keyboard, she felt the pull in her heart. *It's my break time. I'll leave the office and get some air.*

Maybe then I can come back and read through the Ulrich file one more time.

Once outside her office, Olivia smelled the permeating odor of Hello Age. A nurse on the other side of the glass window smiled as she passed. *People must be getting used to me.*

A man with a walker and a lady with a small terrier on a leash smiled at her. "Time for walkies," the woman said with a slight wave.

I like seeing dogs with their people. Olivia turned the corner. She found residents lined up at the reception desk. The woman in the front signed a paper with a Hello Age embossed pen.

Another group of residents gathered in the entryway. Two women stood in front of Flex Million. "Get going now, you'll be late," he chided. The two women turned away, accepting the dismissal without a fuss. They walked together toward the dining hall.

Olivia made her walk toward the entrance of the atrium. She stepped through the door, aware that she could be seen from all four glass walls. *Like a fishbowl where I'll be the only fish.*

None of the residents were seated on the benches, so she took the one farthest from the door. She had a direct view of the entry, where she saw Flex Million standing next to the reception desk. *Gotta keep my guard up. Flex is still creeping me out.*

Seated on the bench, she took out her phone. She clicked on an app she used for centering prayer. Before the gong on her cell sounded to begin the time of silence, she saw palm fronds rustle. *Someone's behind there.* Olivia kept her eyes open.

Her heart pounded. She saw a familiar pair of boots. She called out, "Raleigh."

She stood up as Raleigh disappeared through the door.

I don't want to chase them and draw attention.

With a deep sigh Olivia sat back on the bench. *I have a few more minutes.* She pressed Start on her app and closed her eyes. *Maybe Raleigh is sleeping at Hello Age.* She opened her eyes to glance at her phone. *This isn't working. My fifteen-minute break is over.* She sighed and turned off the app timer.

On the way back to her office she made a decision. *I can make it a habit to sit in the atrium at lunch to see if Raleigh returns. Maybe I'll catch them tomorrow.*

Facing her computer, Olivia felt the restlessness return. She closed her eyes, thinking about dinner with Michael the night before.

"Here's your pineapple rice. You can have most of the chicken satay if you like. I've ordered two entrees," he'd said.

Olivia raised her eyes. "Thank you for bringing the food. It's been quite a day."

"Tell me everything," he said.

"You go first. What were you doing down the hill?"

Michael took a bite and then ducked to look under the table. "Want a piece of chim-ken?" he asked.

"I fed the mayor dinner." She frowned, not satisfied at his deflection.

When Maguire heard his name, he rose, bumping against the table legs. With a shove, he emerged from under the table to stand by Michael's elbow.

"You're staring at my fork. I'll give you bites when she's not looking," Michael explained to the dog.

M&M's big eyes focused on the dangling piece of meat on the end of the fork.

Olivia laughed. "The dog is like you. He ignores everything but what he wants."

"What do you mean?" Michael's eyes twinkled.

"You're taking trips up and down the hill daily and you don't want to tell me what you're up to." She reached for more pineapple rice.

"Go ahead and finish that. So I won't deny I'm keeping a secret from you, but I will tell you as soon as all the pieces fall into place. Can you trust me on that?"

"Can you give me some hints?"

"Let's just say our future will be greatly enhanced if everything goes as planned."

"Now I am intrigued."

"I like a big reveal—you know, when everything is done and then the curtain is swept back."

Before she could respond, Sage entered the room. She wore her hair back in a ponytail, slacks, and a dressy work blouse. "Hey, you two. Any food left?"

"A little of this and that," Olivia mumbled.

Then she turned to Michael. "Better tell the mayor someone else is getting his chim-ken."

Michael leaned toward the dog. "You gotta share, buddy."

A low growl came from the back of the dog's throat.

As Sage reached for the carton of rice, Olivia told them about Cookie's car.

"The thing is, I think Raleigh may have done the damage. I don't want to think that, but they rushed into the bakery, the first to know. I've heard people who vandalize like to be there to see people's shock." Olivia shook her head.

"I don't want to think it's Raleigh," Sage had admitted.

The memory from the night before faded as Olivia stared at her computer.

Sage is right. I don't want to think Raleigh could be a

202

vandal. *But then I never took Raleigh for someone who would break into a cabin. Maybe I've been mistaken about them, taken in with the emotional upheaval of the trans journey and the pronouns.*

Olivia pushed her thoughts away. Without a window, she had nowhere to look except at the computer and blank walls. She brushed a stray piece of hair behind her ear, taking a deep breath.

She sighed. *I'm not getting much work done today.* Then she pulled her lunch bag out of the bottom drawer, making her way toward the door. She walked rapidly to the atrium, where she hoped to see Raleigh again. She sat on the same bench, her eyes on the exit.

The gentle sound of water splashing over rocks came from behind the bench. Intrigued, she left her lunch to walk closer. Only a few feet from the bench, she discovered the source of the sound. Rocks had been arranged to form a waterfall emptying into a pond. Two cymbidium orchids, tucked to the left, waved with large blooms of white flowers, yellow at the center. Surrounding the orchids were ferns. The display made Olivia gasp with pleasure.

Her eyes drifted to a nearby plaque inserted in the dirt. "Designed and maintained by Mother Earth," she read aloud.

Back at the bench, she opened her lunch sack. She'd packed pieces of apple and a peanut butter sandwich along with a napkin. Alternating bites, she kept her eyes and ears alert for any sighting of Raleigh.

It only took minutes to finish her lunch. She folded her paper bag. *Lunchtime is over.*

She stepped through the atrium door into the hallway. The sound of murmuring voices came from the dining room. Passing the reception desk, a volunteer resident stood behind the counter, eating from a plate of food.

Olivia stopped to say hello. "How's the food?" she asked in a friendly way.

"Pretty good," the woman mumbled. "I'm looking forward to dessert." She nodded at the thickly frosted three-layer cake.

Biding her time, Olivia glanced over the woman's head toward the large bulletin board behind the counter. She stopped to read under the Special Activity section. Everything from knitting to poker night were offered for the residents' weekly entertainment.

Then she blinked. "Karaoke," the notice read. "In the community room at four o'clock on Sunday, meet your friends for some fun and then go together to the dining room for supper. Crab cakes, with big lumps, will be served."

Olivia nodded. An idea niggled in the back of her mind.

I can bring the autoharp and volunteer to sing after my work hours. I can also ask Raleigh to join me. We can sing together, and maybe they will stop to talk.

Olivia said goodbye to the volunteer, hurrying to her office. Unable to ignore her work any longer, she opened the Ulrich file. The first page listed all the general patient information about height, weight, and blood pressure. *All that looks normal. In fact, Granddad had excellent numbers for a man who was in his early eighties.*

Robert Ulrich Sr. had appointed Sasha Ulrich as his contact person. *So the daughter-in-law was Robert's go-to in case of emergencies. Would that make her the person who would make life or death decisions should Robert be incapacitated?*

Olivia had no trouble picturing Sasha efficiently pulling the plug if that difficult decision needed to be made. In fact, she had been very eager to tell the emergency services at Mother Earth not to attempt resuscitation. She moved her face closer to the screen. Her eyes grew wide.

"My grandchild, Raleigh Bartholomew Ulrich, will make all health decisions on my behalf, should I be unable to make them myself." *I stand corrected.*

So he wanted Sasha to take care of the paperwork, but he wanted Raleigh to make any big health decisions. *Raleigh, not Sasha.* Olivia's heart beat faster.

Then she glanced at her phone. *It's almost two o'clock.* She closed the Ulrich file. Taking a minute to absorb what she'd discovered, she thought, *Robert trusted Raleigh to make good decisions. He deliberately didn't burden his grandson with the day-to-day paperwork. He left that to Sasha.*

If I walk slowly, I'll clock out just in time. On the way to the elevator, she ran into the kindly woman walking her Corgi. "I love your dog," Olivia said.

The woman smiled while the dog stopped to sniff her shoes.

Olivia petted the dog, then moved down the hall. When she reached the reception desk, she waved at Walter and Sheila, who were on duty. Deep in conversation, they didn't notice.

Olivia stepped up to the counter. "Have either of you seen Raleigh Ulrich around here lately...Robert's grandson?"

Walter smiled at Sheila before he turned toward Olivia. "Funny you should ask, young lady. I stopped and talked to Raleigh this morning."

The hair prickled on the back of her neck. "Really? Do you know why they were here?"

"I do," offered Sheila. "Came to look through some of Robert's belongings."

"I remember their stepmother was busy cleaning out the room. Over a week ago now, when I first came here."

"Oh, the room got cleaned out already. But Robert's valuables have been stored in boxes in the outbuilding at the far end of the back parking lot."

"Where Flex Million's office is located?" Olivia knew the answer, but she wanted to hear what Walter and Sheila thought.

"That Million character keeps all of the residents' belongings out there. I keep asking him about my box of clocks, but he never has an answer. I had some antique ones that were quite valuable. Don't suppose I'll ever see those again." Sheila sniffed.

Walter patted her hand. "Don't worry, dear, who needs an antique clock when you have a cell phone?" He held his in the air. "This little gadget is worth ten clocks any day. Plus you can call me whenever you want. No clock does that."

Sheila shook her head as if not entirely convinced.

Walter looked at Olivia. "Why did you ask about Raleigh?"

"I thought I saw them today, when I was taking my break in the atrium. They aren't good at picking up texts. I want to talk to them."

Eyes narrowed, Walter leaned closer. "What would that message be exactly?"

"'Tell Raleigh to call me." She smiled and added, "'They have my number."

CHAPTER TWENTY-FIVE

When Olivia arrived at Hello Age the next morning, she had her autoharp tucked under her arm. *I'm going to sign up for the karaoke night and maybe, just maybe, I'll have a chance to talk to Raleigh.* Olivia began to hum under her breath, "You are my sunshine." *Everyone will know that song.*

Once inside her office, she put her purse in the bottom drawer, keeping her autoharp on the desk. She continued to hum, "You make me happy when skies are gray." To her surprise, even more administrative work arrived in her email. This time it did not pertain to death. Olivia took a sigh of relief and got to work. *Maybe I passed a trial period at corporate and they feel ready to give me more to do.*

After half an hour she felt the old restlessness return. *I'm going to take a walk. That might help.* With her office key tucked in her hand, she left, passing the nurse's station on her way to the front lobby. She stopped at the reception desk to ask, "How do I sign up for karaoke night?"

Elsie handed Olivia a slip of paper. "Put your name here and the song you want to sing." She watched as Olivia read and checked boxes. "I'm happy you like us enough to share your gifts and talents. Staff who volunteer their own time mean a lot to Hello Age."

Olivia glanced up quickly. "One question about the form. I won't need backup music. I'll bring the autoharp and provide my own."

Elsie shook her head. "That's not how we usually do things. We have electronic music for the vocalists. But I'll tell Flex, he has the final word on karaoke night." She took the slip from Olivia's hands.

Flex has a lot of authority about nearly everything at Hello Age. And then as if she'd conjured him with her thoughts, she heard his voice speaking loudly from the front entrance.

"Step over here, ladies. We'll be leaving in five minutes. I'll bring the bus around."

Olivia turned to watch the gaggle of residents forming a line, preparing to walk onto the Hello Age bus. Sasha and Echo stood in the back together as if chaperoning the elders.

"Where's Flex taking the gang so early in the morning?" Olivia asked.

Elsie leaned over the counter, speaking in a conspiratorial voice. "It's a secret mission. Every three to four months, different people, depending on the specialist's schedule, are transported down the hill for appointments. I have to leave the desk now to join them."

"See you later."

Elsie took off her name tag, dropping it in a drawer beneath the counter. Then she headed toward the back of the line.

Olivia watched as Flex counted heads. He wrote on his clipboard and then glared straight at her.

She made it a point to smile, making her way around the corner and out of sight. Her curiosity increasing, she stopped to listen to the voices from the lobby. A bulletin board gave her an excuse to linger. Her eyes looking intently at the notices, she kept her ears open for more conversation.

"I can only take seven more on the bus," Flex insisted. "You went the last time, Berta. So you can't come this morning."

"Will we be back in time for lunch?" Olivia recognized Elsie's voice.

"Of course we will. Do I ever make you ladies late for a meal?" Flex sounded injured.

"Oh Flex, we love you." An unfamiliar voice spoke in a high-pitched tone. "Here you go, sweetie, I'll put this in your pocket. A little extra for a rainy day." Olivia assumed the resident paid Flex for the inconvenience that vexed him.

A special doctor's appointment for a few select residents. *Maybe I'll mosey down to reception again to observe the residents coming off the bus. I can find out more about Elsie's specialist.*

Back in her office, Olivia turned on the computer. As she waited for the login screen, she felt her edginess return. *Just do the work,* she told herself. Then she typed in her password to read the entire Ulrich file once again. Olivia scratched her head.

I'm going to break a rule and print this file for Janis. If she hasn't heard from the coroner about cause of death, at least she'd see what I see and would realize that Raleigh was their granddad's number one choice to make end-of-life decisions.

Olivia glanced at the printer sitting next to her autoharp.

Of course, I could get fired if I print Robert's file. It's against all the regulations that protect patient confidentiality.

But I have to help Raleigh.

Olivia moved her cursor to the corner and clicked Print. Within moments Robert Bartholomew Ulrich Sr.'s records spewed onto the desk. She secured the papers with a clip in the corner, shoving them into her purse in the bottom drawer.

Since Flex is out with the bus, I could take a look in his office one more time. I may poke around and see if I can find Raleigh while I'm at it.

She put the computer to sleep.

Once in the parking lot, Olivia stopped to catch her breath and look around. She pulled her phone from her back pocket, pointing the camera in the direction of the outbuilding. With her fingers on the screen, she zoomed in, directing it toward Flex's office door to see if he had left it open.

Olivia pocketed her phone and headed across the lot. *If anyone asks, I wanted to talk to Flex about karaoke.* She pulled on the door, stepping inside.

To her surprise someone else was already in the room.

"Raleigh, I wanted to talk to you!"

Bent over a cardboard packing box, Raleigh stood up, face flushed.

Olivia's eyes lingered on an old-fashioned clock that they held in both hands. "What are you doing?" she asked.

Raleigh glanced at Olivia, then back to the clock. "I help Flex out sometimes, when I'm not at work in town." Raleigh put the clock back in the box, bending the cardboard flaps closed.

"Was that one of Sheila's? She told me about her collection."

"Yeah, Flex keeps resident stuff in this building, his office."

"Sheila told me Flex couldn't locate her belongings."

"That's why I came out here. To look around and see if I could help. I like Sheila and Walter."

When Raleigh didn't say any more, Olivia switched to another subject. "I'm glad we ran into each other. I'd like you to sing with me at karaoke night in the community hall."

"Sing with you?" Raleigh's voice sounded confused.

"I miss working with the Tone Rangers and I know what an incredible voice you have."

"I haven't sung since the music academy. What songs do you have in mind?"

"I know we get one song and I signed up for an old favorite that I'm sure you must know. 'You are My Sunshine'?"

To Olivia's surprise, Raleigh's eyes filled with tears. "That was Granddad's favorite. He'd ask me to sing with him whenever we were together."

I'm onto something here. Go gently and don't scare them. Olivia waited a moment, giving Raleigh a chance to harness their tears. "Did you sing that last time, when you met your granddad in the garden?"

Raleigh sniffed. "I did. We sang together before I went back to Thyme Out. Granddad was very supportive of my job at Thyme Out. He thought I'd make a good baker."

Raleigh's eyes filled again. Olivia used her voice to comfort rather than an embrace. "So I'm not supposed to tell you this, but I've been looking at your grandfather's intake papers, the ones he signed when he first came to Hello Age. Did you realize he put you down as the one to consult for end-of-life decisions?"

"He told me a couple of months ago when he wrote up another will."

Raleigh looked perplexed. "I can't find the will, but he might have left it with his lawyer or with someone else."

"Did Sasha come across it by any chance?"

"She might have, but she hasn't spoken to me since the memorial, which is fine with me." Their jaw tightened and their eyes glanced furtively back and forth. "I'd better get going. Flex will be here soon."

"Will you take the clock to Sheila?" She pointed to the box.

"I'm gonna wait. But I'll tell her I found it for sure."

"Be sure you do. I don't want you to be held responsible for it being misplaced. You seem to have a gift for showing up at the wrong time and the wrong place. Maybe Officer Jets can help and get you on the right path."

"I know," Raleigh mumbled. "I'll tell Sheila." Raleigh looked closely at Olivia. "So that's why I'm here, but you never said what you came for."

Olivia scrambled for an excuse. "I needed to iron out some karaoke details with Flex."

They both looked at each other. *I think they knows I'm lying.*

When Raleigh didn't say any more, she swallowed uncomfortably. "This is a complete change of subject, but do you think that telling the truth sets you free?"

"Yeah, but only if you're able to speak the truth without getting the crap beat out of you."

A warning tingle ran up Olivia's neck. The kind that happened when something important had been said. *I suppose if you're trans and you know your truth but no one wants to hear you, you learn to duck and tell lies to keep safe. That may be why Raleigh looks so guilty all the time.*

Of course, they may still be guilty. They broke into a cabin and took up residence. If angry and frustrated, they may have painted the bakery walls with slogans and keyed Cookie's car. They may even have been ready to steal an old lady's clock.

Filled with doubt, she inhaled, reminding herself, *But I believe in Raleigh. I don't know why, but I do.*

The tingling stopped. She glanced toward the exit and then gestured to Raleigh. "Let's go together." Olivia stepped aside, losing her balance when her boot hit against a metal object. Looking down, she stared. *At least it doesn't look dangerous.*

"It's a trap," Raleigh told her. "They call it a have-a-heart trap, when you catch critters without harm, and then release them into the woods."

Olivia felt another tingle up her spine. "Would it by any chance be good for catching, let's say, squirrels?"

"Oh yeah, perfect for that. Flex does it all the time. He traps and then releases them behind the outbuilding."

So that's how Flex did it. Olivia bit her bottom lip. "I'm going to go back to work. If I don't see you, let's meet before karaoke begins. We can run the song and some harmonies ahead of time."

"You are my sunshine," their clear tenor began to sing.

She smiled in response.

Outside, Raleigh lagged behind Olivia, and then abruptly cut around the building without a word. She made her way across the parking lot. She hurried to the lobby, stopping with a sigh, sighting the Hello Age bus pulling away from the curb. All the residents had disappeared.

I must have missed them.

Walter stood at the reception desk by himself. A plate of food lay in front of him. He reached down to pick up the sandwich, smiling at her. "Need any help?" he asked, then took a bite of his food. Dabbing his lips with a napkin, he swallowed. "Sorry about the hasty bite. I'm feeling a bit peckish. Anyway, do you need something?"

"No, I was just wondering if the bus had returned. I have a question for Flex."

"I think he's eating in the dining room today. One of his special ladies always treats him to lunch on Friday. It's part of their arrangement."

"What kind of arrangement?" Olivia asked.

"He takes them off campus down the hill at least once a

month for beauty trips, he calls them. The beauty parlor, the nail salon, and then the skin guy."

"The skin guy?"

"The one who gives Botox injections. Residents visit him a lot."

Walter didn't smile nor did he look perplexed. He just took another bite of sandwich.

So that's why so many of the women at Hello Age have frozen expressions and no crow's feet.

CHAPTER TWENTY-SIX

On Saturday morning Olivia and Michael lingered on the deck, cool breezes rustling the trees above. Michael stretched his arms over his head. "So good to have time to ourselves," he remarked, reaching to take a mug of coffee from Olivia's outstretched hand.

"I think Sage is sleeping in." Olivia balanced her mug in her hand as she sat next to him facing the woods. Leaning back in the chair, she propped her feet on the rail. "Lily Rock is shimmering this morning," she said, admiring the rock formation rising above the tree line.

"So the first week at the new job and you haven't found one dead body," Michael remarked in a matter-of-fact tone.

"Nope," she said.

"That's excellent news." He reached for her hand. "I'm thinking after our dinner date with Janis and Cookie, we could relax in the hot tub."

She felt her pulse quicken. "We've been in the house for months but never gone in the hot tub."

He stood, leaning over the rail. "Marla and I had long talks about the perfect location for her hot tub. I walked the space for weeks until I found a break in the trees. I wanted her to have a clear view of the stars at night. She laughed so hard when I marked a big X with my boot in the dirt." He looked up to smile at her.

"I loved Marla's laugh," Olivia added. "And now the hot tub is for us."

"I guess it is, but it still feels a bit awkward."

"Awkward and sad," admitted Olivia. "It's like borrowing a prom dress from a friend. It never fits exactly right because it was meant for someone else."

"We're alike, you know. Neither of us expected the house to be ours." Before he could expound on his feelings, a voice came from inside the house.

"Hey, you guys started coffee without me. Is there more in the pot?"

Sage stood in the doorway.

"I made twelve cups," Olivia said calmly, "help yourself."

As Sage retreated toward the kitchen, Michael continued to stare at Lily Rock. "Would you grab her a chair?" Olivia asked.

"Will do." His voice sounded serious.

"Anything the matter?" Olivia felt uneasy. *Is Michael upset about something?*

"Not a thing. I'll get the chair."

By the time Sage returned with her mug of coffee, the third chair had been arranged on Olivia's other side. Sage sat down, holding the mug in both hands, looking out at the view.

"How was work this week?" Olivia asked.

"The kids are settling down and ready for spring break. So am I," Sage admitted. "Will you guys be around?"

"For spring break? Since I just started a new job, I don't think I have any time off yet."

"Okay, so you don't mind if I meet up with some friends in

216

Colorado? I'm going to drive. I hope to do some hiking."

Sage didn't look at Olivia, which aroused her suspicion.

"There's lots of hiking in Lily Rock," commented Olivia. "Am I to assume it's the company in Colorado that you seek?"

Sage smiled. "Yes, assume it's the company. I'll know more after I get to know him over spring break. Don't worry, I'll report every detail."

Michael cleared his throat. "Company is important," he said calmly. "Speaking of company, I've been thinking about this place and you two a lot lately. I wondered how you're doing with the living arrangement. You and Olivia, newly discovered sisters and all."

"I love living with Olivia! It feels like we've been connected for years. Plus she's been so generous adding my name to the house deed. How could I not love being here?"

Olivia stomach churned. *We're all happy, the three of us. Two bedrooms on different floors with lots of privacy. We only come together in the kitchen and sometimes out here on the deck. It's like the perfect roommate arrangement. At least I thought so...*

Michael responded to Sage. "So I can see that you and Olivia make great roommates. But I'm like the extra wheel. I'm here all the time, in fact so often that I feel like I might be...kind of a burden."

"You are not a third wheel!" Olivia said instantly. "Isn't that right, Sage?"

When her sister didn't answer immediately, Olivia felt her stomach knot.

Sage finally spoke. "If you must know the truth, I'm the one who feels like the third wheel. When Michael spent most of his time in the cabin, I didn't notice. But now that you live here, I wonder if I should move back with my mom to give you two some privacy."

A rush in her ears told Olivia she'd landed on emotional ground. Her inner voice began to scream. *I want you both. Right here. Together as a family. Maybe I need to talk to Sage.*

"Gotta put this in the trash," Olivia said, rumpling a napkin in her hand and making her way toward the house.

She hurried through the doorway toward the kitchen. Dropping the paper into the trash, she stood at the sink. *Deep breath.* She stared out the window at Marla's garden, wondering why she felt so strongly.

Footsteps came from behind. She felt Michael touch her shoulder. He whispered in her ear, "Didn't mean to upset you."

She crossed her arms in front of her chest, refusing to turn around to face him. "Why didn't you just say so before...the third wheel stuff?"

"If I'm not mistaken, I did just say so right now. And see how you reacted? I didn't want to burst your family bubble. Apparently Sage felt the same. We've both been dancing around your feelings for quite a while now."

"I had no idea. I'm sorry," she mumbled.

"For what? Wanting to have a family with a boyfriend and a sister in a huge house all wrapped up like a Hallmark movie?"

A small smile crept to her lips. "I guess it was too good to be true."

He kissed the top of her head. "Actually, I have an idea that might ease this situation. I'm not quite ready to spring it on you, but now that we're out in the open about our feelings, maybe you could be patient a little longer. I'll talk to Sage some more while you whip up a batch of muffins or something."

"I'll do that," she said softly.

He left Olivia staring out the window into the woods.

I feel so foolish, like I'm the only one who didn't notice their discomfort. I was blind because of Marla. She left me this beautiful house and I thought I had to be really grateful to her. I am grateful. But that doesn't mean Michael and Sage feel the same.

Olivia mixed the muffin batter with a wooden spoon. She spooned enough batter to fill each spot on the tin three-quarters full. Once in the oven she made herself busy tidying the dishes in the sink. Then she pulled the glass carafe away and refilled her mug with coffee.

Once through the glass doorway, she stepped outside on the deck. Michael and Sage were laughing at Mayor Maguire, who chased his tail in an endless circle.

"He showed up while you were making coffee," Michael explained.

The mayor stopped to look at Olivia. His right ear raised as if to listen.

"Hey, M&M," she said softly.

He wagged his tail, coming closer to sit at her feet.

"Stop by for breakfast?"

He rose up on both paws, his tongue darting out to lick her chin.

* * *

Later that evening Janis Jets closed her menu. "So Cooks and I decided you two are our official couple friends." She smiled across the table at Cookie, who winked back.

"Yep, we had a discussion and think that you both qualify as couple friend material," he added.

Olivia smirked. "So how did we qualify exactly?"

"More importantly," Michael placed his forearms on the table, looking earnest, "what do we have to do now that you've bestowed this honor upon us?"

219

"I thought you'd ask that," Jets snickered. "For one thing you have to share food when we go out to dinner. No bogarting your entree and the extras. We give each other access to tasting at least, you know, one grab at a time."

"Spoken like a true foodie," Olivia said.

Janis sighed. "I don't really care about eating from your plate, it was his idea." She nodded her head toward Cookie. "So I guess I'll share. Reluctantly, just so you know."

Michael looked around. "I'm ready to order. Where's the waiter?" While they waited, he redirected his conversation back to Janis and Cookie. "Before we get down to agreeing to be your couple friends, we need to know who else is in the running. Will you be offering Meadow and Thomas a chance at the prize? Or how about Arlo and Cay? They own the pub, and it would be sweet to get a free beer-of-the-day from them."

"Nope, they're not in the running," Janis insisted. "Just you two."

"Plus," Cookie added, "Mike and I are going into business together, so being couple friends is a natural continuation of our connection."

"You are business partners?" Olivia didn't hide her surprise.

"You kind of figured, right?" Michael smiled. "His bakery needs a selection of gourmet coffee blends. Plus I wanted to start a small enterprise in Lily Rock to get into the good graces of the town council. I sort of moved past them with Marla's help on the house. Then Arlo got me over the hoops with the pub. But this is my own idea. They tend to go along with more visionary ideas if you already have a business in town."

Now Janis looked interested. "You have visionary plans? Who knew?"

Michael opened his mouth to explain, but Janis shut him down.

"I don't care about your plans that much. Flag down the waiter again, would you? I need to order my hanger steak before they run out and I'm stuck with a hamburger."

Michael waved his arm over his head just as the waiter stepped up to the table. "I'll take the seafood risotto," Olivia said first, while the others stared at their menus.

"Hanger steak rare," said Cookie.

"Hanger steak well," said Janis, giving him a hard stare. "You know I won't share a piece of meat that's still mooing."

"Eggplant parmesan," said Michael, laughing at Janis.

Once the waiter left the table, Olivia leaned toward Janis. "So I hesitate to tell you, but I've broken the law."

"What, again?" Jets's left eyebrow lifted. "On the one hand you just can't help yourself, can you? But on the other hand, you're boring when you're not in trouble. So spill. What have you done now?"

Olivia looked over at Michael and Cookie, who were already deep in conversation. She reached into her purse and pulled out the folded papers, leaving them on her lap. "Here's a medical report from Hello Age. Mr. Ulrich's intake file," she emphasized. "I'd like you to have a look." She shoved the papers at Janis under the table.

Janis tucked her hand under the tablecloth, her eyes narrowing. "You kept his private health file. There are laws about this, Olivia! What the hell?"

"Shush," she said, her finger on her lips. "I didn't tell Michael."

"He'd be furious if he knew," Janis hissed back.

"He thinks I take too many risks," she admitted.

"That's why you're no longer my assistant."

"What do you mean?" Olivia felt her face flush.

"I mean he was worried about your safety and the way you care about people, plunging yourself into danger without a

221

second thought. Like these papers, for instance. If Hello Age finds out about this, you could have a lawsuit on your hands. That corporation has a cutthroat reputation, in case you didn't know. They'd sue you to make an example for the pure fun of it."

A chill traveled down Olivia's spine. "But everyone seems so nice there, the staff and everything."

"That's their ruse. Four deaths in one month is way over the average for nursing homes. We're looking into it, but in the meantime, keep your head down."

"And the papers?"

"I'll look at them when date night is over. What exactly do you want me to know?"

"It's in the beneficiary part, the details about who is responsible for end-of-life decision-making. By the way, did you hear anything from the coroner?"

Jets groaned. "What is this, girlfriends' gossip hour? I'm not talking to you about the coroner."

"Please tell me. I'm worried for Raleigh. They're in a vulnerable place right now, with the trespassing incident and all of those problems at the bakery. Do you still think Raleigh is innocent, that someone else did the vandalizing?"

"I like the kid, but it looks like Raleigh was there and had access," Janis admitted. "Would you stop worrying about them? The kid will be okay for a while longer. I just wish I knew where they were sleeping. I haven't been able to figure that one out."

Do I tell her Raleigh might be staying at Hello Age?

Olivia looked past Janis's accusing stare, trying to catch Michael's eye. She could tell that he'd detached from the conversation with Cookie by the way he stared at his hand on the table. When he didn't say anything, she looked away. "Oh look, here comes the waiter with our food."

* * *

"Did you enjoy couples' night?" came Michael's lazy voice from the other side of the hot tub.

She closed her eyes, remembering their walk minutes earlier.

Once they were home, they'd made their way outside, stepping gingerly in oversized bathrobes over the stone pathway. "Watch your step," he'd said, his voice all but lost in the dark.

Bubbles came up on the surface of the water with steam hovering above. Michael reached over to slip the robe from her shoulders. She shivered as he helped her step into the tub. The water came up to her neck, feeling warm and welcoming. Still watching her in the water, he dropped his robe, his naked body slipping into the tub right after her.

"I liked couples' night," she said, squinting to see his face through the steam. "I can hear you but can't see you. It's really dark tonight."

His face came closer, his eyes looking mischievous. He reached out to lift her chin, his finger traveling down to trace her neck. He ran his hand over her chest, stopping at the top of her breasts.

"I can see you just fine," he said, leaning in, his mouth soft and warm on her lips.

She reached under the water with her hand, touching his firm belly, moving it lower until he gasped with pleasure.

He pulled her body toward him, lifting her slightly. As the water splashed around them, Olivia thrust her hands on his shoulders to keep her balance.

She looked up to see the stars shining overhead and then buried her face into his wet shoulder. "Don't stop," she told him. "Don't ever stop."

CHAPTER TWENTY-SEVEN

On Sunday Olivia held her autoharp under her arm, watching Hello Age residents assemble in the community room. Unlike when she'd sung for her job interview, all the rows of chairs had been removed, rearranged in small groups around round tables.

There was a portable bar toward the back, where cocktails were being served by Elsie Meyer. A bright pink feather, sticking up from her bejeweled headband, made her easy to spot across the room.

The lights, dimmed to create atmosphere, hid the more institutional aspects of the room. A pseudo nightclub vibe permeated the space. Olivia noted that many of the residents dressed in cocktail attire. Some of the ladies wore black dresses, along with sensible shoes. The men donned sport coats.

Olivia sniffed. *Smells like camphor, probably mothballs.*

Residents with walkers were escorted to tables. Once they were seated, the walkers were rolled away to be stacked against the wall. Residents in wheelchairs were rolled under tables without standing chairs, two per table. Small battery-powered lamps had been set on starched cloths, giving off a soft glow.

Olivia looked toward the back of the room. Echo, wearing a black shirt tucked into black slacks, pushed the wheelchair of a man whose head listed to the right. His eyes closed as if he were asleep.

Echo slid the man's wheelchair under the last available table. She adjusted his lap blanket, placing his hands over the top.

I wonder if that man is a relative of Echo's? Dismissing the thought, Olivia looked around the room, hoping to catch sight of Raleigh. When she couldn't find them, she walked closer to Echo's table to say hello.

"Good to see you," she called out in a friendly voice. "Are you signed up for karaoke?"

Echo's face hardened. "Don't be ridiculous," she snapped. "Are they paying you overtime for some reason, is that why you're here?"

Olivia brushed aside the question. She held up her autoharp. "I'm volunteering. I'm going to sing with Raleigh."

Echo bit her bottom lip. "That pathetic person? They're not worth the trouble, lingering around all the time, looking for handouts. I would have thought you'd have better things to do than sing with them."

Olivia's cheeks flushed in anger. She looked at the man in the wheelchair, hoping he had not heard. Head listing to the side, his eyes were still closed. *Is he even alive?* She held her breath and then felt relief; behind his eyelids she could see movement.

"Is this man a relative?" she asked Echo.

"Oh no, I met Mr. Adams months ago when I was here caring for the atrium plants. He struck up a conversation and I promised I'd be there for him toward the end."

Olivia nodded. "Does that mean he has a terminal illness?"

"That's none of your business," retorted Echo.

"It isn't. You're right. I remember caring for my mother years ago. The last days and weeks are an important time for a dying person."

"He needs me, I'm sure." Her eyes drifted, looking over Olivia's shoulder. A smile came to her lips. "Look who's coming, Michael Bellemare. He's quite the catch. I can only imagine what you had to do to get him."

Olivia's jaw clenched. Aware that she was being baited, she wanted to push back Echo's insinuation. Before she could respond, Michael had made his way across the room and touched her shoulder.

He politely smiled at Echo. "You're the owner of Mother Earth. Nice to see you under better circumstances." He took Olivia's hand.

Echo glanced up at him, coyly batting her eyelashes. "Oh, I've seen you several times since Robert's death. You've been over at Thyme Out with my was-band. I only have to look from the back gate to see you two talking away. You're thick as thieves."

Michael released her hand to put his arm around her shoulder. He gave her a squeeze. "Kravitz and I have a small business plan in the works. I see him a bit, but most of my free time is spent with Olivia, every minute I can get." He pulled her even closer, ignoring Echo.

"You know," Olivia said to the woman, "I'm surprised you still have your ex's last name. Kravitz?"

"I'm Echo Kravitz," came her calm reply. She lifted her chin with a satisfied smile. "We were married and that's my legal name." Venom dripped from her tone.

Olivia felt Michael's body stiffen at her side.

It's time for me to make an excuse to get away.

226

"We have to go and find Raleigh. They're the other half of the duet tonight. Nice to see you again."

"See you later," Michael said offhandedly, steering Olivia away. They inched through the crowd, heading toward the far wall.

"Do you believe her?" Olivia said, feeling more free now that they were out of Echo's hearing.

"There's something wrong with that woman. Cookie told me as much. I believe his exact words to describe her were 'wack job'."

"Cookie may not take her seriously, but I do. She's kind of sinister. Plus she really hates Raleigh. Before you arrived, she couldn't say one nice thing." Olivia looked around the room. "It feels like they're ready to start. Every table is filled, and all the chairs on the back walls are occupied."

He cleared his throat. "I have to admit, I think Raleigh's in some trouble. You have such a soft heart for the vulnerable. Has Robert Sr.'s will been found yet?"

"No, it hasn't. And I'm worried. Raleigh has so little family support. Besides us—you, me, and Cookie—no one else sticks up for them."

"I only met Raleigh's father that one time at the funeral." Michael scratched over his ear. "You said he lets his wife handle all of the business with Hello Age."

"Sasha was around a lot the week after Mr. Ulrich's death. Plus I saw her talking to Echo. Talk about thick as thieves, they seem pretty close, or so it seems." Olivia's eyes glanced to the clock over the entrance. "Waiting for Raleigh is making me anxious."

"Do you know where to look for the kid?"

"They pop up all over the place. I caught Raleigh in Flex's office and, I think, in the Hello Age atrium just this week."

A voice over the loudspeaker called out, "Hey, guys and dolls."

Olivia gulped. Flex Million stood center stage, the microphone in his hand.

When the audience quieted, he continued, "It's time to start our karaoke night. Don't you fall asleep, Mr. Adams," Flex joked.

All heads turned to the back of the room, where Echo waved.

"He's got a pulse?" Flex asked with a laugh.

"Oh, he's listening," she responded in a girlish voice.

Michael leaned closer to Olivia. "I saw the signup sheet. You two are the last act. Let's go look for Raleigh. We'll be back in plenty of time."

Olivia nodded her agreement. With the autoharp under her arm, she led the way out of the community room. They walked down the hallway, heading toward the back entrance. "It's so quiet. I usually see residents and their dogs wandering the halls. The friendly ones say hello. Nice people."

He smiled at her. "Everyone likes you, that's why."

"I guess."

Before they passed the nurses' station, Olivia pointed to a resident's door that was slightly ajar. "I bet that resident forgot to close the door. Probably in a big hurry to get a front table at karaoke night."

She stepped closer. Before she could reach the knob, the door flung all the way open.

Raleigh, hair disheveled, eyes wide, stood in front of them. "Hey, Olivia." They looked past her shoulder. "And hey, Michael," they added.

"What are you doing here?" Olivia asked, alarm clear in her voice.

"It's okay. This is Walter's place. He lets me come and go. I have a key." Raleigh held it up for her to see.

"Why would Walter give you free access to his place?" Olivia asked.

Raleigh hung their head. "Come on inside. I'll explain."

Both Michael and Olivia followed, closing the door behind them.

Once inside the room, Raleigh explained. "This is a two-bedroom unit. I've been sleeping in the spare bedroom on the futon. Walter told me it was okay, until I could save enough money to move out."

"Does the management know?"

"Nope. They don't let people under the age of fifty-five spend the night. That's why I've been hiding. And if family members stay when there happens to be an extra bed in a suite, they have to sign in at the reception desk. There's a three-night maximum rule."

"So that's where you've been," Olivia said. "You know Jets thinks you're trespassing in another cabin."

"Walter wanted me to stay with him. He thinks people are out to get me. He offered the place to give me a chance to continue my search."

"Search for what exactly?" asked Michael.

"Granddad's will. If I don't find it soon, Sasha will get everything. She's probably paying her lawyer to work on the estate as if there were no will, which means all the money would go to my dad and to her. My dad never sticks up for himself."

"Would that be so bad?" Olivia asked. "I mean, you're young and can get a job. We'll help you out and so would Cookie. You can make it in the world without a big inheritance."

I'm one to talk, living the life in Marla's house that I inherited.

"It's not that!" Raleigh raised their voice. "Granddad put aside money. That's what he wanted." Raleigh shook their head. "I don't even know what I'd do with the money, but Granddad told me that wasn't important. He wanted me to have options, you know, for my future, so that I didn't have to rely on Sasha and my dad." Their eyes blazed bright with tears.

Olivia swallowed. "Okay then, that makes sense. Sasha isn't getting the stepmother of the year award. That's pretty clear."

Michael looked at Olivia and then back to Raleigh. "I get it. Things are beginning to make more sense now. So you weren't the one to vandalize Thyme Out, were you?"

"No way! I want to be a baker just like Cookie. I like my job and I'm learning a lot."

"I believe you," Olivia said. She used her free hand to check the time on her cell phone.

"I do too." Michael smiled.

"We have to go now," Olivia said, shifting the autoharp to slide the phone back into her pocket. "Let's lock the door and head to karaoke. They started half an hour ago, so it may be close to our time."

"Sure," Raleigh said.

They made it back just as loud applause poured out of the community hall. "And next," Flex Million announced, "will be Olivia Greer and Raleigh Ulrich."

Olivia took Raleigh's hand, making her way through the doorway, carefully sliding by several tables to the sound of light applause.

"We didn't even rehearse," Raleigh whispered loudly.

She tugged on their hand. "Not to worry. You've got this. 'You Are My Sunshine'."

She watched tears fill their eyes.

"I know you'll be perfect. I'll do the harmony. Wait for me to count you in." Olivia shoved Raleigh to the center of the stage.

She took the microphone from the stand. "We're singing a familiar song tonight. This song happened to have been Robert Ulrich's favorite. You all remember Robert. He passed recently. His grandchild, Raleigh, loved this song too. The two of them sang it every time they were together. Why don't you sing along?"

Olivia replaced the microphone. She lifted her autoharp and looked around.

"I'll just need a chair," she said.

"Here you go." Michael smiled from a few feet away. "I lifted it from the hall. You have a full house tonight."

Olivia sat down, leaning the autoharp against her chest. She reached around with her hand to strum lightly on the strings. "In tune," she told Raleigh. She played three chords to give Raleigh the key.

"Got it," they said. "You remembered my register from before."

"I did," she admitted, strumming the three-chord signature again, leaving no more time for talk.

"You are my sunshine," Raleigh sang out, taking a long pause. The audience grew quiet. "My only sunshine," they continued. Olivia heard a slight tremor in Raleigh's voice. Concerned that they'd break down in tears, Olivia added her voice, giving Raleigh time to compose himself.

Tears brushed away, Raleigh joined in on the second verse. In two more phrases, the audience began singing along. People smiled, their faces glowing with happiness.

By the end of the song, applause filled the room. Olivia watched Raleigh take a bow. She rose to her feet to stand next to them and they bowed together. With the autoharp tucked firmly under her arm, she glanced to the back of the room, searching for Echo.

Her eyes stopped at Mr. Adams. Slumped over from the waist, his face was entirely hidden in his lap. Olivia glanced around the room but could not find Echo. *No one is paying any attention to Mr. Adams.*

And then her eyes stopped on a familiar couple. Walter and Sheila were staring right at Mr. Adams, heads nodding together. *Looks like they've predicted another Hello Age death.*

CHAPTER TWENTY-EIGHT

The following Monday, Olivia arrived at work fifteen minutes early. Unsure what to do with her few extra minutes, she leaned against the hood of the Ford, her eyes inspecting Flex Million's barn office.

From the distance she could see Raleigh standing in front of the door, eyes darting back and forth nervously. Olivia raised a hand over her head to wave. When Raleigh nodded back, she came closer.

"You're here early," she said.

"I like to give Walter some space in the mornings. He tends to talk and then he misses breakfast in the dining room."

"That's not good." Olivia smiled at his consideration for his temporary roommate.

"I just ate a cinnamon bun from Thyme Out. Want one?" Raleigh reached inside a paper bag.

"No thanks. I've just eaten. Are you really just hanging out here to keep out of the way? What if Flex sees you?"

"He doesn't come to his office this early. He's making the rounds of the residents before doing bus errands," Raleigh said.

"Making the rounds...say more."

"He spends most mornings talking to the residents who pay him. He asks them about their stuff or if he can do any extra errands for them during the week."

"Does the corporation know about Flex's extra income?"

"I'm pretty sure they don't. He keeps it on the down-low."

Olivia took a quick glance at her cell phone. "I only have a few minutes before I clock in, so I'd better be going."

"Wait," Raleigh pleaded. "I want to tell you something. You know the other day, when you saw me looking through boxes?"

"I remember."

"I realized later that might have looked suspicious. I want you to know that I wasn't trying to steal anything. I was looking for Granddad's will."

Olivia felt relief. *So Raleigh knows how lots of people assume the worst. Why didn't you tell me that at the time? Why did you hold back?*

"I get that. But I do want to hear your reasons, so start right now."

Words tumbled out. "I've looked everywhere for that will, in all of the boxes, not just Granddad's."

"You're looking for something in writing that's been witnessed, right?"

"Oh, I know I won't find the paper document. I'm not wasting my time looking for that. Granddad left his will and letters on a thumb drive."

Olivia felt shocked. "So many older people aren't that tech savvy."

"Before Sasha moved him to Hello Age, my granddad was on his computer every day."

"Where did the computer go?"

"I suspect Sasha grabbed it when he wasn't aware."

"So no will and a missing computer."

Olivia remembered the day Robert Sr. passed away, how Sasha stashed his cell phone and the other items, the thyme cookie and the herb branch, which were left on his lap.

"Like I was saying, Granddad was pretty smart for an old guy."

Olivia's heart beat faster. "Did he open the drive and show you the information?"

"Not exactly, but he did show me the drive. It was cutesy and unusual. It looked like it belonged to a schoolkid. There was a small yellow sun at the top."

"Wow, Raleigh, that's so incredible." She sighed. "You realize that thumb drive was for you? He left a symbol, the sunshine, because that was your song."

Their eyes filled with tears as Raleigh admitted, "I didn't put that together."

More accustomed to their emotional responses, Olivia waited for Raleigh's tears to stop.

After they wiped their face dry, they said, "I have other people to back me up. Sheila and Walter were the witnesses on the will. They told me when Granddad passed."

Olivia absorbed the information. Then she confided in Raleigh. "I probably didn't tell you, but the first time I visited Hello Age, Sasha told me she was cleaning out your grand-dad's room."

Raleigh scowled. "I bet she found the paper will and destroyed it. But there's a chance she didn't know about the thumb drive."

"Did your granddad give any hint where he'd keep it?"

"I've thought hard about that. I even called his lawyer, but he never called me back." Raleigh's shoulders slumped.

"You told me your father is intimidated by Sasha."

"He won't help! He doesn't even talk to me."

"Has that always been the case?"

"We never got along. He doesn't like my gender fluidity and just makes such a big deal. It feels like they both try to make me look unstable. No one in my family treats me like I'm smart. They judge me on my clothes and pronouns, as if I have a mental illness."

Olivia fidgeted. "By the way, have you looked in Flex's desk or on his computer?"

"I was afraid to do that," Raleigh admitted. "If he caught me, I'd be in bigger trouble."

"The desk would be a good place to continue the search, but I understand you don't want to cross Flex. I've noticed that people shy away, like he has some sort of power over them. Is that your take?"

"People either pay him to do something or owe him for something. No one crosses Flex."

"You confirmed my suspicions. Flex is most likely nervous about his illegal small business at Hello Age. But I have a feeling there may be more."

"You're kind of a detective," Raleigh smiled. "We're alike because we both notice stuff other people don't."

Olivia grinned. "But now I have to go before someone finds me missing from my office and starts wondering." She smiled and waved goodbye to Raleigh, sprinting across the parking lot.

By the time she looked at her computer, she saw one new message in her inbox.

See attached paperwork. Resident Thorgood Adams passed away yesterday. His daughter will be here tomorrow to collect his belongings.

Olivia gulped. *Walter and Sheila must have known, just like they told me. She* downloaded the attachment to her desktop. *I can't concentrate on this right now. I need to find out*

236

about that thumb drive. If I make an excuse to visit Flex's office, I can look through the desk.

Olivia eyed her printer. With the press of a button, the ink cartridge moved front and center. She lifted the black ink cartridge out. With one toss, it landed in the trash.

Looks like I need a new cartridge.

Olivia left through the side door. She walked around the building to the back, down the slope until she arrived in the lower parking area. Instead of taking the direct path across the parking lot, she ducked into the woods, strolling where no one would see her.

When she reached Flex's office, she pulled the door open, leaving the lock hanging in the hasp. With a quick glance over her shoulder, she entered the building.

Flex's desk looked tidy. The Hello Age phone, along with a computer and printer, were the same vintage as the ones in Olivia's office. She stopped to consider. *If Flex gets all the death notices I do, he could get the jump on sorting out a resident's valuables, maybe before their families. It would be so easy to pocket cash or jewelry.*

Olivia looked up toward the loft and then back to the computer. A wave of discouragement came over her. *Flex could have pocketed the thumb drive and hidden it anywhere in this mess.*

I might as well look inside the desk. She opened the long narrow drawer usually reserved for pens and paper clips. She ran her hand to the back, coming up with a few crumbs but no thumb drive.

She pulled out the top side drawer. A set of 3x5 index cards, rubber banded, sat in front. Olivia picked up the pack. Each card held a resident's name at the top. Underneath in block printing, there was a list. *Flex kept a written inventory for himself.*

Olivia found Robert Bartholomew Ulrich Sr's card immediately. A line had been drawn diagonally through the information. *Flex went old-school with this antiquated system of keeping track. Was he afraid an electronic list would implicate him in something illegal?*

Her curiosity aroused, she shoved the top drawer closed. The middle drawer was empty. Finally the bottom drawer held promise. A metal box, the kind used to collect cash, was the only item in the drawer. Olivia lifted it out. The lid was locked.

Looking around the room, her eyes landed on a small workbench with tools. Grabbing a screwdriver, she poked the narrow edge into the lock. *Click.*

She opened the metal lid and found a roll of bubble wrap inside.

Picking away the plastic, a metal thumb drive lay exposed. A small plastic sun had been molded to the end, just as Raleigh had said. She shoved the bubble wrap back into the box, shutting the lid. Sliding the thumb drive into her back pocket, she dropped the box into the drawer, closing it with her foot.

She headed toward the door. Looking across the parking lot, she saw the empty Hello Age bus parked at the entrance. *They must be back from the drive into town.* One quick glance backward assured her that the lock was where she'd found it, hanging open on the hasp. Then she felt a prickle on her neck.

Someone's watching me.

"You come to see me?" asked a voice from the corner of the building. Flex Million, arms folded over his chest, glared at her.

She swallowed back her fear. "I need a new ink cartridge," she said, dredging up her preplanned excuse.

"You get those behind the reception desk," Flex said

matter-of-factly. He walked closer, standing an inch away. "You should know that by now. No more excuses about being a new employee."

This was a new Flex. Not the annoying flirty man who tried charm first to get his way. He seemed more aggressive, setting her nerves on edge. *I can't let him know I'm afraid.*

Olivia looked him in the eye and then looked away. "Okay, you got me. I thought I'd catch you alone and, you know, see what you're doing for lunch."

A small smile started at the corner of his mouth. "So I got something you want?" He leered at her.

Olivia bit her bottom lip. "It's too late now. I have to go." She waved her cell phone in the air. "Maybe another day," she called over her shoulder. This time she deliberately walked through the center of the parking lot, where she could be easily seen. *He's less likely to follow if I'm in plain view.*

It wasn't until her office door slid closed that she reached into her pocket for the thumb drive. *I won't look at this on a computer until I get home.* Instead of returning it to her pocket, she shoved the thumb drive down the side of her shoe. Her cell phone pinged with a text from Raleigh.

Did you find anything?

I did. She added a smiley emoji.

Before she could look at her computer screen, her cell phone buzzed with a call. She glanced at the screen. Janis Jets. She pressed the green icon. "Hey," she said softly.

"Hey yourself. I need to talk to you now," came Jets's voice.

"Anything in particular?"

"I got the coroner's report about Robert Ulrich Sr. Plus I heard someone else died last night, some guy named Adams. Know anything?"

"I got a notice about Thorgood Adams's death."

"Yeah, that's the guy. On the one hand I get that most of

those old people likely die because they're old. But on the other hand that's four people last month plus two more this month. We can ask for the coroner to look at Mr. Adams before they rush him away for cremation.

"I can't believe I'm saying this," continued Jets. "But thanks to you I have the information from the Ulrich guy. It may not hold up in court since you stole the evidence, but I think I can move forward with more confidence and get a warrant to check it out."

"I haven't read Mr. Adams's papers yet," Olivia admitted. "Did you find something suspicious?"

"That's for me to know and for you to find out. Come down to the constabulary after work and I'll fill you in. Don't want to talk anymore over the phone." Jets clicked off.

Olivia smirked. *I guess I can tell her about the thumb drive later.*

CHAPTER TWENTY-NINE

Later that afternoon at the constabulary, Janis Jets looked all business sitting behind her desk. Olivia stood at ease in front of the desk, her tongue in her cheek. "How are things?" she asked innocently, watching Janis's jaw tighten with irritation.

Jets growled. "I've just been thinking. How do you do it!" Her fist smacked against the desk. "You get a perfectly innocent temp job at an old folks' home; what's the harm in that, I would ask?"

"None, I would answer," Olivia said. "Aren't you happy to be rid of me?"

"Your boyfriend is happy, so I'm happy. I hired the drug overlord of Lily Rock..." She rolled her eyes. "Okay, even I admit that's an exaggeration. Brad's not smart enough to be dangerous. But I hired him anyway to be my assistant, because God forbid your boyfriend gets mad at me again."

Olivia sat down in the chair opposite Janis, her curiosity piqued. "Why would Michael be angry at you?" she asked.

"He was furious with me when you worked here, I said as much over dinner. About took off my head after the undercover assignment I handed you at the music academy. Geez, I can't have Bellemare, architect to the rich and famous, mad at me over a temporary hire. So I fired you and grabbed the next warm body. Happened to be Brad. He sacrificed—he put away his weed business to work for me. He's not a bad typist..."

The explanation stopped as Janis took a breath. Her jaw tightened and she began again. "On the one hand, you are good at getting people to confess, but on the other hand? You get right smack dab into the middle of my next investigation. Nobody invited you, Miss Smarty Pants. On the other hand..."

Janis suddenly drew her lips together in silence. She glared at Olivia, who had stopped listening, turning her head to look at the door and around the room. "I'm talking here. What are you looking for?" Janis asked in an exasperated voice.

"The third hand," Olivia said innocently. "I think you mentioned three hands in that last tirade."

Jets's fingers tapped on the desk. "As I was saying," she cleared her throat for emphasis, "on the other hand, I think you may be holding the key to necessary information about my ongoing investigation. All along you've been sitting in the Hello Age back office acting all innocent, poking your nose into the dead guy's life. You don't fool me!"

As Janis continued to rant, Olivia did her best to focus on her words, but the only thing she found interesting was that Michael was worried when she worked at the constabulary. *I had no idea Michael was that afraid.* By the time Olivia tuned back in, Janis had stopped talking and was staring at her.

Olivia lifted her hand from her lap, curving her fingers as if to inspect her manicure.

Jets cleared her throat. She unclasped her fists, stretching her fingers out. "Okay then, I'm not gonna waste any more words on you. I just want to know what you know about this Ulrich investigation. That's all. Plain and simple."

"So you admit that I *am* helpful?" Olivia smiled. "And maybe even a bit clever when it comes to catching people in lies."

"I admit nothing!" Janis shouted back. Then she swallowed hard as if eating a tough piece of meat. "Okay, so you're helpful, I'll give you that. I'm going to fill you in on the autopsy report, just to show you that I'm not above admitting," she paused, her face scrunched as if in pain, "that you have a certain useful perspective."

"And a gift?" Olivia added, taking advantage of Janis while she could.

"People do confess to you. It's like your superpower. I used to think it was about the singing, but now you're on some kind of overdrive. You can't help yourself, something about that innocent face and those big eyes. People want to unburden their souls to you."

Olivia opened her mouth to say thank you, but Janis kept speaking. "Just look at me, letting it all hang out, telling you confidential police information. I don't do that with anyone else," she snapped. She shrugged and added, "It's kind of spooky, the power you have."

"Relax, Officer Jets. I won't tell anyone." Olivia smiled.

"That's the problem. You keep secrets better than I do. How is that?"

Olivia leaned over the desk. "I'll tell you the biggest secret of all. Nothing's a secret to me. Just information ready to be revealed at the right time."

"Not that mumbo jumbo." Janis let out a breath of exasperation. "Sounds like you've been hanging out with Cayenne again."

Cayenne.

Olivia blinked at the mention of her name. She immediately realized what she'd been missing. *Cayenne would be perfect.* Olivia filed away that thought, paying attention to the agitated Officer Jets instead.

"So let's dig in. Tell me about the autopsy," Olivia insisted.

"You're never gonna believe it." Janis flipped open her laptop. "I've got the report right here." She read aloud, "Robert Bartholomew Ulrich died of..." she looked up at Olivia,"... botulinum overdose."

Olivia's eyes grew wide. "What is that exactly?"

"Botox," Jets explained. "The old guy was poisoned with Botox, smeared onto his arm."

"How is that possible?"

"Take a look at this photo." Janis spun her computer around for Olivia.

"There's a big scratch on his arm I didn't notice before."

"Right, no one saw it at first. If they did, they dismissed what they saw. I mean, what person doesn't have a scratch or two on their body? You walk in the woods and a branch catches you. Happens all the time."

"Right, like a branch," Olivia said. *You're just making excuses for not noticing that scratch at the time.*

"Or a rose bush," added Janis.

Olivia kept her face blank.

Jets continued to explain. "So I didn't think about it right away, neither did the doctor. Once the death certificate had been filled out, Ulrich was rushed off to the mortuary. The plan was to store the body, have a quick service, and then bury him immediately."

Jets leaned over her desk. "On the day we found him dead, Ulrich's daughter-in-law scheduled a cremation. But then someone read the fine print on Ulrich's DNR." Janis turned to her laptop screen to read aloud, "It says here that Ulrich requested no cremation."

Olivia's stomach clenched. "Do you think Ulrich Sr. suspected that someone wanted him dead?"

Jets's eyes narrowed. "I thought of that. The obvious people to benefit from his death would be his son and daughter-in-law, and of course your current favorite, the forlorn and lost Raleigh."

Olivia felt offended. "I have compassion for Raleigh, but that doesn't mean I'd ignore any wrongdoing on their part."

"I know you like the kid, what with your Tone Ranger bonding, but admit it. They're kind of nuts. They dropped out of school. Did some breaking and entering instead of renting a room. They had access to the code at Thyme Out and could have easily plastered the place with trans slogans. Plus they were the first on the scene to report the keying of Cookie's car."

Jets continued. "You know vandals often show up afterward to watch people's reactions to their work? That's why Raleigh looks suspicious. They were right there to announce Cookie's damaged car."

"All of that is true," Olivia admitted. "But I think Raleigh's gender fluidity makes them a vulnerable target."

Jets sighed. "I just wish the kid would pick a team. I don't get the in between girl and boy thing, I really don't."

"So your gender sensitivity training didn't take?"

"I'm sensitive enough," mumbled Janis. "I just have trouble getting used to this pronoun crap and you have to admit, the kid looks guilty."

Janis is trying. Maybe the most I can hope for is that she's aware that she's judgmental.

"He doesn't look guilty to me," Olivia said emphatically.

"But back to the Botox. How does the scratch have anything to do with botu-whatchamacallit?"

"Botulinum," Jets said firmly. "The coroner thinks Botox was injected into a tube of antibiotic topical cream, probably with a syringe. Then the cream was smeared onto Bartholomew Sr.'s arm. Wham bam thank you ma'am, he's got an overdose. His heart stops, he takes his last breath, and then he's dead."

"That's diabolical." Olivia shook her head. "I read somewhere that Botox had some dangerous side effects, but I didn't think it could be used as an actual poison. So what happens now?"

"We start interviewing the family members," Jets said. "And I'm thinking of pulling in your pal Raleigh. They'd be my first suspect for sure."

Olivia bit her tongue. She looked down at her shoe, remembering the thumb drive. When she wiggled her foot, she realized it had worked its way up, lodged into the side of her arch. *If I tell Janis about the thumb drive it may get Raleigh into more trouble.*

Olivia heard the door open behind her. She turned around in her chair.

"Hey, Olivia, Officer Jets," Brad drawled. "I've got somebody to see you."

Brad opened the door further. Mayor Maguire trotted inside, stopping to look at Olivia.

"He's been pawing at the glass door," Brad explained. "Can't get my work done."

"Leave the dog and get back to your desk," ordered Jets.

Once Brad left, she added, "The kid is always interrupting me with one problem or the next. Can't help himself. When I took my sensitivity class, they talked about weed and cognitive impairment; Brad's the poster boy."

246

"I'm happy to hear you learned something from the training." Olivia reached over to pat Mayor Maguire's head. The dog ducked, avoiding her hand. He lowered his head as if interested in her shoe. He sniffed and then pawed at her foot, which drove the thumb drive farther under her arch. *Ouch. Stop that, M&M.*

"Why is he pawing at you?" Jets asked.

Olivia curled her fingers around the dog collar, pulling his head away from her shoe. "Good boy, M&M," she said, doing her best to distract him. *And stay away from that thumb drive.*

The dog wrenched away from her grasp, ducking his head to sniff the same shoe. As he pawed, the lace caught on his claws, untying the knot. Before Olivia yanked his head away again, Janis Jets stood up, walking around the corner of her desk.

"What do you have, Mayor? Something in Olivia's shoe?" Janis bent over to inspect as Mayor Maguire continued to paw. "Maybe you'd better take the shoe off and see what's going on. The mayor and I both want to know."

Olivia leaned over to slip off her shoe. The thumb drive dropped away from the bottom of her sock, falling to the floor.

"And what do we have here?" Janis Jets swooped her hand down to pick up the drive. She walked back to her chair, holding it in front of her. "So do you want to tell me why this was in your shoe, or do I just plug it in and find out for myself?"

Mayor Maguire watched Olivia. A smile appeared on his lips.

She glared at him. *Dang it, M&M. Why did you have to out me to Janis?*

Mayor Maguire, no longer interested in her shoe, curled up at her feet. She took a deep breath. "The thumb drive belonged to Robert Ulrich Sr. Raleigh knew about it but couldn't find it in Granddad's belongings after his death."

"And how did it come into your possession?" Jets asked.

"I found it just this morning, in Flex Million's desk at Hello Age. Residents' belongings are stored in that building."

"If I remember correctly, he's the handyman and bus driver at Hello Age."

"That's him," Olivia agreed. "I found the drive in a locked box in the bottom drawer of his desk."

Jets leaned forward as she stared at Olivia. "Now that's interesting." Janis held the drive in front of her, staring at the sun. "It looks like something I'd buy my ten-year-old niece, with the thingy on the top. More like a kid's toy, if you ask me."

"Sunshine, that's what Robert called Raleigh. It was a thing between them. You know the song 'You Are My Sunshine'? Anyway, Raleigh knew about the drive and that it held their grandfather's most recent will."

"That's what Raleigh told you?" Jets sounded skeptical.

"Why won't you believe what Raleigh says?"

"I already told you, they look suspicious. And I think Raleigh is manipulative. They conned Cookie into a job before the bakery was even open. And then they've brought Cookie nothing but bad press ever since. Since the slogan event, Thyme Out has lost nearly every customer. Cookie is quite frustrated. That's why Raleigh won't get an award for best Lily Rock citizen of the week."

"I get that," Olivia admitted.

For a moment her confidence in Raleigh faltered. *Maybe Janis and everyone else is right. Maybe Raleigh is manipulative and they've hooked me like a big plump gullible fish.* Olivia glanced at the thumb drive in Janis's hand. *Am I being gullible?*

She grew quiet, attending to the inner turmoil with calming breaths. Then she shook her head.

I believe in Raleigh. Everything in me tells me they're genuinely grieving the death of their granddad. Janis doesn't see things from my perspective. It wouldn't be the first time.

"Are you going to plug that thing in?" she asked Jets.

"I suppose I am." Jets pulled her laptop closer, sliding the thumb drive into the slot. She leaned forward to peer into the screen. "We've got a last will and testament right here," she announced to Olivia. "I'll have a quick look."

Olivia knew better than to ask to see the document. "That's what Raleigh said. Their granddad showed them the thumb drive before he passed away."

Jets ejected the thumb drive. "The problem is, this document only makes Raleigh look more guilty. He had motive. Pushed to an untimely death, the sooner Ulrich Sr. died, the sooner Raleigh would inherit. I just need to find out where Raleigh was that afternoon, when Ulrich Sr. was discovered dead in the garden.

Olivia inhaled. *I know Raleigh was right next door at Thyme Out. But I can't tell Janis, or she'll arrest them.*

"I'd better get going," she told Jets.

"Don't you go and warn that kid." Jets glared.

Instead of answering, Olivia patted Mayor Maguire. They walked toward the door together. "I'll take the mayor with me. He can have dinner at our place."

"You do that," Jets said with a distracted wave of her hand. "I've got some calls to make. Thanks for coming in."

On the way down the hall, she realized, *I did just what I didn't want to do. The thumb drive only made things worse. Now Janis has enough proof to arrest Raleigh for Robert's death.*

CHAPTER THIRTY

The next morning Olivia stood at the sink. She reached over to open the window and inhaled deeply. A recent rain had brought out the fresh scent of pine and earth. Holding two mugs full of coffee, she walked to sit across from Michael at the kitchen table.

"I'm mad at you," she said as calmly as she could.

His head rocked back, his forehead wrinkled. "What did I do?"

"You made Janis fire me at the constabulary," she said.

"I did not," he retorted. "Did nothing of the kind. I may have mentioned how nervous it made me when you went undercover that time, but I never suggested she fire you."

Olivia leaned forward. "And you didn't consider that Janis would just as soon fire me rather than upset you?"

Michael shook his head back and forth. "Did she tell you that?"

"In so many words," Olivia mumbled.

Michael reached across the table for her hand. "Okay, I'm going to explain myself. You have no idea how nervous you make me when you turn all amateur sleuth. The last time, I admit, I started acting like some kind of overprotective boyfriend, which may have caused Jets to get tense. Considering she's already one trip wire away from an explosion on the best of days, I see why she fired you. Janis is nervous for your safety. She doesn't want to admit her feelings, so she used me as an excuse."

Olivia's eyes widened.

Michael continued in a softer voice, "You may not realize, but that's what love looks like. People get concerned and sometimes step into your business. It's not easy loving someone who's putting herself in danger all the time."

"I never thought about it like that, you know, from your perspective." Olivia paused to take in his admission.

I feel overprotective about Raleigh. It's not that different. No one thinks about how it would be to be a they/them. How you probably wake up every morning wondering who you're going to be that day. How other people look at you as if you don't belong. And how your family might think you're just a big inconvenience.

"So I'm sorry if I had anything to do with you losing your job at the constabulary. I'll talk to Janis." Michael still held her hand.

"Janis told me that I'm the problem, not the constabulary. I'm in just as deep at Hello Age. I think I'm a common denominator for trouble."

Michael's eyebrows raised. "I don't want to believe that. But I must admit you've caused me a certain number of sleepless nights since we met, so maybe you have a point."

"I do," she said.

"But think on the bright side. If you didn't care so much about people, investigating every emotion and perspective, Jets would have to solve her own crimes."

"Which brings up my next point," Olivia said. "I need to tell you all about the missing will and the thumb drive."

Michael stopped smiling. He patted her hand. "I need more coffee." He took a long sip from his mug.

Olivia stood up to grab the coffeepot. She refilled his mug and then hers.

"Remember good ol' Flex Million?" she began.

* * *

At noon, three rapid knocks came from her closed office door. *I wonder who that is?*

"Door's unlocked," she called out.

To her surprise, Janis Jets stuck her head inside. "Got a minute?" she asked crisply.

"Perfect timing." She shut down the computer. "It's my lunch break. Do you need privacy or can we walk around?"

"We can walk and talk." Looking all business, Jets wore her navy blazer over a white button-down shirt. The blazer grazed the khaki slacks below the belt.

"I see you have your weapon." Olivia pointed to the slight bulge near Janis's right hip.

"I used to think these old people were benign, but now I'm thinking they are as nefarious as anyone else. So in answer to your question, I'm packing heat."

Olivia laughed. "That may be the first time I've ever heard that expression in real life, not from TV or a movie character."

Jets ducked her chin in embarrassment. "You got me. I've been watching old Humphrey Bogart movies on Netflix. I may have picked up some of the lingo."

"Oh, the lingo." Olivia kept her face straight. "Makes sense."

"Not like you have any room to talk," Jets said, opening the door for Olivia. "Your whole life is one Nancy Drew adventure with an unending series of dead bodies and eavesdropping."

"You know that Nancy often packed heat?"

Jets looked surprised. "I had no idea. You've actually read those old books?"

"I read them all when I was a kid." *And I read them now when no one is looking.*

"That explains everything. Stories have a huge impact on how we look at things."

"Look at you, going all psychological," laughed Olivia. She closed the door behind them.

Standing in the hallway outside her office, Olivia nodded toward the back exit. "Is there anywhere in particular you'd like to go? I have half an hour for lunch. Please say you brought me a sandwich."

"I didn't bring your lunch. I'm a cop, not a fairy frickin' godmother."

"Okay then, no lunch." Olivia shrugged. "I assume you came to have a look at Flex's office and the storage area?"

"You assume correctly. Plus one more thing. I want to know more about the guy who died a couple of days ago."

"Would that be Thorgood Adams?"

Jets nodded. "Not a name you'd forget."

"I'm still inputting his paperwork," Olivia said.

"And that would be protected by HIPPA?" Jets said.

"It would."

"I don't suppose you'd break the law again..."

"I never make decisions on an empty stomach." Olivia patted her middle.

"You only break the law when it suits you, is that it?"

"Stop complaining. You got Mr. Ulrich's paperwork hand-delivered." Olivia pushed open the door that led outside. *And the thumb drive that you kept.* "If we walk out this exit, we can head toward the parking lot to have a look at Flex's office. He'd be back from the daily bus trip by now, probably having lunch with his ladies."

"I can wait for a few minutes," Janis said, her eyebrows raising. "Any chance you've seen Raleigh Ulrich today?"

"Like I'd tell you!" Olivia protested.

"So as a warning, I called Raleigh's parents last night to let them know that I wanted to talk to them again."

"Raleigh's nearly twenty-one and considered an adult. Why call his parents?"

"Since Sasha and Robert Jr. are the next of kin in my investigation, it would be wrong not to let them know." Jets turned her inscrutable face toward Olivia. "Plus if they know I'm still on the case, then they may trip up under the pressure."

Olivia's stomach churned. *Is Janis distracting me while one of her cops is searching for Raleigh?*

Olivia stopped to catch her breath at the top of the incline. "There's the building." She pointed toward the woods.

"Looks like an old barn," Jets observed. "So why don't we pay Flex Million a visit? I bet he's back from lunch."

"Sounds good to me. I'm happy you have a weapon. He gives me the creeps, especially when I'm alone with him."

"Yet you keep breaking into his office," Jets commented. "No wonder Michael's always worried about you."

"And he says you're also worried," Olivia replied. "I talked to him this morning."

"What? Give me a break! My biggest worry is how you obstruct my investigations."

They arrived at the front of the building. The door had been flung wide open.

"Anyone here?" called Janis from outside.

Flex appeared in the doorway. Ignoring Olivia, he looked at Janis, a sheepish grin coming over his lips. "How can I help you, Officer?"

"I'm looking for Raleigh Ulrich."

Instead of answering her question, he pointed at Olivia. "Why is she here?"

"Don't change the subject. Have you seen Raleigh Ulrich?" Jets pushed.

Flex shrugged. "I see the kid around. Come on in, I know you want to look around for yourself." Flex stood aside as Janis then Olivia walked through the doorway.

To Olivia's surprise Sasha Ulrich stood in the middle of the room, wearing tight black jeans and a white cowl-necked sweater. Sunglasses were perched on her head.

Janis spoke first. "Mrs. Ulrich. Looks like you came right over after our phone call. Seen Raleigh anywhere?"

Sasha's cold stare took in Olivia, then returned to Janis. "I was here to ask Flex the same question. He always knows where people can be found at Hello Age."

"But I haven't seen Raleigh," Flex insisted.

Jets rocked back on her heels. "So no one has seen Raleigh." She glared at Flex. "At least no one who cares to admit to seeing them."

"I also want to find Raleigh," Sasha said, her voice sounding harsh. "They have a lot of explaining to do, not just to me but their father. They don't answer any of our texts or calls. We want to get together with an attorney to sort out Robert Sr.'s estate. We haven't found a will, you know. Raleigh is stalling and holding up our progress."

Janis didn't tell her about the thumb drive. I wonder if she's mentioned that Mr. Ulrich Sr.'s death has been determined a homicide...

Jets took out her cell phone. "Got a text from the office,

just a minute." Everyone watched as she scrolled with her thumb.

She's taking forever. Olivia looked away from Janis.

She saw Flex glance back toward his desk. Her stomach clenched. Flex looked at Sasha from the corner of his eye. Then he stepped cautiously closer to his desk. Olivia held her breath as his hand moved to the bottom drawer, where the drive had once been hidden.

Flex pulled open the drawer, right as Sasha said, "Stop looking for stuff in your desk and come closer. I want to tell you something." Her eyes flashed, but Flex didn't flinch. He looked around to Janis. She was composing a text.

Janis tapped on the cell, then looked up. "Come back here and answer a few questions, Mr. Million. You can play with those drawers later."

Olivia silently exhaled her relief.

Was he going to hand over the thumb drive to Janis? It's like Flex is playing cat and mouse with Sasha, only I'm not sure who is the cat and who's the mouse...

Janis said, "I told Sasha on the phone earlier, new information has come to my attention, so I'd like to question Raleigh again. If either of you know where I can find them, then give me a call." She reached into her jacket pocket, coming out with a business card.

"Mrs. Ulrich, you have my number, and Mr. Million, here's my card." When Flex didn't hold out his hand, Jets dropped it on his desk. She'd turned to stand between him and the desk. Using her heel, she kicked the drawer shut.

Flex's eyes narrowed. "I wanted to show you something in that drawer," he explained, a side glance directed toward Sasha. She nervously fiddled with the cowl neck on her sweater.

"You don't need to do that," Janis assured him in a calm

voice. Her cell phone pinged. She looked down to open the text.

"Why not? Don't you want to know what I have to show you?" Flex demanded.

Janis looked up. "On the one hand, I like it when people volunteer testimonies and evidence and even an occasional opinion without my having to ask. But on the other hand? People who volunteer information usually have something more important to hide, otherwise they wouldn't bother. Is that the case with you, Mr. Million?"

His face fell. "I see I may have underestimated you," he said quietly.

"Oh, that wouldn't be the first time I've been underestimated," Jets assured him with a smile. She held up her phone. "Plus I'll get all the information I need. Right here on my cell phone, I have a warrant to search this entire office—shed, barn, whatever you call it. My officers will be here shortly to begin the process." She appeared to ignore Flex's shocked expression.

Turning calmly toward Olivia, she added, "So you get back to work and these two will follow you out the building. I have things to do. Skedaddle now."

"But you can't toss my place of business for no reason!" Flex insisted.

"But I have a reason, Mr. Million." As if explaining to a child she continued, "I don't have to include you in my ongoing investigation. I informed Hello Age's corporate office about the warrant early this morning. They've given me the go-ahead to look in any office I want." Jets nodded at Flex, a smile on her face.

Without an argument Olivia headed outdoors. Her stomach growled. *Lunch break over and no food.* On the way across the parking lot, she thought about her next step. *I'll go*

*back to my office for that granola bar in the bottom of my purse.
Then I'll look around Hello Age for Raleigh while Janis is
turning over Flex's office.*

Sitting behind her desk, Olivia reached into her purse to
snag her emergency granola bar. The first bite in, she gave a
sigh of relief. *Janis just saved me. She dragged out the conversation with Flex until she got the electronic warrant. She didn't
mention Mr. Ulrich's autopsy report, so Flex and Sasha are still
in the dark. She kept it calm so her team could sweep in and do
the search. I bet she'll drop that thumb drive into the evidence
box, as if her team discovered it.*

That way I'm off the hook.

Okay, I forgive her for not bringing me a sandwich.

Olivia crumpled the granola bar wrapper in her fist,
tossing it into the trash can.

CHAPTER THIRTY-ONE

Early the following morning Olivia lay in her bed. *I smell coffee. Michael must have gotten up earlier. I bet he's already showered.* She shut her eyes, drifting back to sleep. She'd spent most of the day before avoiding Janis Jets, looking for Raleigh at Hello Age. When her phone pinged, her eyes fluttered open. By the third ping she grabbed her cell from the nightstand, holding it in front of bleary eyes. Raleigh had sent a text.

Got your message. I'm with Walter.

Raleigh sent the text early in the morning.

Okay then, Raleigh. Janis will find you today for sure, but at least I warned you.

The next message was from Michael.

Had an early meeting down the hill. Coffee made. Stay safe at work. xo

Olivia smiled, selecting a unicorn emoji blowing a heart as her response.

The third text, from Janis Jets, caused her to sit up in bed.

Got Raleigh at the constabulary. Caught him at Hello

Age this morning. He's been sleeping there. Like you didn't know. Don't show up here. I've got this.

Olivia texted a one-word response.

Damn.

* * *

That afternoon she sat alone in her office in front of the computer. She spent most of the morning inputting data and checking her work. A succession of emails and attachments had come her way in the last two days. The work had become easier for her. By lunchtime she'd opened all her files and completed all of her tasks.

Okay, I'm getting the hang of this job.

She reached for a sandwich that she'd packed at home. Ham and cheese, with a little mustard, slapped together and placed hastily in a plastic bag. Taking it along with her cell phone, she left her office, making her way to the atrium. The tranquility of the trickling water fountain and the greenery made the space a perfect location for her to think and eat.

Pushing open the glass door, she stepped inside, spotting her favorite bench. The smell of moist air and earth filled her nostrils. She sat down and admired a selection of palm tree varieties a few feet away. Planted in enormous black ceramic pots, two of the trees were over six feet tall, their branches stretching across the fountain.

I hear footsteps. Someone is behind the waterfall. She stopped chewing to call out, "Hello?"

Echo Kravitz stuck out her head from behind the palms. "Oh, it's you."

"This is my favorite lunch spot." Olivia raised her voice to reach Echo on the other side of the path. "How often do you come here to tend the plants?"

"I work here two days a week, pruning and replanting," Echo answered briskly. She dropped her spade into a pocket on her apron and then patted her gloved hands together to remove excess soil.

I haven't seen her since karaoke night.

Olivia called out again, "I'm sorry to hear about Mr. Adams."

Echo walked across the path. The gardening apron around her thin waist held the spade, a spray bottle, and some packets of plant food in the front pockets. "He was ready to go," she said, a detached tone to her voice.

"I looked for you after singing that night."

"I had to slip out. I didn't get back until they called the paramedics." A slight smile came to her lips. "I suppose since you work here, I can explain my opinions freely. Most of the residents at Hello Age are on their last leg, just holding on. Sometimes it's nothing but a blessing when they pass away. The families can move forward with their grieving, unhampered by the costs of health care. It's not cheap to live in one of these places." Echo looked around at the garden. "Just take a look at the atrium. Looks nice, but that's to increase sales, not to improve health care."

Olivia felt her stomach clench. "I tried to ask how much it costs to live here one time and they refused to tell me. There's no price listed on the brochures."

"That's because they raise and lower the prices depending on the circumstances. If the resident has the money or if the family feels guilty enough, they add on extra fees like turn-down service and mints on the pillow."

"Or a beautiful tropical atrium," added Olivia.

"I'm not saying they ever do anything they can be prosecuted for. It's all in the name of serving the elderly. People who work here feel very good about themselves, slightly superior, if you want my opinion."

"I suppose that's true. Not everyone has the patience to work with the elderly."

Echo spat out, "Most people don't realize caring for old people is a for-profit business. The basic price for independent living at Hello Age is seven grand a month. Can you imagine paying that much for someone who's only going to die anyway?" Echo shook her head.

"I hope you don't mean that," Olivia protested. "I'd pay anything to have my mother still with me. Have you not lost someone you loved?"

"My job is to take care of the plants, but just so you know, I'm not one of those people who stand helpless in the face of death. Everyone dies, it's just a matter of time. I take charge of my life and I wouldn't let a relative of mine linger indefinitely, especially with a terminal diagnosis." She turned away.

Olivia shook her head in disbelief. "Feeling the loss of a loved one is a natural expression of love."

"Wait until you've lived longer and see what I've seen. You'll change your tune." Bitterness oozed from Echo's words.

"You've got to admit it seems odd that you love plants but don't like people much. I'm just saying."

Echo faced Olivia again, her expression frozen. Then she shook her head. "I'm really quite consistent with plants and people." She walked over to a group of lilies that grew next to the pathway. A few leaves had turned brown. Blooms hung limply on dried-out stems.

With several swift yanks Echo removed the dead leaves. She flung them to the path in repeated bursts. "I'll pick the debris up later. People and plants deserve respectful treatment. When they stop growing, it's time to be recycled."

Olivia felt her gut twist.

Seems awfully harsh to me.

She finished her sandwich in silence, watching Echo trim back a batch of overgrown ferns. Then Olivia called out, "I was wondering, how long have you worked at Hello Age?"

Echo swung around. "Why do you care?"

"Just trying to make conversation here." Olivia smiled, folding her paper lunch sack.

Echo stepped closer. "I've worked here for around six months. Before I opened the Mother Earth garden, I found a small cabin to rent. Then my friend recommended me for this job. The Hello Age corporation wanted to pay an actual horti-culturalist. I told them I was a professional plant keeper. Then I showed them my living design for the atrium, how they could bring in more exotic indoor plant varieties. They hired me on the spot." Echo smiled. "I got a raise just last month."

Olivia inhaled in the beauty of the indoor courtyard. "I bet residents love to come out here and visit with families."

"They do love it here. And it works for employees to take a break in a more natural environment. Some of those offices down the hall are more like cells, small spaces with no windows."

"Tell me about it. So who recommended you for the job anyway?"

"My friend, Sasha Ulrich."

Olivia's hand dropped to her lap.

Echo hastily explained, "Sasha isn't a friend really, just an acquaintance. I met her in town and we got to talking. She told me about her father-in-law living here. Later she put in a good word."

"I only met Sasha the day Mr. Ulrich died in your garden."

"It happened for a reason," Echo said flatly. "And I bet that grandchild helped his death along."

Olivia felt alarm. *One more person pointing the finger at Raleigh.* "Why would you say that?"

"Because of the cookie he was holding. Someone had to bring him the cookie with the sprig of thyme."

Olivia shook her head. "I don't think Raleigh wanted their granddad to die. A couple of residents told me how often Raleigh visited Robert at Hello Age."

Echo shrugged. "You're not a pragmatist like I am. I call them as I see them. That kid visited their granddad in my garden and was probably the last person to see the old man before he died. It wouldn't surprise me if Raleigh helped the old guy along, you know, brought him a dry cookie on purpose. Once he took a bite, then all Raleigh had to do was hold a hand over the old man's mouth and nose. Not that difficult with a Parkinson's patient, weakened from the disease. They have trouble breathing anyway."

Olivia stared at Echo, both confused and mesmerized by her words.

Echo continued to speak, lowering her voice as if sharing a deep secret. "One slip of the hand, a slight hesitation, only for a minute or two, and then the person stops breathing. Put out of their misery once and for all. Just like that."

Olivia's throat constricted. She held back a gasp and then knew: *Something is wrong with this woman.*

"Lunch hour is over," Olivia said, abruptly standing from the bench. "See you around."

Walking out of the atrium, Olivia stopped to lean against the nearest wall. She needed to catch her breath and think about what just happened.

Echo sees herself as a good person but also a pragmatist. As she continued to talk, she spun a web of logic around me that I had trouble resisting. She believes that killing an old person before their time is an act of mercy. She almost had me, to the point I would agree, lost in my confusion and brain fog. She had me and then...

I remembered my mom, how we'd laugh, right up until the end. I felt my mom as if she were standing next to me, her breath warm on my cheek.

Her love surrounds me even after her death. Those experiences are still alive inside of me. And that's why I believe that Raleigh couldn't have killed their granddad; they loved Robert just like I loved my mom.

Echo is wrong.

Olivia stopped in the public restroom on the way back to her office. She washed her hands and then looked in the mirror. *I'm going to the constabulary right after work. I don't care if Janis objects. I have to support Raleigh.*

She slipped her wet hands under the electronic dryer, listening to the rush of air coming from the wall. Then with a dry hand, she sent a message on her cell phone.

Meet me at the constabulary after 2 o'clock. I need your advice. There's also someone I want you to meet.

Olivia hit send.

I'll be there, came the reply.

* * *

By ten after two, Olivia parked in front of the constabulary. She twisted her key out of the ignition, taking a moment to breathe. *Look out, Janis Jets. I'm coming for Raleigh and I'm bringing the perfect defense.* She stepped out of the car and turned to lock it, glancing toward the constabulary entrance.

Her friend Cayenne stood outside the door, looking lean in black jeans, a black T-shirt, and black leather boots. She'd braided her long hair in one strand, which hung over her shoulder. Cayenne wore sunglasses, looking inscrutable yet elegant.

"You're here right on time," Olivia said.

"Your text worried me," Cayenne commented dryly.

"Have you met Raleigh Ulrich, the kid working at Thyme Out?"

"I have not had the pleasure."

I like the way she pronounces every word distinctly.

"Raleigh is nearly twenty-one and identifies as they/them," Olivia explained.

Cayenne removed her sunglasses, her face showing concern. "That is good to know."

"And I think Janis is going to arrest them today—at least I was told they're in the constabulary. I'm not sure about the arrest part."

"Have you invited me to raise my tomahawk, escape with the victim, and take them back to my wigwam?" The corner of her mouth turned up as she stared at Olivia.

Olivia knew she was being teased. "No Native American stereotypes this time. I want your insight into Raleigh's situation. I've become too involved to be objective."

"Does this mean you do not trust your inner sense of knowing?"

As usual, Cay cut to the exact place where Olivia felt uncomfortable.

"I guess I'm doubting myself."

"I see," Cayenne said.

"That's it exactly, you do see. Plus I'm wondering, assuming you were so inclined, if you'd listen to Raleigh and maybe help them. I don't know if they're Two-Spirit like you, but I do think Raleigh is struggling."

"I'm not the only voice of wisdom. I also think Janis Jets is very wise. She must have taken Raleigh in for a reason."

"Oh, she did take Raleigh in for a reason. She thinks they killed their grandfather."

Cayenne scanned the horizon, her eyes coming to rest on Olivia's face. "Shall we go inside and find out, or should we stay out here and imagine the worst?"

Olivia reached for the door handle. "You first," she said, stepping aside.

CHAPTER THIRTY-TWO

Once inside the constabulary, Olivia found Officer Jets sitting behind the reception desk, a large grin on her face.

"Where's Brad?" Olivia asked. Then she answered her own question. "I know, he's getting your coffee?"

Why is she grinning at me? I thought she'd be angry.

"My new assistant, competent as hell, is in the back room chatting with my suspect, while I sit here and think about my mortal coil."

"Is your mortal coil in need of contemplation? If so, I have some news for you. Raleigh is not guilty!"

Jets kept smiling, unfazed by Olivia's vehemence. "You're preaching to the choir, Nancy Drew."

Olivia turned to Cayenne. "I asked Cay to come with me to meet Raleigh."

"And how are you today?" Jets asked Cayenne.

"I am well. I am intrigued." Cayenne remained unsmiling and calm.

"Are you now?" Jets laid her tablet on the desk. "I'm glad you're here to meet my suspect. This could work out very well for me."

"I didn't invite Cayenne to help you out," Olivia argued. "You're the problem."

Cayenne stepped closer to Olivia. She leaned to whisper in her ear. "Janis is not your enemy."

Before she could disagree, Jets interrupted. "I think Raleigh may be a wrong place at the wrong time kind of kid."

Olivia's eyes grew wide. "Are you finally convinced that Raleigh is innocent?"

"I think Raleigh may be confused and has probably been set up to look like the guilty party," Janis confirmed. "So far as I know, I can't arrest someone for being confused about their gender and out of cash."

"Then why don't we go talk to this Raleigh. Maybe some of the confusion will be lifted," suggested Cayenne in her matter-of-fact voice.

Jets looked Cayenne up and down. "Sometimes you irritate me with all that logic. It takes away my fun of getting down and dirty. Anyone ever told you that?"

Cayenne spoke calmly. "No one has ever dared, until now."

Olivia nodded at Janis. "So you'd better reconsider your mortal coil after we find Robert's killer. I'm just saying, you might be in trouble now that you've crossed a Two-Spirit." She glanced over at Cayenne, who looked disinterested.

"Sure, whatever. Let's see what Raleigh has to say." Jets stood up from the chair, taking steps toward the glass door. Olivia followed with Cayenne close behind.

They discovered Raleigh and Brad in the break room, sitting at the round table. Both had a soda can in front of them. Brad was the first to look up. Raleigh scowled at Janis Jets.

"Olivia and Cayenne are here," Jets announced.

Cayenne stepped forward. She held out a hand to

Raleigh. "I am honored to meet you." She stood tall and regal, as if greeting an equal.

Raleigh stood and then took Cayenne's hand. "I've seen you around Lily Rock. One time in the bakery when you were talking to Cookie."

Cayenne let Raleigh's hand go. She drew her arms behind her back. "I've seen you around as well. Olivia invited me to speak to you about the death of your beloved grandfather."

At the mention of his granddad, Raleigh's eyes instantly grew shiny with tears. They raised a hand to cover their face, chin tucked to their chest. When Raleigh's shoulders began to shake, Cayenne made no move to comfort or interrupt. She stepped back to give Raleigh space, watching the disintegration into grief without a word.

Olivia's heart beat wildly. *Do something, Cayenne.*

Cayenne took her eyes off of Raleigh for a brief moment. She smiled at Olivia.

Warmth instantly filled Olivia's chest, bringing her heart back to a steady slow pulse. She saw what Cayenne was doing.

She's allowing Raleigh to feel their grief.

After a while Raleigh sniffed. They scrubbed at their eyes with the back of a hand. Cayenne remained composed, an observer but not a participant in Raleigh's grief. She offered no word of comfort. She stood calmly as if time had stopped.

Are Janis and Brad watching this?

Olivia turned to see them standing quietly by the table.

Cayenne has cast a spell around all of us.

Olivia inhaled.

I kept interrupting his crying and it made things worse. Cayenne is doing the opposite. Staying close but out of the way, proving to them that their grief is perfectly natural.

Raleigh removed a hand from their face. Olivia watched as eyes, swollen from tears, rose to look at Cayenne.

"Inhale," Cayenne told him in a firm voice. "Exhale through the mouth. One more time."

In that moment the spell was broken.

Olivia placed her arm around Raleigh's shoulders. Jets grabbed tissues from a box on the counter, and Brad filled a glass with water from the sink. He placed it on the table.

"You'll be all right now," Cay stated. "You can tell Officer Jets everything you know to be true without fear. You've touched your sadness, you are no longer a victim."

Olivia squeezed Raleigh's shoulders, surprised when they did not recoil. She pulled them closer to her side. Cayenne turned as if to leave the break room, but stopped at the sound of Raleigh's voice.

"Wait," they called out. "Thank you."

Cayenne turned back around. "You are welcome. It is brave to feel. Remember that. The warrior honors all emotions in the moment."

"I feel like I know you," Raleigh added quickly.

"We are of the same spirit." Cayenne nodded. "When the time is right we'll meet again." She turned to Olivia to add, "I know you have questions. Follow your gut feelings about Raleigh." Then she walked through the door without another word. Olivia watched her long braid bounce against her back as she disappeared down the hallway.

"Okay," Jets announced. "Enough indigenous chitchat. You've got some explaining to do." She pointed at Raleigh. "Here's a tissue." Raleigh dabbed at their face.

Olivia sat at the table. Jets sat next to her. Brad pulled out a chair and then stopped when Janis pointed toward him.

"You need to go out front, I've got this," she ordered.

"But we were just getting to the good part," Brad complained.

"And you are not invited," Jets asserted. "Get going."

Brad left the room.

"Now, where to begin." Jets set her tablet on the tabletop. "You can sit down over there," Jets told Raleigh. "Drink more water so you don't get dehydrated," she added.

Olivia glared at her.

"Are you recording?" Raleigh asked, sitting across from Jets.

"I am not. I'm going to listen and then if we get anywhere, I'll write some stuff down. It won't be official unless I print it up and you sign it. Deal?"

Raleigh nodded, reaching for the glass of water. Once they drained the glass, they placed it on the table.

Jets began the session by asking, "How would you describe the relationship you had with your granddad?"

"Granddad and I have always been close," Raleigh began. "When I was small he'd talk to me like I wasn't a child. He had that way with me, as if he knew I was not just a kid but an adult.

"When I got older, I was eleven or so, I told him I wasn't like everyone else. When my parents were out, I would wear different clothes—not boy clothes, but dresses and skirts from my stepmother's closet. Granddad never looked surprised. He just seemed interested, you know, like I was fascinating him. One day I showed up at a recital wearing a skirt and blouse I got at the second-hand store. That was when Sasha went ballistic."

"So your granddad was supportive, even from the beginning..."

"He called me brave, which infuriated my dad. Sasha didn't want any attention paid to me. I was an embarrassment to her. They both turned their backs on me after that recital. Dad never could stand up to Sasha."

Jets cleared her throat. "Okay so far, but now let's talk about your granddad's death. The rest you can tell your support group or a shrink. Tell me about the day your granddad died."

"I'm getting to that part," Raleigh insisted. "On my sixteenth birthday Granddad took me to lunch. He told me he was gay. I was so shocked. At first I felt mad, as though I'd been lied to my whole life. But Granddad explained. He told me that he'd married Grandma to make other people happy. He always hid his identity from the family. Even after Grandma died, he kept up the act.

"Granddad understood me because he'd kept his own identity a secret. That's why he provided for me in his will. He wanted me to know that there would be money so that I could see a therapist, for one thing. He wanted me to feel supported to fully become who I am."

Tears filled Raleigh's eyes again. They wiped them away with the palm of a hand. "So that's how I know that he made a will and what his intentions were. Plus, I was there the day he died. I took him some thyme cookies that I'd just baked. We talked for a while and then I had to go back to work. He loved smelling the fresh herb, something about reminding him of his mother's garden." Raleigh swallowed. "That was the last time I saw him alive."

Janis reached for Raleigh's empty glass. She got up from the table to refill it, placing it close by their hand. Then she spoke.

"I admit, I may have been overzealous in my assumption that you killed your granddad. Your gender thing makes me uncomfortable." She glanced at Olivia and then continued.

273

"When I put that bias aside, I thought differently. But I have to ask you directly, did you help your granddad die?"

Raleigh's eyes widened. "No. I loved Granddad. He was my only family."

Jets nodded. "Good clear response, and for what it's worth, I believe you. But there's something else. Did you vandalize Thyme Out or key Cookie's car?"

"No," Raleigh insisted. "I love baking, why would I want to hurt Cookie? He gave me a job."

Jets nodded. "Okay, that sounds sincere. Who do you think is trying to frame you?"

"Someone wanted to undermine Raleigh's credibility," Olivia interjected. "Somebody who would benefit from Robert Sr. dying sooner rather than later."

"Do you think my dad would do that to me?" Raleigh asked.

Jets did not respond to the question. Instead she reached for her iPad. "I'm going to write down Raleigh's testimony. I'll print the document for you to read and sign later. And then I'm going to get a court order to look at some bank statements. I have a feeling about some of this."

Olivia kicked Janis under the table.

"What do you want?" Jets asked.

"Tell Raleigh about the cause of his granddad's death and the thumb drive."

"On the one hand, I don't need to share that information, especially with a suspect. But on the other hand, I think Raleigh may be in danger."

She opened a document on her tablet. "You remember how we snatched the body right from the funeral at Hello Age? We did an autopsy that revealed that your granddad did not die from complications of his disease. He was poisoned."

"I knew it!" Raleigh shouted. "Granddad was just fine

when I left him. Plus he was talking. They always said he didn't speak, but he talked to me all the time."

"I asked about that. The doctors told me the medication he was taking wears off. Parkinson's patients become less vocal until the next dose. That might explain why he could talk to you but was nonverbal at other times."

Jets cleared her throat. "I also want you both to know that my guys found a copy of Robert's will. I won't tell you where we found it, but let's just say it's now in safe keeping. You were right. Robert Sr. listed Raleigh as his sole beneficiary. You were to inherit the estate on your twenty-first birthday.

"So then my next question becomes, who benefitted from hiding the will and where was everyone the day Robert Bartholomew Ulrich Sr. died? I have yet to get everyone's alibi."

As Olivia and Raleigh stared at each other, Janis pulled out her cell phone. Olivia watched as she scrolled to recent calls, clicked on a name, and started barking orders on her cell.

"Brad, listen up. I want you to get on the phone and tell certain people to meet me tomorrow afternoon at Mother Earth. I'll text you the list. Make it for three o'clock. Tell them there will be consequences if they don't show up. Of course they can bring an attorney, but I don't think it will be necessary." Jets glanced over at Olivia.

"I'm bringing Olivia, and I'm pretty sure she'll get a confession out of the culprit. If it doesn't happen right away, I'll make her sing a song for them. That always works." Jets tapped to end the call. Olivia looked at Janis's screen to see her text: "Raleigh Ulrich. Robert Ulrich Jr. Sasha Ulrich. Echo Kravitz. Charles Kravitz. Flex Million. Michael Bellemare." Janis touched Send.

"I'm keeping Raleigh at the constabulary until the meeting at Mother Earth," Jets said. Before Olivia could object, she added, "For Raleigh's safety, not because I think they are guilty of murder."

Olivia nodded.

"I put everyone on the list, including you and your boyfriend and that Flex Million character. Everyone who was there or close by when the body was discovered. And even though Robert Jr. wasn't at the death scene, he's the next of kin and needs to be questioned. Got it?"

Olivia nodded again.

"Then get out of here. I have work to do."

CHAPTER THIRTY-THREE

A full moon illuminated Olivia's house. As the wind picked up, swirling dry pine needles drifted to the ground. After parking her car, she stood for a moment looking toward the night sky, inhaling deeply. She saw a waft of smoke from the chimney and smiled.

Inside the house, the pleasing tang of garlic and marjoram greeted her. "I'm home," she called out.

Michael appeared from the kitchen, a chef's apron tied around his trim waist. "Hello, honey, how was your day?" he asked.

Olivia swept the back of her hand against her forehead. "I had an exhausting day at the office. What's for dinner?"

He grinned. "Rack of lamb."

She dropped her purse on the floor, running toward him, her arms open for a hug. He enveloped her into his soft flannel shirt, as she inhaled his woodsy aftershave.

She lifted her face for a kiss, which he reciprocated.

When he pulled back, he said, "I am not your average boyfriend. Take a look around. I've been busy."

In a glance she saw that he'd set the table in the dining room. A navy-blue cloth covered the surface, with white dinner plates and silverware on both sides. He'd even folded cloth napkins on both plates.

"We're eating in the dining room?"

"It's a special occasion," he said.

"You even got out the fancy goblets?" He'd set the table with crystal glasses, hers filled with ice and water, his with a deep burgundy wine.

"I have a lot to tell you and thought a good dinner would help me sound convincing." Michael raised a plate stacked with carrot and celery sticks. "You can dip them in the hummus," he instructed, clearly pleased with himself.

"Oh thanks." Olivia reached for the celery. "Yum, you added roasted peppers to the hummus."

"How about you change clothes and I'll finish up the potatoes. The rack of lamb will be done in half an hour."

She looked toward the stairs and then back at Michael. "Should I be nervous about this conversation?"

"I've been working on a plan for some time. I want to let you in on what I've done. I'm the one who's nervous."

"That's why you've been spending so much time down the hill?"

"I had to consult with attorneys and do some research. But now I'm ready for your opinions and critique."

She sighed with relief. "I thought maybe you had bad news."

"If I had bad news I'd blurt it out. This is more like a long-range plan kind of thing."

"Oh," she said softly. "Are you proposing marriage?"

"Would that be a bad thing?"

"Honestly this is the first time I've thought of it because you're being very mysterious."

A hopeful look came over his face. "It's not my plan to propose tonight. But that doesn't mean it won't happen another time."

She felt relief. "Then I'll go take a quick shower and come right back."

Olivia kissed his clean-shaven cheek, making her way toward the stairway leading to their suite.

* * *

She returned in twenty minutes smelling lightly of gardenias, a scent she'd received as a gift for her birthday. She'd piled her hair on top of her head, a clip tucked into her curls. Without makeup she felt refreshed. "It smells heavenly in here," she said, taking a carrot from the plate. "I could make an entire dinner of the veggies and hummus. Thank you, by the way. I now get it why people like to come home from work and have dinner prepared for them. It's pretty awesome."

Michael nodded. "Let's chat over the hummus. Then I'll take the lamb out of the oven so we can talk further."

He escorted her to the table, pulling out her chair before he circled around to stand on the opposite side. With a flick of his wrist, he lit a match. Reaching over, he lit two white taper candles, which brought a warm glow to the table setting.

He cleared his throat and sat down.

Olivia sat in rapt attention.

"When I designed this house," he paused to look around the room, "I did it for Marla. She hired me to create an architectural wonder, the likes of which Lily Rock had never seen. We had fun with the project," his eyes clouded for a moment, "but I never intended to live in the house I created. It was always for Marla, my client."

Olivia nodded. "I remember the first time I walked in the

front door. Such amazing vaulted ceilings, with the light and the glass walls. It took my breath away." Her voice caught as she spoke. "That day, finding Marla dead in the garden and meeting you..."

"A challenging time that brought us together," Michael said. "I've been aware that for the past year and a half we've been feeling our way. Maybe that's why I ignored my feelings, a certain discomfort I had about the house. It wasn't until recently that I had to admit to myself that this house was always Marla's. And then I wondered if you felt the same, but I was afraid to ask. I didn't want to bring up the memory of Marla's death."

Olivia took a sip of her water before speaking, absorbing not just his words but his tone. "I sensed you were uneasy. I thought maybe you were tired of living with Sage and me. When you disappeared for a few days I figured you were thinking about a way to tell me that you'd be moving out."

"I never thought of moving without you," he said quickly. "But I admit I was hesitant to talk to you. I love Sage. I know you two had a lot of time to make up for, being newly united sisters and all. I didn't want to interfere with your bonding time. But then I dug deeper and I realized it wasn't you and Sage."

"So you're not mad at Sage?"

"I'm not mad at anybody," he insisted. "It's just that I'm an architect and I design for other people. I've never lived in one of my own designs before and it feels different."

Her skin prickled.

Michael took a deep breath, his words coming more quickly. "I thought it was just me, but Olivia, I think you have some trouble living here. I've watched you look out that kitchen window. You get really quiet. I think you're remembering Marla. Is that true?"

"Yes, I think about Marla all the time. This was her house. She died in the garden out back. It does make me sad."

"Okay then, I wasn't too far off. That's what I thought. So now for my plan." Michael reached under the table. "My big reveal for dramatic effect." He lifted a long tube of papers from under the table, holding them in both hands. Slipping a rubber band from the center, he unrolled the papers in the air. Then he stood, walking around the table. He spread the papers out at the far end.

Olivia watched with fascination.

"I've been working on a new design for a new house. It's a cozy place, not as grand as Marla's, but lots of square footage." He watched her face. "I even have a plan for a sound studio." When she didn't speak, he softly added, "Come over here and I'll show you."

Olivia stood up, walking closer to his side. Her eyes filled with tears as she realized what he was telling her. She blinked rapidly to clear away the tears.

Michael pointed to the draft. "See, this is the front of the house, and here's the first floor."

She looked where he pointed but had trouble focusing on what he said. She felt overwhelmed with emotion, watching his face, intent on his creation. She gulped. *Two years ago, I ran away, but now I think he's the most beautiful, interesting, and loving person I've ever known. He's designed a house for us.*

Michael continued to explain. "I also picked out a lot. I had to move fast and I didn't speak to you about the location. The town of Lily Rock has so many rules and regulations, it took me a bit to figure things out. Can you forgive me for that?"

She stared at the plans. "Of course I can."

"After a lot of searching I found the perfect spot, up in the hill toward Lily Rock, off the beaten path, and I made an outright offer. Makes me feel really nervous now that I'm saying all of this to you." He looked at her again.

Olivia didn't flinch. "I understand artistic license. I mean, I never ask you to pick out music for a gig. I get why you went ahead on the property."

Relief showed on his face. "I never thought of it that way." He ran his hand through his hair. "I was so worried. Okay then, here's the house." He pointed to the plans. "I designed it for you." He looked at her and then hesitated. "And for me. I want this to be our home."

Suddenly there was a lump in her throat. She looked around the great room, taking in the beauty of the space, the glass wall, and the roaring fire. Then she turned to him. "I love this house. It was love at first sight, the beauty and graceful design, the way you bring the outside inside." She closed her eyes to hold back tears. "But I never imagined anyone would design a home for me."

"I know most men give other kinds of gifts, like flowers and jewelry." He shrugged.

She smiled, her eyes still shiny with tears.

He cleared his throat. "You're probably concerned about Sage."

"I don't think she wants to live here by herself," Olivia admitted.

"Maybe it's time to have a talk about her expectations and the idea of us moving. She will have plenty of time to catch up emotionally by the time the project is completed. Just so you know, it takes a long time to get all the permits in place. And then I have to hire a crew who either lives here or is willing to move up to Lily Rock for the project. It won't be for at least a year, maybe two for this house to become a place for us to live."

"I want to appreciate your plan, at least for tonight, without worrying about Sage. I want to feel happy without any complications. This is an unexpected gift and a bit overwhelming." Threatened by tears again, she swallowed. "Plus I'm hungry. The lamb smells so good."

Michael grinned. "I'm going to carve the meat in the kitchen. It will only be a minute."

Once Michael left the dining room, Olivia listened to him move about the kitchen. She gazed into the candlelight, her heart full. *He designed a house for me.*

* * *

"Is this mint jelly?" she asked, pointing with her fork.

"It's a must with lamb," Michael said.

She admired his clean jawline and dark eyes from across the table. "Did you make dessert?"

"I am a full-service boyfriend and of course I made dessert."

"Yourself?"

"Okay, you got me. I had Cookie make a cheesecake with strawberries."

"My favorite!"

"There you go, I'm also a mind reader."

He offered her a serving bowl with a large fork. "Green beans almandine," he said. "Here, have some."

She spooned a helping of beans to her plate.

Michael asked, "Did you learn anything new from Janis today?"

"I took Cayenne with me to meet Raleigh."

"How did that go?"

Olivia looked up, her fork poised in the air. "I think

Cayenne is a spell caster. She has this way of putting everyone in the room on pause while she works her magic."

"That's her Two-Spirit persona I suppose."

Olivia chewed the last bite of lamb slowly, savoring the flavor.

Michael stood up. "Take your time. I'm going to get the cheesecake."

"Lots of strawberries, please," she called after him.

After dessert Michael cleared the table. Olivia stood at the sink, rinsing dishes. "I can't remember the last time I ate such a delicious meal," she called to him from the kitchen. She pumped dish soap on her sponge. "I forgot to ask, did you get a message from Janis Jets this afternoon?"

He called back from the other room. "The one about her meetup tomorrow at three o'clock?"

"I wouldn't exactly call it a meetup." Olivia laughed, closing the front of the dishwasher. "More like her usual question-and-answer grilling, followed by an arrest."

She dried her hands on a dish towel, her eyes looking out the window over the sink. He came through the door. Standing behind her, he encircled her waist with his arms.

"Let's look at the house plans more carefully tomorrow. In daylight I'll have your undivided attention as I explain how amazingly clever I am, so that you can ooh and ahh at appropriate intervals."

She turned in his arms. He lifted her chin with his hand, staring into her eyes.

"That does sound good. I'm ready to ooh and ahh."

He removed his finger from her chin to pull her closer. "We should get an early night, don't you think? We need to be alert for the gathering of suspects."

She ducked her head, bumping playfully into his chest.

He reached over with one hand to flick off the kitchen lights. "We could go into the other room and sit in front of the fire..."

Olivia took his hand, leading the way.

CHAPTER THIRTY-FOUR

Olivia yawned and then stood up from bed, looking out the open window. The sun rose in the distance. Clouds raced across the sky, puffy and promising. From the open window she smelled balmy, rich earth. The wind from the night before had settled into a slight breeze.

The voices of Michael and Sage came from downstairs. Pulling on a robe, she searched for slippers under the bed. She hurried toward their laughter.

"I smell coffee," she announced, entering the warm kitchen.

"I'm hearing about Michael's plans for the new house," Sage said. "Does that mean I'll get this place all to myself?"

Olivia felt a surge of relief. The night before, she couldn't have predicted how Sage would take the news. *She doesn't mind at all.*

Michael handed Olivia a full mug of coffee. She took it from him with a smile. "Even if we don't live together, we'll still have coffee in the mornings, right?" She looked over at her sister and then back to Michael.

"I've planned a breakfast nook that will fit all of us with

room to spare," Michael assured her. "And there will be a massive deck with a view of Lily Rock for our afternoon get-togethers."

"You see, the man's thought of everything." Sage nodded. Olivia smiled back at her. The three sat in companionable silence.

Olivia, placing her empty coffee mug on the table, was the first to speak. "I have to get ready for work in a few minutes. Did Michael tell you we have a Jets-style meet-and-greet at Mother Earth?"

"I hadn't heard." Sage's eyes grew wide with interest. "I've been too busy with the school to listen to the Lily Rock grapevine."

"Let's just say Janis has rounded up the usual suspects and we're part of the crowd," Michael said. "The old guy they found dead at Mother Earth? Turns out he was murdered."

Sage's jaw dropped. "You two get into the darndest situations."

"Oh, you haven't heard the half of it. You remember Raleigh, one of your old students?"

"Sure, Raleigh was the tenor in the Tone Rangers. What do they have to do with all of this?"

Olivia filled Sage in on Raleigh as Michael refilled their coffee mugs.

"You two have been busy. I hope everything goes okay this afternoon."

Olivia stood up. "I'm taking my coffee with me. Time to shower and get ready for work. You coming?" She glanced toward Michael.

"Oh yeah," he said, a grin on his face. "I'm not going to miss a chance to see you naked. My day just got so much better."

Olivia felt her cheeks flush. She looked over at Sage, who stared at her cell phone pretending not to hear.

Okay, maybe having our own house would be best. A little more privacy for everyone. All of her doubts about a new house the night before had been swept away in the light of day.

After a quick shower and getting dressed, Olivia drove up the hill to Hello Age. Once parked, she ignored Flex's office, heading straight into the back entrance to clock in. She took a deep breath to clear her thoughts as the elevator door closed. *I'm going to spend my breaks gathering more information for Janis's meeting at Mother Earth. I can stalk the Hello Age halls and listen for gossip.*

She passed her office, walking down the hallway toward the front entrance. Both Walter and Sheila stood behind the counter, chatting and laughing.

"Good morning," Olivia greeted them.

"You're just the person we wanted to see. Walter told me that Raleigh's still in jail. Do you know anything?"

"They're completely safe, at least for now. I think Raleigh will have to find a more permanent place to live once released from the constabulary."

Walter looked away, his neck flushing red.

"I told Walter that Raleigh couldn't stay in his room forever. It's against the rules, you know," Sheila remarked.

"I do know," Olivia nodded. She waited for Walter to recover from his embarrassment before asking, "Remember Mr. Adams? I suppose you've heard that he passed away on karaoke night."

Walter and Sheila nodded together. "We know." Sheila spoke for them both.

Olivia continued, "I've been inputting the paperwork. And while I was typing I remembered what you told me about making those bets."

"That's right," Walter said. "We have that little game we play, don't we?" He smiled at Sheila.

"About which resident will be the next to die," Sheila said. "I won the bet on Thorgood. Walter didn't think he was sick enough, but I saw all the telltale signs."

"So the pattern of death has become that predictable..." Olivia mused aloud. "I guess I have one more question—was Echo the volunteer caregiver for all of the people who died over the past month or so?"

Walter reached up to scratch behind his ear. "Well now that you mention it, I think Echo pushed the wheelchairs of a couple of those residents who recently passed. I never put that together."

Sheila looked at Olivia intently. "I'm not sure that matters. I mean, all of the deaths looked like natural causes to me."

Olivia took a quick intake of breath, aware that she'd asked one too many questions. *I'm not supposed to give residents any cause to worry about their safety.*

"I don't want to speculate anymore," she added hastily. When Sheila didn't smile, Olivia added, "Let's keep this conversation between the three of us. I was just wondering, that's all."

Sheila extended her pinkie finger to Walter. "Pinkie swear. That's what we need to do."

After they each partook in the gesture, Olivia nodded. "I'd better get back to my office. I have an interesting afternoon ahead." She extended a small wave and turned to leave.

The morning passed quickly. By the time her break rolled around, Olivia had already shut down her computer. *I'm going to take the elevator downstairs and walk around.* She headed out of her door, directly to the elevator. The door swished open, revealing Flex Million.

"Need a ride to Mother Earth after work?" he asked.

Her heart raced. "I've got a ride," she said, pushing the elevator button, keeping her back turned to Flex. "I'm surprised to see you this time of day."

"I didn't take the old people into town. Too much to do," he grumbled. "I don't know why Jets wants me there. That day he died, I only stopped by Mother Earth for a restroom break. I had to get back to the bus to calm everyone down and take them back to Hello Age."

"Janis Jets has her own way of doing things," Olivia commented.

"You can say that again. She took something that belonged to me in that search."

Olivia's shoulders stiffened.

"I'm only telling you because everybody should know that cop isn't trustworthy."

Olivia changed the subject. "Speaking of trustworthy..." The door swept open. She stepped out, Flex following right behind. "I've been thinking about that day, when that squirrel got caught in my car and you showed up to help me out."

"Lot of good it did me. You never said thanks," Flex said defensively.

"But then when I was in your office, I saw one of those special traps, to catch small animals without causing harm."

"So?" Flex slipped his hands into the pockets of his jeans.

"So did you catch that squirrel and put it in my car just for the fun of it?"

"Now why would I do that?" Flex glared at her, the corner of his mouth twitching.

"Don't gaslight me," Olivia retorted. "You put that squirrel in there so that you could save me and then what? I'd be grateful and you'd get something back?"

His eyes narrowed. *He's reassessing my gullibility.*

"So what, your car was unlocked and I wanted to get to know you better. What's the crime in that?"

She did not dignify his question with an answer. Instead she asked him something that had been nagging at her for days. "You messed with my cell phone too, that time I had you put in your number."

Flex stared up, avoiding her eyes.

"You blocked my boyfriend's texts." She didn't add how upset she was at the time. She didn't want to give Flex the satisfaction of knowing he'd gotten under her skin again.

"I probably hit the block button by accident," he said, a glint in his eye. "How else would I get to know you better? What happened, a little trouble in paradise?"

"Not on your life," she said. "We're better than ever."

Turning on her heel, she headed toward the parking lot exit, leaving Flex to his own devices.

After a brisk stroll outside, Olivia felt better. She walked toward the first-floor entrance. Once inside she took the elevator up to the second floor.

Olivia walked down the hall and looked into the atrium. From her favorite bench, she could see through the lobby to the entrance. The Hello Age bus was parked alongside the curb.

She rose from the bench, making her way through the door to the empty lobby. She heard voices from the dining room. Olivia looked toward the reception desk. On a hunch she walked closer, making her way around the counter to the mailroom and back offices.

Heated voices came from the workroom. Her heart beat rapidly. She backed against the wall to listen.

"I'm done keeping your secrets," came Flex Million's voice. "That cop is looking too closely at me. Not worth it at any price."

"We have a deal. I pay and you keep things hidden," came the familiar voice of Sasha Ulrich. "That cop is stupid. When she doesn't find enough evidence, she'll move on to someone else."

"You left before they searched my office," Flex whined. "They found all the boxes with the valuable stuff."

"You're exaggerating. That Jets woman has no idea what that stuff is for. As far as she knows, you're storing it for the residents. I'm pretty sure the cops couldn't find their backside with both hands."

"I wouldn't be too sure of that. They found the flash drive."

Olivia heard a quick inhale of breath. "Why didn't you tell me sooner?" Sasha's voice turned harsh.

Olivia sank farther against the wall, her breath coming in short gasps.

"I don't have time to deal with your incompetence right now. I have to go to the little meeting that Jets woman planned this afternoon," Sasha warned.

"So I won't tell them about the thumb drive and where it came from. I'll back you up with the cops," came Flex's wheedling voice. "You'll have to pay for my silence. It will cost you."

"I don't need you. I already have a plan B. Get out of my way. I have to go."

Olivia felt a tingle up her neck. *I better get going before one of them catches me listening.* She took slow steps, then began to hurry. Stepping through the doorway, she slipped around the desk and into the main lobby.

I'm going to sit on one of those sofas. I can look busy with my phone.

Once seated, she held her cell in her lap. Instead of checking her texts, she waited. Flex Million stomped through

292

the doorway. He walked around the counter, followed by Sasha Ulrich.

Sasha's pale face turned her lipstick into a shocking red. She stopped in front of the counter. Flex hovered nearby, his eyes on her oversized tote bag slung over one shoulder.

From the dining room, Elsie Meyer called out, "I'll be right there." Olivia watched from the corner of her eye. When Elsie realized it was Sasha standing at the counter, she quickened her step.

"Hello, Mrs. Ulrich, nice to see you today. Sorry I wasn't here earlier. They're serving crab cakes in the dining room and I wanted to get there early. How can I help?"

Sasha's hand opened, revealing a key. "I forgot to return my father-in-law's room key after the memorial service. I don't think I'll be back." She sniffed and then dabbed at her eyes with a tissue. "Too many memories here, I'm afraid."

Elsie took the key from her hand. "I do understand. You will be missed. By the way, Robert was beloved by all of the residents. I'm sorry for your loss."

Sasha gave a faint smile.

Flex Million edged forward to join her at the desk. "We sure loved Robert," he said in a soothing voice. As he spoke, he placed his hand over Sasha's open tote bag. Olivia saw an object drop from his palm into the bag. As Sasha turned to leave, Flex snatched his hand away, stepping to the right to give her room.

What is he up to?

Olivia ducked her head, pretending to be absorbed with her cell phone. A quick glance told her that Sasha Ulrich headed toward the front parking lot, the tote bag tucked under her right arm.

Flex Million ignored Sasha, leaning over the desk to say something to Elsie that Olivia didn't catch.

"You're so funny, Flex," Elsie said with a laugh.

In half an hour I'll be able to clock out. Not wanting to attract Flex's attention, she stayed seated on the sofa. Finally he smacked the counter with his hand and turned. Olivia watched the entrance doors swish closed behind him.

On the way to her office, she thought about what she'd heard. *Sasha and Flex are nervous about that thumb drive. Now that Janis has it as evidence, there shouldn't be any questions about who inherited Robert Ulrich Sr.'s estate. Everything goes to Raleigh.*

Olivia felt her gut clench.

Except what did Sasha mean about a plan B? I hope Raleigh is ready for a fight. That woman feels dangerous to me.

CHAPTER THIRTY-FIVE

In town, Olivia circled the block looking for a parking space. To her surprise, Robert Ulrich Jr. stepped out of the constabulary. She waited at a stop sign as he paused before crossing the street. Without seeing her, he shoved his hands in his pockets, walking briskly toward Mother Earth.

Did Janis call him in for an early interview? Olivia drove around the block one more time before she found an empty parking space on the other side of the park. She stepped out of the car and inhaled deeply, willing her nerves to calm down.

Picking up her pace, she crossed through the park. She could hear a couple standing just a few feet away. "Here doggie," the woman called. "Look at me." Olivia watched as Mayor Maguire turned toward the camera, his jowls lifting up in a huge grin.

As soon as the woman lowered her cell phone, he caught sight of Olivia and bounded toward her, tongue falling out of the side of his mouth.

She kneeled in front of the mayor. He came to a sudden halt and then blinked. He tilted his head to the side, his tail wagging in the air as if to say, "Want to play?"

"I can't play right now, buddy, but I'd love for you to come with me to Mother Earth. I could use a canine companion with a nose for crime."

He lowered his front legs, his rear end raised in the air, his tail waving frantically. He gave a yip.

"I'll play later. Promise. Let's go," she begged.

He obediently stood and walked around Olivia, sitting on her right side. Olivia reached down to give him a pat. "Thanks, M&M." They crossed the street toward Mother Earth, walking side by side.

The gate stood ajar. A sign reading "Private Event" had been taped right above the wooden Mother Earth plaque. Olivia walked in, the mayor right behind her. She pulled the gate partially closed. Voices came from the back of the garden.

Mayor Maguire bounded off, leaving Olivia to follow close behind.

"Hey, Maguire," Michael called out. When he caught sight of Olivia, he grinned. "Sit here." He patted the chair next to him.

Olivia glanced around the circle of chairs as Mayor Maguire went to explore the area behind the greenhouse. She noted Raleigh, sitting with arms crossed over their chest, face set in a scowl.

"As soon as Mr. Million shows up, we've got everyone," Janis Jets announced. She stood next to the raised bed over- flowing with herbs. Janis didn't acknowledge Olivia.

"Let's get this party started," came Flex's voice from the back gate of the garden. He arrived out of breath.

Jets scowled at him.

He sat in the empty chair between Echo and Sasha, smiling at both women before crossing one knee over the other.

Jets wasted no time. "Everyone has arrived. Introductions

aren't necessary, but I'm going to check you off my list. This is Raleigh Ulrich, grandchild of the deceased, and then Charles Kravitz, owner of Thyme Out. Over there we have Carl Million, employee of Hello Age, and Echo Kravitz, owner of Mother Earth. Next to her is Sasha Ulrich, wife of Robert Jr., stepmother to Raleigh and daughter-in-law to the deceased. Then of course there's Michael Bellemare and Olivia Greer. Olivia works at Hello Age and Michael is a famous architect who lives in Lily Rock. Why don't you move closer to Olivia, Raleigh?" Janis gestured with her hand to the empty seat. They reluctantly complied.

"That's everyone. With the exception of Robert Jr., sitting over there, you were all here at the time Robert Bartholomew Ulrich was found dead."

"He was old and sick," Flex mentioned casually. "Poor old dude."

"Old people die," added Echo, looking closely at the nails on her right hand.

Jets ignored their comments. "Some of you might already know that Ulrich Sr. did not die because he was old or sick. An autopsy revealed he died because he was poisoned."

Olivia glanced at the faces in the circle. *No one looked that surprised.*

Echo spoke first. "Murdered or not, what does that have to do with me?"

Jets turned to face Echo. "Since you were the first to speak, maybe you can tell me where you were at the time of death, right before noon on March fourteenth?"

"I was here at my garden. Everyone saw me." Echo looked at Cookie for confirmation.

He cleared his throat. "I did see Echo off and on all morning. She ducked in and out of my shop with questions. And then close to noon she ran into my bakery saying she

needed help. She claimed she'd found Mr. Ulrich unconscious." Cookie pointed to the spot where Janis stood, next to
the raised planter boxes. "When we got here, we saw him
there."

"Okay then, what about you, Mrs. Ulrich?"

"I was shopping in town," Sasha said immediately. "I left
my father-in-law with Echo while I did the errands. I already
told the police that." She glared at Janis Jets.

"Before I get into that," Janis looked from Sasha to Echo,
"what is your relationship?"

"We're friends," Sasha said immediately. "We met a few
months ago at Hello Age. We both volunteer."

Jets's eyes narrowed. "Okay then, let's get back to your
statement. I know you, Mrs. Ulrich, were shopping at Lady of
the Rock and then the Marvelous Moose souvenir shop. I also
know that you came back to the garden around eleven thirty,
through the back entrance."

"I did no such thing." Sasha glared at Jets, who glared
back. Sasha was the first to back down. She fluttered her
eyelashes. "Now that you mention it, I did stop back for a
minute to check on Robert. He was asleep by then, so I left to
finish my errands."

"My witness says you stayed longer. My witness was
smoking in the back alley and he saw you, both when you
arrived and when you left. Care to amend your statement
with those times?"

Olivia felt puzzled. *Does Janis really have a witness or is
she just pushing Sasha's alibi for holes?*

Sasha shook her head. "Why don't you question one of
these other people instead?"

"As you wish," Jets replied. She turned to Flex Million.
"So Carl, aka Flex, where were you between eleven and noon
that same day?"

"That's easy, I was on the bus helping the old folks off and on." Flex smiled at Janis, daring her to disagree.

"Except for the ten minutes you asked us to watch the bus," interjected Michael. He nodded toward Flex. "He was gone, disappeared into Mother Earth, and then came back the same way. Both Olivia and I waited for him out front by the Hello Age bus."

"I was just using the little boy's room," whined Flex.

Janis moved on to Raleigh. "If I remember correctly, you were working at the bakery that morning."

"That's right." Raleigh nodded.

"The entire time from eleven to noon?"

"Not the whole time. I knew Granddad was next door because Sasha stopped to talk to me at Thyme Out. She told me to keep an eye on him while she was doing her errands. You know, drop in and say hi. So I walked over on my break."

"Was he alive?"

"Oh yeah. We talked at least ten minutes. I brought him a lemon thyme cookie from the bakery. It was still warm. He smelled it and then saved it to eat later. Then I left. That was the last time I spoke to him..." Raleigh's voice dropped away.

"And then you three," Janis waved her hand over Cookie, Michael, and Olivia, "didn't show up until Echo told you about the body."

"That's correct," Michael said. "We can alibi each other. Olivia and I were waiting for at least ten minutes to talk to Cookie. He was finishing up his class with Hello Age."

Jets placed her tablet on an empty chair. She stood to face the circle, her hands held at her back as if standing at ease. She looked around at each person, pausing before moving to the next. "So the only one left is Robert Jr."

All eyes swiveled to Raleigh's father, who looked stoically into the distance.

Jets cleared her throat. "The rest of you probably wonder why I invited him at all." She held up her right hand. "On the one hand, he's not a suspect." She held up her left hand. "But on the other hand, he holds a key to the motive for murder."

Sasha spoke up first. "Robert wasn't close to his father." She glared at her husband. "I did everything for Robert Sr. I placed him at Hello Age and took him for outings—"

Jets shut her down. "I said murder. Has it sunk in yet? You all should be asking yourselves, why would someone want to murder an old sick man who was dying anyway?"

Olivia glanced at Echo. *I'm going to pretend I agree with Echo, just to see how she reacts.* "Some people get tired of paying the bills for health care. Caring for the elderly is an expensive proposition."

Echo turned to glare at her.

Olivia continued, "Sick people can run up costly bills. Not everyone can afford that expense. Think of the families. Sometimes there's not enough money left, even for the funeral expenses."

Jets looked back and forth from Olivia to Echo. "That's not the case with our victim," Janis insisted. "He had plenty of dough—stocks, bonds, investments. His estate, worth more than ten million, was left entirely to his grandson, Raleigh. We found the will on a flash drive in the bottom of Flex Million's desk drawer."

All heads turned toward Flex.

"I have lots of stuff from the old people in my office. I have no idea how the drive got in my drawer, just an oversight. How was I to know it had the only copy of the will?" Flex shook his head.

"That will is invalid," Sasha said. "Wills on computers with electronic signatures must have paper backups. The courts are filled with cases without proper authentication. In that case they side with the next of kin, which would be my husband." She stamped her foot. "We will argue this in court and we will win. No one wants my father-in-law's estate going to them." She pointed directly to Raleigh.

"Raleigh is an unstable person, not of sound mind, anyone can see that, what with their gender issues and the break-ins. They even destroyed their employer's business next door. Who else would vandalize the bakery with those ridiculous slogans? Plus Kravitz's prized automobile was vandalized because of Raleigh's irrational temper. I know they poisoned my father-in-law to get his money. Probably put something awful in that cookie they baked themselves."

"Interesting," Jets said. She looked at Raleigh, whose eyes had turned dark and threatening. "Except there's a problem with your information. As of this morning I've been handed a written document, a copy of Robert Sr.'s will. The document includes the signatures of witnesses. So there's no need to alert your lawyers or go to court. It seems Raleigh will inherit all of the estate on their twenty-first birthday in just a few months."

Sasha Ulrich's shocked face made Olivia cringe. Instead of looked defeated, she screamed across the circle at her husband, "How could you ruin our future by giving up that paper! I warned you not to do that and now, that, that boy or girl or whatever has our money!"

Assuming her traffic cop persona, Janis held up her hand again, the palm toward Sasha. Robert Jr. sat staring straight ahead, not uttering a word.

Janis lowered her hand and continued in a calm voice, "And then about the cookie. The poison was not in the cookie. Nor was the sprig of thyme anything more than a sprig of thyme. After some confusion, the coroner found where the poison came from." Jets took out an enlarged photo, displaying the body of Robert Sr. slumped over in a wheelchair. Olivia reached over to take Michael's hand. He squeezed back, offering her support.

Jets pointed with her index finger. "Right under his sleeve you can see a bandage on his arm. Underneath the bandage is a two-inch scratch, right there. If you look closely enough, the skin looks red and infected."

Flex spoke quickly. "He got that a couple of days before his death. Ran his wheelchair too close to some wood siding at Hello Age. I helped him get the splinter out and got the cut bandaged up."

"Was someone pushing the wheelchair when it happened?" Janis asked.

"Echo, she was pushing him to breakfast. After the scratch, she headed to the nursing station. On the way she ran into me, and I went with them to the nursing station. I wheeled him back in time for breakfast." Flex smiled.

"Apparently Mr. Ulrich got more than breakfast," Janis said dryly. "He got a significant dose of botulism. The toxin finally caught up with him at the garden. Got into his system and his lungs shut down and he suffocated. That's how Robert Ulrich Sr. died—not from Parkinson's disease but from toxic bacteria administered through an open wound."

Olivia's stomach twisted. Her heart began to race. She saw Raleigh's look of horror and their father's grim expression. Michael squeezed her hand again.

"Who would do such a thing?" Flex demanded.

Jets turned toward him. "Who would do such a thing?" she mimicked. "According to your employers, you take residents to the dermatologist every week, some of them for injections. When we spoke to the receptionist, she admitted that you convinced her to remove ampules of Botox and give them to you about a month ago. Apparently you paid her to steal them."

"Sasha wanted the stuff. I stored it for her until she picked it up," Flex said, flashing Janis a slight smile.

"You 'store' a lot of stuff...like Hello Age residents' valuables and flash drives, for example. You get people to pay a hefty price for that storage privilege. We checked into your bank accounts and found lots of electronic deposits from residents and even individuals here today." She pointed to Sasha. "The payment that interested us the most was for five thousand dollars from you."

"I paid him to store my father-in-law's belongings," Sasha insisted.

"And to store the Botox and probably to hide the flash drive with the will," added Jets. Then she turned toward Echo. "But you were the one with the opportunity to administer the poison."

Echo squirmed in her chair.

"Did you get that toxin from Flex and rub it into the old man's arm?" Jets asked.

"I did nothing of the sort," Echo said. "And you can't prove anything. Those other dead people have been cremated."

"All except for Robert and Thorgood," Jets said. "You didn't get to Ulrich soon enough and Thorgood's report is still pending."

Olivia blinked, feeling confused. "I don't understand how the toxin got into the wound. Did you say it was injected?"

Jets nodded. "It took us some time to figure that one out. It seems the botulism toxin from the doctor, usually used to make lines on the face disappear or in some cases to stop migraine headaches, was used, but not on its own. The forensic specialist found traces of antibiotic ointment in the cut. The same brand anyone can buy over the counter.

303

Rubbed into an open wound, it travels through the bloodstream and then to the lungs."

Olivia could see where this was going as Janis continued.

"From what we can tell, someone most likely squeezed the ointment out of the tube, and then carefully, with gloved hands, mixed the bacteria with the ointment. Then they injected their concoction of ointment combined with Botox into the antibiotic tube. So we're looking for a tube of generic-looking ointment that's been tampered with. It's still fatal because the toxin lives up to six months."

Olivia felt a jolt. *And I know where the ointment is.*

She rose, pointing to Sasha Ulrich's tote. "I heard Flex arguing with her in the mailroom and then watched him slip his hand into her tote when she wasn't paying attention. I bet you'll find the evidence you need right in there."

Michael leaped to his feet to snatch the tote from Sasha's hand.

"Flex did it! He did the poisoning!" Sasha raised her fists, her eyes wide with anger.

Echo jumped to her feet, blocking Flex from Sasha. "He may have stolen the Botox, but he never put it in the old man's arm. That was you. I saw you that day, standing over him, rubbing it into his skin. I thought you were just being nice, playing the beloved daughter-in-law, taking time out from shopping to look after the old man. You poisoned him then, right in my garden!"

Sasha stood and slapped Echo hard across the face. "That's a lie!" she screamed, raising her arm to strike again.

"I was only storing the tube for her. I never went near the old man's arm," argued Flex.

"Sit down, everyone!" hollered Janis Jets.

Two uniformed police officers appeared from behind the greenhouse. One forced Sasha Ulrich's hands behind her back. The other snatched her tote from Michael, opening it wide to look inside. With a gloved hand, the officer reached into the bag, coming up with a half-filled tube of pharmacy ointment wrapped in plastic. "I've got it, ma'am," she said to Jets.

Janis pointed to Sasha Ulrich. "You have the right to remain silent." Then she turned to Flex Million. "And you too. Keep quiet if you know what's good for you."

Flex's eyes grew wide as he pulled his hand away from the police officer. "Don't touch me," he screamed.

Ignoring Flex, the officer jerked his other arm behind his back, pushing him toward the exit where Sasha stood, her jaw clenched in defiance.

Only Echo remained, watching the scene before her as if it were a play and she was the audience. Jets stared her down, taking out a pair of handcuffs from her back pocket. "And you need to be silent as well. Imagine helping old people die to save money." She took the woman's hands behind her back and cinched them together, edging her toward the others.

As Janis recited the entire Miranda rights to all three, Raleigh burst into tears.

CHAPTER THIRTY-SIX

Olivia and Michael drove together up the hill toward the town's namesake. Lily Rock shone in the distance, her surface glimmering like alabaster. Michael pointed to the left. "I almost bought that property," he explained, "but they wanted too much money."

As he steered onto a dirt road, she looked up. "I feel like I can touch Lily Rock from here."

"The closer the better, right?" He drove along the bumpy stretch of road, pulling the truck next to what looked like an abandoned farmhouse. "So that's the place we're tearing down," he explained to Olivia. "We're in escrow, which should close in a couple of weeks."

She nodded, admiring the clear blue sky overhead. "Will you keep any of the original dwelling?"

"Some of it," he explained. "I plan to keep just enough so that my work counts as a remodel, not an original plan. That's the compromise that took so long with the Lily Rock town council. This house has a history, and they want to preserve part of their heritage."

"I like the wraparound porch. Can we keep that part?"

"Once we lift the house and establish a new foundation, we can build another wraparound. I only need to maintain one bearing wall and the rest is up to us. I kinda figured you'd like the porch. So I included an expanded version in my plans. We could put a dining room table out there and have friends over for a meal. Mayor Maguire will have his own house entrance from the porch." He stopped the truck and pulled the emergency brake.

"M&M will like that a lot."

"Wait until you see the back." He jumped from the driver's seat, running around to her door to help her out.

She stood next to him, looking at the old farmhouse. He took her hand, moving closer to the porch. "Don't walk up those steps," he warned. "The stairs may collapse. The wood is rotting and there are termites."

Tempted as she was to get a look inside the house, Olivia followed Michael around the corner toward the back. Lush pine trees nestled against the hillside. "It's so green back here," she commented. "Lots of shade."

He led her toward an opening in the woods. She gasped. A deer with two fawns nearby stared at them. Only a few feet away, the deer lowered her head to drink from the creek, her fawns nibbling grass close by.

Olivia smiled and pointed. Michael stood by her side, inhaling deeply.

As the doe and her fawns wandered away, Michael tugged on her hand. "There's a waterfall on our property," he whispered in her ear. "Come look."

Olivia listened for the sound of a waterfall as her eyes wandered up the hillside. One tree grew tall in the midst of a rock formation. Its branches shaded a cascading flow of water that splashed over the hillside. She broke the silence. "This is a sacred place," she said to him. Stepping closer, she bent to touch the water with the tip of her finger.

"My plan is to work with this waterfall, you know, incorporate it into our house. I want the water to flow into the house from underneath the deck. We'll have an inside water source. An engineering challenge that I welcome." He smiled, his eyes bright with anticipation.

Olivia nodded as he continued to explain. "The engineers on the Lily Rock building committee gave me a run for my money, but now they're satisfied. They signed off on my proposal just last week."

He ran his hand through his hair, the corner of his mouth tightening. "Lily Rock doesn't accept many plans for new housing construction. Luckily I proved myself worthy."

"You did? How was that?"

"I reminded them how Marla's place earned several awards in prestigious architectural journals, and I also told them you'd be living in the house."

Olivia scoffed. "Please, no one cares about me."

"That's where you're wrong." He turned a serious glance in her direction. "You've gotten quite the reputation in just over a year with your crime-solving genius."

He bent down, lips brushing against hers. Then he took her hand, walking closer to the house. "So over there, beyond the waterfall, look toward the mountain range. You can catch a glimpse of an old barn that's part of the property. I'm going to move that building closer and then renovate it. It will be your new state-of-the-art recording studio for Sweet Four O'Clock."

Olivia shook her head. "I can't believe this is what you've been doing, planning a new house for us and a studio. You're really something, Michael Bellemare."

"I wanted to surprise you. But now I need your advice, especially about your studio space. I did contact an engineer who specializes in sound studios. We can use him as a consultant."

A look of surprise came over her face. "I've been so busy at Hello Age, I nearly forgot about rehearsals. Sweet Four O'Clock starts again in a week."

"I'm fast but not that fast. The barn won't be ready for a couple of years," he joked.

"Don't worry. Sage says the band can use the music academy facilities for as long as we want; a perk of her being the principal of the academy."

He looked back at the house and then at her. "So what do you think?" He waited, watching her face for clues.

Olivia inhaled deeply, searching for the right words. "I feel peaceful here. It's the land and the waterfall." She looked upward. "And of course, the closeness of Lily Rock. I can't believe you can do this—take something old and imagine its next life. Then you translate your vision into plans that other people can read, so that they can execute something real and tangible." She shook her head. "You are amazing."

Michael grinned. "I don't think anyone has ever described what I do better." He pulled her to his side, an arm around her shoulders. "So you think you can get behind this plan and leave Sage with the other house?"

"No problem," she said nonchalantly. "I'm all in. When do we start?"

"The council gave me trouble for months. It took a lot of talking. They were a big hurdle. Now that I have the agreement in writing, I'm fine-tuning the plans. We can start pulling this place down maybe early next fall."

"That will give me plenty of time to adjust to the idea and work things out with Sage," Olivia added.

They walked toward the road hand in hand. As Michael began to explain the details of pitched roof construction, Olivia found her thoughts wandering. She let his words grow distant, thinking about the day before, when Janis made her arrests.

With all three in custody, the cops had left, sirens blaring. Janis had invited Michael, Cookie, and Olivia to Thyme Out for a wrap-up conversation. Sitting at a round table with a plate of cookies between them, Olivia spoke first. "I thought Flex Million killed Robert."

"He looked so suspicious," Jets agreed. "Turns out Flex is one of those guys who gets joy from causing other people problems. Just like that squirrel incident you told me about, and the cell phone sabotage.

"Flex stuck the squirrel in Olivia's car to make a problem for her so that he could fix it, hoping she'd feel indebted. He wanted Olivia to turn to him for help with her computer. When none of that worked, he sabotaged Olivia's cell phone to cause trouble between her and Mike. I think he hoped to step in if they broke up. He wanted people to be dependent on him. The residents need him for rides on the bus. He told them their property wasn't safe and that he'd store their valuables—for a hefty fee, of course. As soon as they passed away, he'd cash in before the families knew what happened. And then Sasha? She needed him to get the Botox and then to store it in a safe place."

Janis folded her hands on the table. "When I looked at Flex's financials, I found the evidence. Residents sent him money to keep their stored belongings safe. I also found payments from Sasha. I think she knew how Flex operated and that he'd be a good resource to procure the Botox. After she poisoned Robert Sr., she asked him to store the concoction until she needed it again, though she probably didn't tell him

310

exactly what she was using it for. I think we can arrest Flex for accessory to murder and even fraud."

Michael got up to get more coffee. Cookie removed his apron and then joined them, listening to Janis explain. "So we got Sasha. Such a greedy piece of work, that one."

"Will Echo's evidence be enough to convict her?" asked Olivia.

Janis smirked. "Okay, so Echo is not that reliable of a witness but I'm happy to tell you that after some pushing and shoving, I got Hello Age to give up closed circuit footage of the week prior to Robert Ulrich Sr.'s death. Our girl Sasha can be seen rubbing that ointment into his arm several times over several days. So we have plenty of evidence against her."

Olivia nodded, feeling satisfied and oddly more relaxed. She took the last bite of her cookie. "All she wanted was the money."

Cookie spoke up, standing next to Janis's chair. "I suspect Sasha planned to kill her husband next. Once she got the estate from Raleigh, it wouldn't be long before Robert Jr. would be found dead."

Olivia's eyes grew wide. "That makes perfect sense. Sasha was on a one-woman mission to pocket as much cash as she could, eliminating whoever stood in her way."

"Not anymore," Jets said. "She's in jail now and I'm pretty sure a judge will keep her there."

"But what about Echo?"

Michael looked uneasily at Olivia. "She told you her feelings about hastening an old person's death, a terrifying admission."

"I know, I was horrified as I listened to her," Olivia admitted. "Especially when she described how to strangle a person, like she had experience."

"No wonder. She's a scary woman, just ask Cookie," Janis said as Cookie sat down next to her.

All eyes were on him as he took a thyme shortbread from the plate. Reaching his hand under the table, he paused and then pulled it back. The cookie had disappeared.

A few seconds later, Olivia felt a tongue lick her ankle. "The mayor appreciates a fresh bake," she told Cookie.

"Not to take away from the murder, but the good news," Cookie said, "is that I'm going to get my name back."

Janis patted his arm. "I'll get to that part in a minute. Back to Echo. I had to release her. There wasn't enough evidence to hold her accountable for the other Hello Age deaths. For the record, I'm not sorry she's leaving Lily Rock. It turns out she's the one who arranged to have the bakery vandalized and Cookie's car keyed. Motivated by Sasha, together they figured they would kill two birds with one stone. Raleigh's reputation would be ruined and Cookie's new business would be vulnerable, at least for a while."

Michael's jaw dropped. "I didn't see that coming. I thought it was all about Sasha wanting Raleigh to look bad and that she hired Flex to do the dirty work."

"It looked that way at first, and you're not far off." Janis nodded. "But then Echo admitted to using Flex Million. He did the Thyme Out vandalizing for the right price."

"No wonder he showed up the next day at the bakery," Olivia said. "He was so early. He gave me some flimsy excuse, but it just felt wrong. He came to see how people would react. He was proud of his dirty work."

Cookie leaned over the table. "So as I was saying, before releasing Echo, my lady here texted me to come over and make an official complaint."

"I suggested to his ex that he wanted to press charges." Janis smirked.

"But instead I offered to buy out her business. She had to agree to end the spousal support since I paid more than she asked for. And then my final request was that she get a legal name change and stop using mine."

Jets said, "It wasn't until I did some background research on Echo that I got a bigger picture. Her credit history was disturbing."

"She was in debt when I met her," Cookie added. "Something about her father. I forget the details."

"Maybe she lost her money caring for him? She probably took her frustration and anger to her volunteer job. She was on a self-righteous mission to push old sick people into an untimely death. She as much as told you so." Jets nodded to Olivia, then shrugged. "Because the people were old and sick, no one cared if the end came in an untimely way. Echo relied upon cremation and quick burials. She made it her business to find out what people had put in their wills. Casual conversations with families helped. Unfortunately I don't have enough evidence to convict her. She slipped through my fingers on that charge." Janis looked glum.

Cookie began to chuckle. "I think she may have escaped a legal process, but from what I could see, she was ready to track down the next husband."

Olivia nodded. "I thought I saw Echo looking at Robert Jr. pretty carefully. Because of what Sasha did, he'll probably divorce her. Maybe Echo wants to cozy up to Robert."

"Robert is Echo's type," muttered Cookie. "I guess I should know. Maybe a new husband and a new life could steer her in another direction, away from the elderly."

Jets stared at him. "Should she decide to apply for another job at a residential care facility, I have my ways of putting a stop to it, and I can promise you that any background search will red-flag her previous work history."

Olivia snatched one more cookie from the plate as the door to the bakery opened. Everyone looked up. Raleigh smiled.

"Come join us," Cookie offered. He pulled over another chair, scooting his own chair over to make room.

Raleigh sat down. "I just talked to my dad. He's pretty sad about everything."

"I'm happy he finally stood up for you," Olivia said. "I can't imagine what it would be like to be Sasha's spouse."

"He kind of said the same thing to me," Raleigh agreed. "I'm not feeling it yet, but I might get there in time, you know, to forgive him."

"So what will you do while you're waiting for the estate to settle?" asked Olivia.

They smiled. "Cayenne set up a place for me to stay, a bedroom and bath."

"Did she now. Where would that be?" asked Michael.

"I'm moving in tonight with an older woman who lives alone. Do you know her? Her name's Meadow McCloud."

A collective chuckle came over everyone at the table.

"You'll be fine with Meadow," Olivia assured him, flicking a crumb to the table. "Just make sure you brew your own tea."

Jets snorted, coffee spraying from her nose. "Meadow's a good home baker. I bet you two will get along just fine."

Olivia felt a nudge to her knee. She looked under the table. Mayor Maguire bumped her leg with his nose.

"No more cookies for you," she told him in a stern voice. "Too much sugar. Wait until we get home. I'll feed you a nice healthy dinner."

The mayor edged his way out from under her feet, his body bumping the table leg. Cookie grabbed the cookie plate before it fell to the floor.

Mayor Maguire looked beseechingly at Olivia. When she didn't offer him a cookie, he dropped his head in protest, tail drooping.

"I need to have dog bones available on the counter," Cookie said. He looked over at Raleigh. "See if you can get a good recipe going. Make it healthy."

Raleigh smiled. "Finally something that makes sense. Why wouldn't Lily Rock have an original cookie recipe for a psychic dog who happens to be the mayor?"

"You got that right," Michael said.

Back to the present, Olivia looked toward Michael, who was still talking about concrete foundations. "And then the new foundation would pass earthquake standards..." He turned to her. "You're not listening to me."

She grinned. "I caught most of it. I was just thinking about yesterday at the bakery, all of us together."

Michael opened the passenger side of the truck for Olivia to step in. She reached to pat his cheek before he closed the door.

He walked around to the driver's side.

Once he'd settled behind the steering wheel, he turned to her. "If I had curly hair and floppy ears and was a politician, would you listen to me then?"

She laughed loudly. "Only if you were psychic. Then I'd pay full attention."

Michael nodded, flashing her a smile.

She patted his knee while he drove down the highway toward town.

* * *

Thank you for reading *Getaway Death*! For the latest Lily Rock news join my VIP newsletter. PS signing up also gets

you a copy of *Meadow's Hat*, a short story set before book one
:).

Sign up on bonniehardywrites.com/newsletter

Continue the series with *Deadbeat Dad*

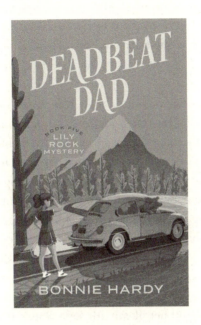

Chapter One

"To what do I owe this pleasure?" Arlo smiled at Olivia as he wiped the bar with his cloth.

"I'm meeting someone here, so I thought I'd hang out with you to catch up." She looked over her shoulder and then back to him. "I don't have to ask about business, the place is packed."

"It's been like this all summer. I thought the crowd would back off a little after Labor Day, but if anything more people showed up. Hold on a minute. Have to take this to the table over there." He held a tray with three beers and a bubbly soda.

Olivia watched his tall lanky frame move effortlessly through the crowd. He carried the tray aloft, stopping to speak to a couple. Then he moved on to the next group. Four young adults sat at a high-top table near the small stage. The man looked up as Arlo approached.

He must be asking for IDs, Olivia observed. Three of the four handed over their driver's license before he set the glasses on the table. *I've never seen those people before. Probably up from LA.*

Arlo returned with an empty tray at his side. With deft efficiency, he slid the tray under the counter and then checked his iPad for the next order. He poured a flight of beer, four samples from the pub brewery, then checked his order again before putting the flight on the tray and hoisting it in the air.

After a few minutes Arlo returned, the empty tray under his arm. He polished a glass and looked at her with a smile. "The usual?" he asked, using his tongs to drop ice in the glass.

"Thanks." When he didn't keep talking, she realized he was looking over her head at the busy room filled with customers. She ducked to give him a better view. He reached for the hose to fill her glass with soda water. Pulling a lemon from under the bar, he gave a skillful squeeze, sliding the drink closer.

"Waiting for Mike?" He reached for another clean glass.

"He's been staying late at the construction site." She eyed the slice of lemon he'd balanced on the rim of her glass. "I'm actually here to meet up with a potential new percussionist for Sweet Four O'Clock."

At the mention of her band, Arlo nodded. "The other one didn't last too long."

She took a long sip. The liquid hit the back of her throat with a tingle. Olivia stopped drinking to explain. "We took on a drummer for our tour this summer. But she had another gig for fall so we're looking for someone new. A guy named

Malone contacted me on Gig Masters. He said he'd meet me here at five to talk."

Arlo leaned over the bar. "Malone..." His face looked quizzical. "You don't mean Beats Malone, the old drummer for The Eclectics?"

"That's him." Olivia's eyes grew wide. "He's famous in certain music circles."

"He's well known to a lot of people, plays old-time music and rock and roll. He got a mention in a recent percussion documentary on Netflix. I call that *really* famous."

Olivia grinned. "Am I supposed to be honored with his presence or something? Do we roll out a red carpet when he shows up and then stop everyone and make a big introduction? That kind of famous?"

"You gotta admit, it doesn't take a lot to be famous in Lily Rock. But I think we can forget about the red carpet. If he stays even a weekend, I'm so naming a beer after him, probably an IPA."

Olivia held up one finger to temporarily halt their conversation. She looked over his head at the bar clock on the wall. *It's a little past five.*

"He's late," she told Arlo. "I'm not impressed."

"He's a drummer. Being late goes with the territory," Arlo said with a smirk.

"Actually coming in late can be catastrophic for a drummer and the entire band. We depend on the percussionist to come in right on time." Olivia put the phone on the bar top. She took another sip of her soda water. "So do you think Beats is his nickname? I mean, he's a drummer and all."

Arlo reached under the counter again and refilled her glass. "I thought his name was weird the first time I heard it. But then I read an interview in *Rolling Stone.* Apparently

Beats is his given name. His family comes from Switzerland and Beats is as common as naming your kid John."

Olivia's eyebrows raised. She checked her phone again. "Okay, I'm not an expert but culturally speaking, the Swiss are even more particular than the Germans about time, and if that's the case, where is our potential new drummer?"

Arlo didn't answer. He moved to the other end of the bar to take an order. Olivia sipped on her water, thinking about the phone call she'd received the day before.

"This is Olivia Greer," she'd answered.

"Saw your ad on Gig Masters," came a male voice. "Thought I'd call about your job. My name is Beats Malone. Heard of me?"

"I can't say that I have," she'd responded.

"You're in Lily Rock, right? I want to make sure I have the right band, Sweet Four O'Clock?"

"We rehearse here. Are you familiar with the town?"

"Yeah, I read up on it: a couple of hours from LA, in the mountains. Small-town vibe, something about a dog who's the mayor. I know a few people who live up there. I'm a percussionist, by the way. It said in the ad you were looking for one."

Once she realized he was a drummer, she'd dropped her guard. "Give me an idea about other bands you've played with." After a salvo of name dropping, they'd arranged for a meeting the next day.

Olivia glanced to her left and then to her right, waiting for Arlo to return. People stood at the bar, beer glasses in hand, chatting loudly. She felt people standing behind her as if ready to pounce on her chair when she stood up.

I wish Sage were here to meet Malone. Then the decision could be made by both of us. When I told her he was coming up to talk, she pulled away from the conversation so fast. I suppose she has a lot on her mind, what with...

Arlo called out, "I'm going to check on that table again." He glanced over her shoulder, his eyes narrowing. "Those kids drink fast." A ding from the kitchen cut through the sound of loud voices. Olivia saw four plates slide under the warming lights.

Arlo grabbed the plates, stacking them on his arm. "Food for the table over there," he told her as he hustled past. She watched as he placed the food in front of the young people and then reached back to grab a bottle of catsup off another couple's table.

When Arlo returned to the bar, his mouth was drawn in a tight-lipped expression. Olivia raised her eyebrows, waiting for him to explain. "They wanted me to speak to the people leaning on the wall waiting for their table." He raised his voice to explain further. "The boy said, 'They keep staring at us. It makes me feel uncomfortable.'" Arlo shook his head. "We got people waiting for seats because it's Friday night. I can't afford to turn away customers. My motto is: drink a beer, eat the food, and then go."

"So who is that group anyway?" Olivia asked.

"Three of them are siblings. I only know that because they live with their mother up by us. The fourth one may be the boy's girlfriend. I don't know that for certain." He slid his towel over the counter again. "They moved here six weeks ago. Cayenne keeps her eye out. I don't think she feels quite right about all those older kids living with their mother in a mountain cabin."

"Cayenne's intuition is kicking in again," Olivia agreed.

Before Arlo could say more, a loud bark pierced the crowd of voices, most likely coming from the parking lot downstairs. "Is that the mayor?" Olivia set her glass down.

"Sounds like him." When the barking continued, Arlo focused his gaze toward the railing. Every barstool at the long counter was filled with people drinking, the forest providing atmosphere from a distance. Those who liked the view of the trees came early to grab seats. Plus it was a good place to start up conversations with strangers.

The barking continued as the pub grew quieter, more and more people pausing to listen. One man shoved the shoulder of his companion, holding his finger over his lips.

"That is Mayor Maguire!" Olivia spoke loudly and then stood up from her stool. She snatched her cell phone off the bar, slipping it into her pocket. She began to push past people standing in the way, heading toward the exit.

"Let me get this," Arlo shouted after her. "I don't want you going all hyper-sleuth on me. You're always getting in over your head."

Olivia paused. "Why don't we both go together to see why he's barking so ferociously?" She waited for Arlo to untie his apron and walk around the bar as people resumed their conversations.

"See anything?" Arlo asked as they passed people sitting on the rail looking over.

One man shook his head. "Whose dog is making all the racket?"

Arlo took Olivia's elbow. "It's not someone's dog, that's the mayor of Lily Rock you're talking about. He doesn't bark for no reason." Arlo made his way through the remaining crowd with Olivia close behind. When people began to follow them, Arlo turned around.

"Stay put. We'll figure this out. You just keep drinking." The crowd did not need a second invitation. Those who stood now sat back down as the voices grew louder in conversation.

Once outside, Olivia followed Arlo down the metal stairway. At the foot of the stairs, she stopped to listen. "I think

M&M is over at the end of the parking lot near the woods." She followed Arlo as they made their way closer.

The barking grew louder as they passed parked vehicles and reached the area where the pavement ended and the woods began. "Stay behind me," Arlo insisted. "I'll go first and see what the commotion is about."

"Okay," she agreed.

"Hey, Mayor," he called out. The sound of his voice only made the dog bark louder.

"It's me, M&M," Olivia shouted. As soon as Mayor Maguire caught sight of her, he jumped up and down and then stopped barking. His tail wagged, urging them forward. He turned his back on them, his head bowed, sniffing something on the ground.

The closer they got, the more her stomach tightened. Arriving at the same time, they flanked Mayor Maguire.

"I see now," Olivia said, her voice filled with concern.

A body lay on the ground, facedown in the dirt.

"This doesn't look good," Arlo said.

The body was awkwardly posed, with one arm folded underneath, blood oozing on the dirt from under his body.

Arlo grasped Mayor Maguire's collar with one hand and spoke in a calm voice. "Good dog," he said. Once he'd secured the dog, he stooped down to look more closely at the body. Olivia came up next to him.

"Looks like a male; he seems to be unconscious," Arlo stated flatly.

She felt her heart beat in her throat. "That's a lot of blood. Can you check his pulse?" Taking Mayor Maguire's collar, she moved him back so that Arlo could look more closely.

His fingers wrapped around the exposed wrist of the unconscious man. After a moment he dropped the hand and then backed away. "I can't feel a pulse. You'd better call 9 1 1."

Olivia let go of the mayor's collar to reach for her cell phone. Her hand trembled and her breaths came in short gasps. She tapped in the numbers. Mayor Maguire gave one sharp bark as if to hurry her along.

"We've got this, Mayor," she assured him.

The labradoodle lifted his head, round black eyes looking directly at her. He seemed to be considering her words as if seeing for himself whether she had the situation under control. Satisfied that she meant business, he nudged her knee with his nose.

Olivia patted his head with one hand as she spoke into her cell phone. "There's an emergency at the Lily Rock pub. We've found a body at the edge of the woods."

End of Sample
To continue reading, be sure to pick up *Deadbeat Dad* at your favorite retailer.

GET A FREE SHORT STORY

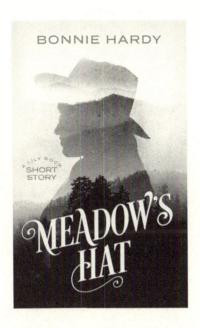

Join my VIP newsletter to get the latest news of Lily Rock along with contests, discounts, events, and giveaways! I'll also send you *Meadow's Hat*, a Lily Rock Mystery short story.

Sign up on bonniehardywrites.com/newsletter

ACKNOWLEDGMENTS

Just a note to thank all the friends of Lily Rock. I am filled with gratitude for this mystical town where there's always an opportunity for a second chance.

Writing about Hello Age returned me to a time when I was employed by a retirement community filled with delightful residents, who shared their zest for living and memorable conversations.

I hope I've represented my small experience with authentic grace.

And then I would like to thank **Christy at Proof Positive.** She holds me accountable for every twist and turn, every piece of punctuation, and for the words I forget to write.

To Kate Tilton of Kate Tilton's Author Services LLC who's shown me the joy of writing for a community of people who love a good mystery, a delicious romance, and a setting to die for.

I also would like to thank **Ebook Launch** for their captivating and artistic depiction of Olivia and Mayor Maguire on each book cover. When I don't know what to write next, I just stare at the books on my shelf and think, "Look at those beautiful books, all in a row. Jump back in and see what they're up to today."

And most of all thanks to Bill, who listens to my ideas every morning when we walk our dogs. He also reads the final proof with his eye for detail and ducks when I get fussy about the corrections. Husband, I love you madly!

ABOUT THE AUTHOR

Born and raised in Los Angeles, Bonnie Hardy is a former teacher, choir director, and preacher. She lives with her husband and two dogs in Southern California.

Bonnie has published in *Christian Century, Presence: an International Journal for Spiritual Direction,* and with Pilgrim Press.

When not planting flowers and baking cookies, she can be found at her computer plotting her next Lily Rock mystery.

You can follow Bonnie at
bonniehardywrites.com
and on Instagram @bonniehardywrites.

facebook.com/bonniehardywrites

instagram.com/bonniehardywrites

goodreads.com/bonniehardy

bookbub.com/authors/bonnie-hardy

amazon.com/author/bonniehardy

Made in the USA
Las Vegas, NV
16 November 2023

80930505R00198